PRAISE I

"[Russell] has a gift for dialogue."—*New York Times*

"Really special."—*Denver Post*

"A crime fiction rara avis."—*Los Angeles Times*

"One of the best writers in the mystery field today."—*Publishers Weekly* (starred)

"Ebullient and irresistible."—*Kirkus Reviews* (starred)

"Complex and genuinely suspenseful."—*Boston Globe*

"Credible and deeply touching. Russell has us in the palm of his hands."—*Chicago Tribune*

"He is enlightening as well as entertaining."—*Tampa Bay Times*

"Enormously enjoyable."—*Ellery Queen Mystery Magazine*

"Russell is spectacular."—*San Diego Union-Tribune*

"This work by Russell has it all."—*Library Journal*

"Grade: A. Russell has written a story to satisfy even the most hardcore thrill junkie."—*Rocky Mountain News*

L.A. WOMAN

BOOKS BY ALAN RUSSELL

Gideon and Sirius Novels
Burning Man
Guardians of the Night
Lost Dog
Gideon's Rescue
L.A. Woman

Hotel Detective Mysteries
The Hotel Detective
The Fat Innkeeper

Detective Cheever Novels
Multiple Wounds
The Homecoming

Stand-Alone Novels
Shame
Exposure
Political Suicide
St. Nick
A Cold War

Stuart Winter Novels
No Sign of Murder
The Forest Prime Evil

L.A. WOMAN

ALAN RUSSELL

A GIDEON AND SIRIUS NOVEL

THREE TAILS PRESS
NEW YORK, NEW YORK

To my three sibs, and to my three children. In chronological order: J.R., Bret, Ronni, Luke, Hart, and Brooke.

PROLOGUE

CRIME SCREAM

The Four Corners
692 miles from Los Angeles

Sergeant Rick Eveleth of the Colorado State Patrol arrived late to the party. He pulled his Chevy Tahoe off the road and parked in a washboard gully well away from the human activity going on in what was normally a deserted area.

What Eveleth saw didn't improve his mood. "FUBAR," he said.

The cop had enlisted in the army right out of high school and done two tours of duty before switching one uniform for another. He had been with CSP for a dozen years now, but old habits die hard. In an effort to avoid cursing, or at least to somewhat curtail it out of respect for his wife, Eveleth frequently used military euphemisms. His wife was a preacher's kid and didn't want their children growing up under the influence of her husband's not infrequently blue vocabulary.

Even from a distance, the crime scene looked chaotic. Under his breath Eveleth muttered, "What a Charlie Foxtrot." That was army talk for CF. Sometimes he got creative and used the phrase "cluster fork."

Eveleth got out of the Tahoe, and though he was at least fifty yards from the yellow police tape cordoning off the scene, he was still mindful where he walked. He carefully navigated the rutted road, following the tire treads of vehicles whose drivers had chosen to park closer.

You'd think law enforcement would know better, Eveleth thought, but I guess that's what happens when you're afraid of arriving too late to get a seat at the table.

There were no structures around them, no buildings or homes. Eveleth looked to the east and could just make out the outlines of a few buildings. This spot was a third of a mile from the Four Corners Monument operated by the Navajo Nation. For five bucks a head, tourists could stand on a marker that delineated where the four states of Arizona, New Mexico, Utah, and Colorado were originally thought to come together.

Eveleth heard footsteps and saw Carl Bates hurrying his way. Bates was a CSP trooper assigned to Colorado's District 5. It was Bates who had called in requesting assistance at the crime scene. The Colorado Bureau of Investigation had also been summoned, but it would be at least another half hour before a criminalist joined them.

The sergeant held up a hand to the fast-approaching Bates, motioning for him to slow down. "The body isn't going anywhere, Carl," he called. "Let's not take chances about further contaminating the crime scene."

Bates nodded, even if his expression appeared skeptical. Eveleth thought the trooper was probably right. Judging from the activity at the scene, that ship had sailed. Still, Bates slowed his approach, the ground crunching under his feet. They were in the high desert of the Colorado Plateau, but that didn't mean the ground was sandy. Limestone and sandstone formations had broken down to form the soil, with the area sculpted over time from the elemental forces of wind, and water, and ancient volcanoes.

Eveleth looked beyond the trooper to where everyone else was gathered. Most wore law enforcement uniforms, but of different colors and tailoring. Even from a distance, he could hear them jawing to one another.

"Everybody and his uncle," said Bates, stepping into the sergeant's line of vision.

Snafu, thought Eveleth. No, that military acronym wasn't quite right. This was not situation normal. But it was fu—that is, fouled—up.

"What the hell is going on?" Eveleth said.

His wife wasn't quite as censorious of the words "hell" and "damn."

"I'd summarize it as a jurisdictional issue," said Bates. "Six different departments are claiming they should have authority over the investigation of what appears to be one divvied-up body."

Eveleth wasn't sure which question he should ask first, but settled on saying, "Six?"

"There's law enforcement from Arizona, New Mexico, Utah, and Colorado," said Bates.

"That's four," said Eveleth.

"The Navajo Nation Police are also here," said Bates, "as well as the Southern Ute tribal police."

"Fuck me," said the sergeant.

Sometimes you just can't settle for a euphemism, thought Eveleth. Sometimes mouthing anything less than a good curse word is just wrong.

CHAPTER ONE

AT THE INTERSECTION OF FOUR CORNERS

I was about to take the first sip of my morning coffee when my cell phone rang. The display told me Ben Corning was calling. With reluctance, I set aside the hot mug. I knew the news wasn't going to be good.

"Where?" I said.

The FBI Special Agent wasn't surprised at my inquiry. "That question requires a two-part answer," he said, "or perhaps more accurately, a five-part answer. The victim was killed in southwest Colorado. His remains were then transported to the Four Corners."

"What four corners are you talking about?" I asked.

"That's what they call where Colorado, Utah, Arizona, and New Mexico come together."

I'd driven through the Southwest several times and knew the area in question was an easy two-day drive from LA. With every murder, the All-In Killer was getting closer to me. He was only around 700 miles away now.

Corning continued. "The killer left four small vinyl sacks containing some of the victim's remains, perfectly equidistant, about a foot apart—one in each of the four states. The centerpiece of his arrangement was a leather pouch situated so that it was arguably in all four states."

"That sounds seriously messed up."

"It was. It is. For once, local law enforcement was glad to relinquish control to the FBI. No way they could resolve who had jurisdiction with six different police forces involved."

"Six?" I said.

"The Navajo and the Utes both have tribal claims to the land where the remains and the leather pouch were left."

"Tell me there are security cameras in the area," I said.

"Afraid not," said Corning. "The remains were left at the true location of the Four Corners, not the Four Corners Monument run by the Navajo Nation about a third of a mile east."

"Why the disparity?"

"The spot for the monument was chosen in the 1860s. Later, the geographically correct location was identified, but since no one wanted to move the monument, the states and tribal nations retroactively legitimized the monument marker as the official meeting point of all four states. Our killer apparently didn't approve of that gerrymandering."

"Not to mention that the true location probably made for a better dumping ground, away from any prying eyes around the monument."

"There is that," said Corning.

"I'd like to look at the case file as soon as possible."

Corning made a noise that was neither affirming nor denying, then said, "We'll see if we can work out a mutually agreeable accommodation."

"'Accommodation'?" I said, trying to keep the heat out of my voice.

"We need you to visit Ellis Haines."

It had been months since I'd seen Haines in San Quentin State Prison, but it wasn't as if the serial killer known as both the Weatherman and the Santa Ana Strangler hadn't been on my mind. I was working with Las Vegas Metropolitan Police, trying to pin Haines to at least one Nevada homicide.

"I'm under doctor's orders not to see Haines," I said. "He's bad for my health."

The headshrinkers and behavioralists at the FBI thought Haines could assist them in a program designed to pick the brains of serial killers. That was a sewer I didn't want anything to do with, but Haines insisted he would only talk through me. More worrying was that he seemed to be in touch with the All-In Killer. How and why, we had yet to determine.

"*We're* just asking for a few hours of your time," said Corning. He was doing his best to sound understanding and concerned. I was confident that if he made a career change, he could do very well selling timeshares. "Since Haines won't talk to us, *we* feel it's important that you reopen the lines of communication."

I'd heard enough of the royal *we*, and said, "*We* don't think much of that idea."

Sirius and Emily were both snoozing in the living room, but I didn't think they would mind me speaking for them. Dogs are generous that way.

"I'm sorry to hear that," said Corning. "As you know, *we* have been supplying you with our All-In Killer information out of professional courtesy. Since *we've* been doing you that service, *we* were hoping you could help us out."

"It's not like I'm a bystander," I said. "There's a murderer out there who's dropping not-so-subtle hints that I'm a future target. For that reason alone, I should be looped into what's going on with your investigations."

"I can understand how unsettling your position must feel," said Corning. "But I've been advised that you'll have to give in order to get, Detective."

"'Unsettling'?" I said. "This isn't some minor inconvenience."

"You know I didn't mean it that way."

I sighed. "Can you at least tell me if you've found anything at this homicide that appears to be directed at me?"

"You were definitely in the killer's thoughts," Corning said.

"Can you offer more in the way of specifics?"

He took a long moment before answering. "That leather pouch that I referenced contained some very interesting items. We believe those items were specifically meant for you to see."

"Then let me see them," I said.

"I'm sure they'll become available to you in time," Corning said, "but right now *we* are carefully cataloging everything."

"Let me guess," I said. "If I agree to see Haines, I won't have to wait for that information to trickle my way."

"*We've* already begun a preliminary analysis," he confirmed, "but you can understand how *we* don't want to be premature in releasing any information."

He didn't need to add the word "unless." Even unsaid, the bait was hanging there. I did a slow burn while waiting to hear more.

Corning decided to dangle even bigger bait. "*We've* determined that the leather pouch straddling all four states is what is called a charm bag, or a gris-gris bag."

He pronounced the word *gree-gree*. I had a vague recollection of what that was. "Are we talking like a voodoo thing?"

"Right ballpark," he said. "Its contents are supposed to ward off evil."

"I could use one of those."

"Eleven different items were placed in the bag," he said. "Apparently, it's important to have an odd number of items in a charm bag."

Eleven. Eleven potential clues. Eleven puzzles I wanted to work on.

"Okay," I said, "I'll play ball. Send me everything you've got."

"Can you be a little more specific than that?" said Corning.

"I'll meet with Haines."

"Within the next forty-eight hours?"

It was my turn to dissemble and be contrary. "I've got work stacked up that needs my immediate attention. The earliest I could meet with him would be next week."

My ploy bought me a little time. "We need you to see him no later than three days from now. There's no wiggle room in that timeframe."

With unfeigned reluctance, I said, "All right. When can I expect to see what you've got?"

"We're processing information from two different crime scenes—where the remains were left and where the victim was killed. We're still in the preliminary stages."

"I don't want to wait a year for the finished report. Today I'm expecting pictures of both scenes and the contents of that charm bag, as well as whatever you have on the victim."

When Corning didn't respond, I quoted his own words back to him: "There's no wiggle room in that timeframe."

"I'll get you some pictures and the raw gris-gris data later today," he promised.

Maybe my hearing was going bad. Maybe my years of being a dog handler had led to partial deafness. Whatever the reason, when he said "gree-gree," to my ears it sounded like "flee-flee."

At the conclusion of our call I was finally able to take a sip of coffee. I wasn't surprised to find it was cold.

CHAPTER TWO

SNAKEBIT

"A watched cell phone never rings," I told Sirius and Emily, once more checking my cell phone.

Neither one paid any attention to my lament. Dogs are too smart to own cell phones. Mine were busy playing a game of tug of war with a small rope whose looped ends made it easy for big jaws to clamp down on.

It had been several hours since my conversation with Corning, and my file from the Feds still hadn't arrived. I have never found it easy to occupy that spot which exists somewhere betwixt and between, something I refer to as betwenxt. It was hard for me to kill time when someone had announced they wanted to kill me.

My sweat-soaked shirt betrayed my torment. Like it or not, denial seemed to be my best recourse. For now, I had to tamp down any response, because there simply wasn't anything I could do. My mind—and my body—wanted to go into fight-or-flight mode, but at this time neither made sense. Letting the situation prey on me was a sure prescription for madness, so I put my phone away and tried to tell myself the file would arrive in its own good time—hopefully before my wannabe assassin turned up. In the meantime, I'd enjoy the faux fighting being waged right in front of me.

The tug-of-war was being hotly contested in the family room, with the back-and-forth accompanied by sound effects worthy of a WWE bout. When Emily first became a part of our household, Sirius essentially had to teach the gentle pit bull how to play. In those early days her wagging stub of a tail showed that she wanted to play, but it was almost as if she needed permission to have fun. I supplied toys and balls, and Sirius demonstrated how it was done. Now there was no holding her back.

Naturally, my pocketed phone chose that moment to begin ringing. "Hail to the Chief" announced the identity of my caller.

It was time for the referee to call for an end to the contest. I shouted, *"Halt die Klappe,"* which is German for *shut up*. The German shepherd knew the command was meant for him. Sirius stopped his mock growling, but his look my way said, "Killjoy." It took another German command—*"Lass es fallen"*—for him to drop the rope. Emily rubbed it in a little, triumphantly displaying her prize while doing a victory lap around the room. At least she did it quietly.

"Braver Hund!" I said to Sirius, but he was too busy sulking to acknowledge my telling him he was a good dog.

"Poor loser," I muttered, and then used the relative quiet to answer the phone. "Git-E-und," I said, with a bit of a Teutonic accent.

"Good afternoon, Detective," said LAPD Chief of Police Gene Ehrlich.

"How are you, Chief?"

"Fair to middling," he said, and I tried to picture in my mind where on the map such a place would be. It was likely sandwiched between Okay and Not Bad.

Our pleasantries didn't last long. The chief had marching orders for me.

"The body of a young woman was discovered this morning," he said. "Although her death has not yet been ruled a homicide, the circumstances make me believe the investigation should be under the purview of SCU."

SCU is the acronym for Special Cases Unit. While it might sound official, SCU consists of Sirius and me. Emily is now a charter member as well. When you live in La-La Land, you have to deal with the unusual in both life and death. SCU was the chief's answer to cases that were not run-of-the-mill. In fact, I was generally the recipient of any cases that were strange, bizarre, and/or aberrant. I'd finally found my calling in life.

"Is this a good time for you to take down information?" he asked. "If not, I can have Captain Brown call you back."

A day without the captain known as Brownnose, I thought, is a good day. "Now is fine," I said.

"The name of the woman who died is Carrie Holder. She was twenty-seven years old. Ms. Holder died at her residence in Bel Air."

Bel Air is one of the most affluent areas in Los Angeles. Along with the wealthy enclaves of Brentwood and Beverly Hills, it's known as one of the "three Bs"—or "killer Bs"—of LA. In 2018, work was finished on a Bel Air home described as the world's most expensive residence. The property supposedly cost half a billion dollars. Billion. Maybe that will one day be the requirement for the fourth B.

"Was this Carrie Holder royalty?" I asked. The subtext was: *How in the hell could a twenty-seven-year-old afford a house in Bel Air?*

"I'm told the property was not owned by Ms. Holder," the chief said, "but by her employer. It was used for the occasional social gathering. Ms. Holder lived there as its caretaker."

"Who was her employer?"

"She worked for the Church of the Gate."

The Church of the Gate was LA's latest and greatest spiritual haven for the stars. That was enough for me to say, "I've got nothing against God, but some of his fan clubs I can do without."

The chief cleared his throat, which proved to be a much more effective silencing tool than shouting, *"Halt die Klappe."* He knew better than to comment on religion. Even though the Church of the Gate was relatively new to the LA scene, it had made a big splash in a short time, using multimedia to spread its message around the world.

"Ms. Holder was found dead in the garden," he said. "The cause hasn't been definitively determined, but her death appears to be the result of multiple bites by a rattlesnake."

"Snakes and religion," I said. "Never a good combination, according to the book of Genesis."

The chief ignored my commentary. "Ms. Holder's colleagues at the church tried to contact her yesterday. After not being able to reach her, a coworker went to the house this morning. When there was no answer at the front door, the coworker went through a side gate and found her body in the backyard."

"Is Ms. Holder's house located on a canyon?" I asked.

"It is," said the chief.

Even within the heavily populated boundaries of LA, there's no shortage of rattlesnakes, especially in the city's canyons. Of course, that doesn't mean those rattlesnakes always stay in the canyons. They've been known to turn up everywhere from playgrounds, to golf courses, to parks. Every spring the California Department of Fish and Wildlife hits the airwaves, warning Californians that it's that time of year. "Bite season" typically runs from April to October. Carrie Holder's snake encounter had occurred on the fourth of June.

"There have been news reports that the drought has brought lots of uninvited wildlife into backyards," I said. "Rodents and birds have taken up residence so as to have access to water sources, and snakes have followed right behind them."

"That's very true," said the chief. "And that has also caused an increase in snakebites. Fish and Wildlife is estimating that there will be in the neighborhood of eight hundred rattlesnake bites in California this year. But only one or two fatalities. On average only five people in this country die of snakebites in any given year. Statistically, I find that interesting."

Before taking his post as top cop of LA, Ehrlich had been an academic. He enjoyed lecturing.

"Any other red flags, aside from the statistical improbability of a person dying from a rattlesnake bite?" I asked.

"You said it yourself, Detective: snakes and religion are not a good combination. In fact, there's a history in this area of snakes having been weaponized by cults."

"I was referring to the Garden of Eden," I said. Or even Gethsemane, I thought. "I wasn't aware of any LA connection."

"Then you'll have to research Synanon. I want to make absolutely sure history is not repeating itself."

Sin-anon, I thought. It would be easy to remember, as its sound translated to *sin later*, or *sin shortly*.

"I've cleared it with the West Bureau that you're to head up this case," Ehrlich said. "They have detectives on the scene who will get you up to speed."

"I'll wear boots," I said.

Not only for the snakes, I thought, but for what I'd probably have to step through.

"Do you happen to know what kind of work Carrie Holder did at the church?" I asked.

"The church said she was one of their penitents. A spokesperson referred to her as Sister Carrie."

"Her job title was 'penitent'?" I asked.

"As I understand it," said the chief, "most of those who work at the church are referred to as penitents. I was told Sister Carrie was a performer in the church's weekly television and media broadcasts, but I'm sure you'll be ascertaining her duties."

"Has any background been done on Sister Carrie's life before she became a professional penitent?" I asked.

"I'm told she attended the Theatre Academy at Los Angeles City College and volunteered at the Audubon Center at Debs Park."

"Any priors," I asked, "or active wants or warrants?"

"Before working at the Gate, Ms. Holder had a job as a dancer at an adult entertainment club on Cotner Avenue. During her time there she pled to a misdemeanor. Disturbing the peace."

A misdemeanor conviction for disturbing the peace tends to get a cop's attention. It usually means a more serious charge was pled down. Given her job, it was likely that Sister Carrie had been arrested for soliciting or prostitution.

"Student, actor, stripper, penitent, and environmentalist," I said.

"What can I tell you?" said the usually politically correct Ehrlich. "She was an LA woman."

CHAPTER THREE

I SEE DEAD PEOPLE

As I was readying to leave the house, my cell phone chimed. I scanned the screen and saw Ben Corning's file had arrived. That was enough to start my heart pounding. Death was on the move, and it was coming at me. I wanted to hole up in a bunker and pore over the file, but I had to resist that inclination. As much as I wanted to study what the FBI knew about the latest All-In Killer murder, my new case took priority, and I resisted opening the file.

"Let's roll," I told the dogs.

Now that I was taking two dogs out on a regular basis, I had wangled a Ford Explorer SUV for a work car. With the three-row seating, each dog could have his or her own space, but most of the time they liked to sit together and breathe down my neck. Backseat drivers.

As we began our drive, I asked, "Any tune requests?"

Sirius nudged me, as if the answer was obvious. "Good choice," I told him.

I did my search for one particular oldie classic. Chief Ehrlich had put the tune into my head, and its psychedelic blues were calling to me. It had been some time since I'd last listened to the title track of the Doors album *L.A. Woman*. As Jim Morrison began singing about LA as the city of night, a prickle ran down my spine. If I'd been superstitious, I would have said someone was walking on my grave. Although "L.A. Woman" was released in 1971, the music sounded all too contemporary. Its lyrics seemed eerily reminiscent of the death of Carrie Holder, and my investigation.

"Cops in cars," sang Morrison, "the topless bars. Never saw a woman so alone, so alone."

I was the cop in a car, and Carrie Holder was an aspiring actress who'd formerly worked in a topless bar. I wondered if Sister Carrie had been as alone as the LA woman of song.

It had been years since I'd spent any time in Bel Air. My work seldom takes me there, and neither does my world. F. Scott Fitzgerald got it right when he said the very rich are different from the rest of us. Being driven by a single-minded pursuit of wealth doesn't leave much time for a life well lived. Then again, the same might be said of being a cop.

Morrison decided to be alliterative, and spoke of a motel, money, murder, and madness. Which was worse, I wondered, Prufrock's measuring out his life in coffee spoons, or Morrison's four M's? *L.A. Woman* was Morrison's swan song. He died three months after the album was released. After his death, the Doors made two more albums without him, but the void of Morrison's absence couldn't be filled. The group needed their enfant terrible.

In the LA area, the most direct route is often not the fastest. According to the GPS, I was only ten miles from Carrie Holder's house if I took mostly residential streets. Taking 101 East and 405 South would add two miles onto my route, but supposedly get me there sooner. The empirical evidence didn't sway me; I decided to take the more scenic route. It would be up to my companions to smell the flowers, and whatever else they could sniff. At the moment, Sirius seemed to be particularly interested in the aroma de Sherman Oaks. Something definitely had his attention.

We made our winding way up into the hills. Every so often the view revealed itself, and below us the expanse of LA spread out. I didn't need the GPS to tell me when we were getting close. Marked and unmarked law enforcement vehicles, as well as news media vans, lined the street around Carrie Holder's residence. There were about a dozen onlookers clustered on the periphery, neighbors talking among themselves.

I parked down the street, availing myself of some shade trees. Even though my vehicle is equipped to provide AC and ventilation for the dogs, I still wanted them to have shade from the sun. Before taking leave of the pack, I passed out snacks and filled both their water bowls. My girlfriend, Lisbet, had gotten Emily her own pink water bowl with her name on it. When it was presented to Emily, the skeptic in me was ready to point out that she could neither read nor distinguish the color pink, but such an explanation didn't take into account the dog's apparent happiness that the bowl was meant for her.

"I'll be back when I can," I told the dogs.

Sirius was used to a cop's life of hurry-up-and-wait, and settled down for a snooze. Emily followed his example. I wished I could join them for a nap of my own, but I stifled a yawn and started toward the house. It was large, set on what I guessed was at least half an acre, although it looked small compared to nearby homes. The front yard was ungated, unlike most of the walled fortresses on the street. If forced to play real estate agent, I would have described the house as being in the style of a Mediterranean villa, with its plaster walls showcasing a Tuscan earthy palette. Lisbet's profession as a graphic design artist had certainly improved my color sense. For too long I had only been aware of the canary yellow that came with crime scene tape.

Such a color was not often showcased in Bel Air, nor was it on display today. In its stead was a uniformed cop who stood out front, discouraging the uninvited. I waved my wallet badge his way, got a nod, and followed a flagstone walkway to the entrance of the home, where I found a front door open. The house had been designed to take advantage of the views. Large bay windows opened up to the backyard and the canyon beyond. That was the view anyone would normally take in, but not when you have a body in the backyard. Carrie Holder's still form seemed to be the eye of the storm; half a dozen people worked around her, processing the scene.

Despite all the activity, this LA woman looked alone, so alone.

I walked through the French doors that opened to the back, staying on the periphery of those working. There were two detectives I didn't know and some familiar faces, techs from the LAPD's Forensic Science Division (FSD) and Technical Investigative Division (TID), busily taking photographs and measurements. Any field investigation into a potential homicide is painstaking, with lots of boxes to check.

Everyone knew I was standing there, but for now I was being ignored. The chief might have cleared my being lead detective with the West Bureau brass, but that didn't mean the detectives working the scene had to like it. I was Bigfoot, cop talk for someone who takes over a case.

Sooner or later I knew I'd have to be acknowledged. In the meantime, being persona non grata allowed me time to study the victim. Carrie Holder was spread out on a checkerboard-pattern patio of stone and dichondra. There was a relaxed expression on her face, or at least on the half I could see. Her brown hair was tousled, as if waiting for her to reach out a hand to smooth it down. She was wearing a lightweight floral dress with spaghetti straps. Apparently, Carrie was the kind of penitent who didn't have to wear a habit. A few inches above her left ankle, I was able to make out what appeared to be several sets of puncture wounds. There was swelling and redness around the bites. Red streaks extended up much of her calf.

I looked around. Beyond the patio were mulched pathways bordered by birds of paradise, banana plants, and passion fruit. On the southern border of the property was a small orchard of mostly citrus trees. While the neighbors had erected fences encircling their entire property lines, Carrie's backyard followed a gentle slope down into an extensive canyon. The only boundary between her yard and the canyon could be seen in colors: her garden was watered, and it showed in the green foliage. The flora of the canyon was browner and more rugged, with the usual chaparral offerings of chamise, California buckwheat, coastal sage, manzanita, and toyon. A footpath led from the backyard down through the chaparral.

One of the detectives must have decided he'd made enough of a point pretending I wasn't there and approached me. He was a heavyset man with salt-and-pepper hair, a bushy mustache, swarthy skin, and one of those broad, beaked noses featured in Mayan stonework.

"Duarte," he said, offering a hand.

I shook it and said, "Gideon."

"Didn't bring Fido?" asked the detective.

I think Sirius is better known than I am in the ranks of LAPD, not to mention among LA's citizenry. He certainly got more media coverage than I did when we arrested the Weatherman. Television newsbreaks offered updates on "K-9 officer Sirius's fight for life." It was only fair. Both of us had extensive burns, but he was the one who'd taken a bullet. My partner has a habit of saving my life.

"He's sleeping in the car," I said.

"Good place to be," said Duarte. "Every time the wind stirs up the leaves, I jump higher than LeBron. Damn rattlesnake could be anywhere."

While he was talking, the second detective decided to join us.

"Anything on the scene that would lead you to believe something other than the snake contributed to her death?" I asked.

"Nothing I've noticed," said Duarte.

The second detective gave a little nod of agreement. Prominent frown lines dominated his face, making me wonder if he'd ever smiled.

"Sometimes the obvious is the obvious," he said, and then reluctantly decided he should offer his name and a hand.

"Grier," he said, and we shook.

"I'm okay with pinning it on the snake," I said, "but we need to make sure all the facts align with that. It's always been easy to blame the snake. Humans have been doing that for a long time. Let's work the scene without thinking we already have all the answers."

I pretended to not see the two of them rolling their eyes. With their unenthusiastic nods, they pretended that what I was saying sounded sensible.

"Snakes give me the creeps," Duarte said.

To spare myself any more eye-rolling, I didn't advocate on behalf of the role of snakes in the ecosystem, and how they keep down the rodent population. Logically, that was true. When you're on the other end of a shaking rattle, though, logic goes out the window.

"Was there anything to suggest that the victim might have done a Cleopatra?" I asked.

"Say what?" said Grier.

"Death by asp," I explained. "Cleopatra killed herself with a snake."

"That doesn't seem likely," Duarte said. "You can see a few fang marks on her calf just above the ankle, which is about where you'd expect to get bitten by a snake in the grass."

Grier offered his approval with a nod. Snake in the grass, I thought, and wondered if there was a complimentary snake expression in any language. Probably not.

"The DME ought to be arriving any minute now," Duarte added. "I'm sure he'll have an opinion on how the victim died."

It would have been more accurate had the detective said, "*She* will." Seconds after he spoke, Dr. Linda Frank, the deputy medical examiner for LA County, joined us at the scene.

Though I had never been introduced to Dr. Frank, I'd attended a talk the board-certified forensic pathologist had given a few months earlier. Still, I was pretty sure she didn't know me from Adam. Dr. Frank surprised me when she looked my way and asked, "No dog?"

Instead of wearing a button-down shirt and tie, maybe I should have been wearing a T-shirt with the words *Second Banana*. "He's busy giving an interview to the media," I said.

"Better him than me," said Dr. Frank. "I loved that picture of your boy receiving the Liberty Award."

"Ever since then, Sirius has been a prima donna," I said.

She knew I didn't mean a word of what I said. The doctor stuck out her hand and said, "Linda." I shook her hand and formally introduced myself, as did the two Western detectives.

"That's quite a display Metropolitan K-9 devoted to you and Sirius," she said, adding, "I help train cadaver dogs for rescue-and-recovery teams."

It was necessary work, I knew, but going out with cadaver dogs was a duty I avoided. I never wanted a job where the best possible outcome was finding a body.

The four of us chatted for a minute, and then the doctor excused herself. She made a slow approach to the body, pausing to put on latex gloves. Before beginning her examination, she gently patted Carrie's hand. I found myself unexpectedly moved by the gesture. In a setting typically devoid of humanity, the doctor personalized the victim.

Although I didn't intrude on Dr. Frank's space, I couldn't help but study her. She didn't speak while conducting her examination, but her furled and unfurled eyebrows seemed to provide commentary. In their various displays I could read question marks as well as exclamation points. I was reminded of John Belushi's eyebrows, which could say as much as semaphore flags.

My hope, as I'd told the two other detectives, was that Carrie Holder's death wasn't a result of any human interaction. I walked around the backyard looking to prove or disprove that theory. I found rabbit pellets, as well as fecal droppings from rats or mice, or both. Not far from where Carrie lay was an active water fountain that also seemed to serve as a birdbath. Hummingbirds hovered and drank. There were no game trails in the backyard, or none that could be seen through the groundcover and foliage. The trail into the canyon was hard-packed earth, and not a good palette for footprints, or to show the serpentine movements of snakes. While there was nothing proving a rattlesnake had slithered through the area—other than a body—there were certainly indications that Carrie Holder's backyard might have looked inviting to any predator searching for a meal.

That was further confirmed when Duarte and Grier waved me over. Detective Duarte was talking on speakerphone and looked excited by what he was hearing. When I drew near, I heard him say, "Can you please repeat what you just told me, Sister Hannah? I'd like Detective Gideon to hear it."

The woman on the other end of the line cleared her throat. When she spoke, I thought I caught a hint of a Southern drawl. "I was just saying that about a week ago Sister Carrie sent all of us here a picture of a big rattlesnake that she said was curled up on a path just off her backyard."

It sounded like the trail into the canyon that I had observed. "And you said this was just a week ago?" I asked.

"I think it was last Tuesday or Wednesday," she said.

It was a good smoking gun, I thought. Duarte signaled me that Carrie's cell phone was already bagged for evidence.

"Was Sister Carrie upset by her encounter with that rattlesnake?" I asked.

"Not at all," her coworker said. "In fact, she thought we were all overreacting after we suggested she call animal control or hire a service to have the snake removed. I even gave her the name and number of a pest removal specialist who attends our church."

"Do you know if she contacted this individual?" I said.

"I'm pretty sure that she didn't. Sister Carrie seemed very unconcerned about the serpent, notwithstanding what was written in Genesis."

"Remind me of what was written," I said.

"In Genesis, God curses the serpent and proclaims that it must forever crawl on its belly and eat dust."

"What's your position at the church?" I asked.

"I don't have an official title other than penitent," Sister Hannah said. "None of us do. The staff refer to each other as Sister and Brother."

"There's no hierarchy?" I asked.

"There is a division of labor," she said, "with an understanding of what tasks need tending to. I report directly to the returned prophet Elijah and his wife, Sister Joan."

"Has Elijah been informed of Sister Carrie's death?"

"He has," she said. "The news saddened him, but he knows Sister Carrie has passed through the gate."

"How well did you know Sister Carrie?" I asked.

"Everyone at the church works together very closely, so I'd like to think I knew her well. Sister Carrie was a very talented performer who was beloved by all."

"Tell me about her job as a performer."

"Every week the church broadcasts a service. It's seen around the world. Sister Carrie was one of its principal performers. Perhaps you've seen some of our broadcasts?"

"I haven't," I said. "But just to be clear, what you're saying is that Carrie's primary job at the church was performing in these shows."

"In our *services*," she said, offering a gentle correction. "That occupied most of her time, yes."

"Would you know who hired her?"

"All personnel decisions are made by the returned prophet Elijah and Sister Joan."

"Any idea how long Ms. Holder was living in the Bel Air house?" I asked.

"I would guess that it's been more than a year."

"I understand the property is owned by the church."

"It is," she said. "The residence is used for retreats, as well as for special spiritual gatherings of our flock."

"How often do such gatherings take place?"

"It varies, but on average perhaps once or twice a week. Why do you ask?"

"It's the job of LAPD to investigate any unusual death, and we don't get many deaths by snakebite. Because of that, we'll need to visit your workplace to get some background on Sister Carrie."

"I'm sure that can be arranged," she said.

"I'd like to do it tomorrow," I said, "and at that time I'll need to talk to Elijah and Sister Joan."

Sister Hannah sounded surprised. "Elijah's time is very precious," she said.

"In that case I'll try not to waste any of it. But I will need to speak to him and his wife."

Sister Hannah said she would check on their availability. I provided her with my contact information, and she promised to get back to me by the next morning.

It was apparent that Dr. Frank had finished with her examination of the body when two men appeared with a gurney. As Carrie Holder was being wheeled away, I approached the doctor and said, "I'm surprised to see you making house calls."

"You do that when the chief makes it known that he has a personal interest in the case," she said.

"That's what got me here as well," I said. "Do you have a minute to talk?"

"The answer to that question is yes, but I am afraid that will likely be the only definitive answer I can provide you."

"Nothing conclusive in your exam?"

"I can state with a relatively high degree of certainty that the victim did die from physical complications associated with snakebite wounds, but the question is, why did she die?"

"I'm not following," I said.

"The western diamondback rattlesnake is the most common pit viper in the county of Los Angeles," she said. "Pending analysis of the venom, let's assume she was bitten by a western diamondback. Judging from the puncture wounds, there appear to be three bites on her lower calf. While a certain small percentage of people do succumb to such bites, the victim doesn't meet the profile. She was young and appeared to be in good health. The location of the punctures also should have been in her favor. Snakebites in the chest can compromise pulmonary function and more readily result in cardiovascular events. In the movies people are bitten by a poisonous snake, only to take a step or two and drop over dead. In real life, that would rarely happen."

"What would happen?"

"She shouldn't have been immediately incapacitated, so how was this snake able to bite her three times? And what stopped her from getting to a phone and calling for help? I'm not saying the enzymes and toxins injected into her body wouldn't have resulted in physical trauma, but how is it that these snake-bites were so instantly debilitating?"

"Are you saying that's unprecedented?"

Dr. Frank tilted her head to one side, then the other, and sighed. "I wouldn't go so far as to say that. It's possible the snakebites resulted in severe and immediate shock, causing the victim to have convulsions or pass out. There have even been instances of snakebites causing paralysis. It's also possible she was suffering from some underlying cardiovascular, or neurolog-ical, or renal condition. In such a case, the snakebite could have quickly brought on a fatal event."

"Are some people allergic to snakebites?" I asked. "A bee sting to most is an annoyance, but to a few it's fatal."

Dr. Frank offered a tentative, or perhaps reluctant, nod. "There have been instances of snakebites resulting in anaphylax-is."

"We're still processing the scene here," I said. "I know very little about the victim's personal life, but is it possible the snake-bite could have proved fatal because there was some kind of ad-verse drug reaction?"

The doctor thought about that for a moment before saying, "If she had taken depressants or painkillers, such an interaction with the snake venom might have had severe consequences."

Maybe, baby. That seemed to be the non-answer du jour. "You know what my next question is," I said. "When will you be able to provide me with some definitive answers?"

"I wouldn't hold your breath, Detective," she said. "We'll have to do blood work and run a number of tests. And that doesn't even take into account the autopsy." She shrugged and said, "From start to finish, that will probably mean at least six weeks."

"You're killing me," I said. It was an unwitting pun, but the doc didn't know that.

"Think of me as the Haley Joel Osment character in *The Sixth Sense*," she said. "Like him, 'I see dead people.' Altogether too many dead people."

CHAPTER FOUR

FLIGHT FROM THE FIGHT IN THE NIGHT

Because it wasn't definitive if Sister Carrie's death was accidental or had some sinister component, the case needed to be investigated as a potential homicide. That was the reality, even though judging from the sighs and side-glances coming from Duarte and Grier, they seemed to think they were wasting their time and that the killer was a rattlesnake. Beginning and end of story.

Despite their posturing, I had the two detectives work the case by the book. After they did an inventory of what was in the house, I assigned them to make a log of any calls Carrie had made or received, then question the neighbors. Because the home had no security system in place, they would need to take stock of the surveillance cameras in the neighborhood so as to see who might have recently visited Sister Carrie. They were okay with that assignment after I told them they could monitor the security footage remotely, and put off reviewing the tapes until the next day. That meant, for tonight at least, they would be getting home at a decent hour.

I didn't have that latitude. Since Sirius and I comprise the entire Special Cases Unit, and since paperwork is not my partner's strength, it was left to me to do an inventory of the house and its possessions. I needed to identify anything that might be suspicious. Being in charge of the Carrie Holder casebook required me to document what had occurred that day and what was in process. I wanted to do the write-up while everything was fresh in my mind. Carrie Holder's death might have also allowed me some escapism. Making her the priority gave me some distance from the All-In Killer.

I took several breaks where I went out and visited the dogs, taking them on short strolls. Their dinner came from emergency food provisions I keep in the car. They ate better than I did, as is often the case. My meal consisted of a package of stale oyster crackers and an old protein bar that I doubt the dogs would have deigned to eat.

Day turned to night, and I found myself alone in the house. Since I was the detective in charge, I wanted to leave as few things hanging as possible. As the old saying goes, when you work for yourself, you better have a son-of-a-bitch for a boss.

Even though a dozen hours had passed since Chief Ehrlich had called me, his reference to the weaponizing of rattlesnakes continued to intrigue me. Sin-later, I thought, recalling my word association with the name he had cited.

"Tell me about Sin-anon," I said to my phone.

The electronic genies must have divined what I wanted to see, as an image of a large rattlesnake appeared on my screen. The photo had been taken in 1977; the dead rattlesnake was being held up by a man identified as an LAPD detective. The tip of the snake's tail was missing; its warning rattle had been chopped off.

Synanon, I read, had been founded as a drug rehabilitation program in 1958, but over time the program's original purpose changed, and in the 1970s it became the Church of Synanon. It wasn't long after that when Synanon gained the reputation of being a cult that brainwashed its membership. A group inside the cult known as the Imperial Marines carried out mass beatings of those who dared to challenge church doctrines or were considering trying to leave. The intimidation was also carried out on the legal front, with Synanon's attorneys suing, or threatening to sue, anyone or anything critical of the church. That didn't stop attorney Paul Morantz from bringing suit against the church on behalf of some former members. In retaliation against Morantz, a derattled rattlesnake was placed in the mailbox of his Pacific Palisades home. Morantz was bitten by the snake and had to be hospitalized for six days. That was the beginning of the end for the Church of Synanon. It disbanded in America in 1991.

The article referenced LAPD's investigation into the attack on Morantz, which helped bring down Synanon. Now I knew what Chief Ehrlich had meant when he'd talked about snakes having been "weaponized" in the past. It annoyed me that I'd been unaware of this not too distant history in my own backyard.

"Those who do not learn history," I said, offering up my mea culpa, "are doomed to repeat it."

Snakes and sects, I thought. How they intersected in this new case deserved a hard look.

It was almost ten o'clock when I decided to call it a night. I rubbed my neck and rolled my head from side to side. The cracking noises wouldn't have sounded good at any time, but in the stillness, they were even more pronounced. Now that I had given myself permission to take leave of the scene, my blinders fell away and I suddenly noticed the view. Below me, the Los Angeles parade of lights was on full display. With all its seductive twinkling, it was easy to understand how the unwary could be bewitched by the city's grand illusion. To the west the Queen's Necklace—the nickname locals gave to the sparkling lights that followed the coastline of Santa Monica Bay—showed off its glittering royal jewels.

For me, work is often like sleep in that my consciousness is muted and gets lost in the background. Now that I wasn't working, I remembered other obligations. Cursing under my breath, I grabbed my cell phone and called Lisbet. She picked up on the first ring.

"Are you all right?" Lisbet asked.

"Other than feeling stupid," I said, "yes. I know it's no excuse, but a lot of things hit me today, including a new case I was assigned."

"I texted you several times," she said. "I was getting concerned when I didn't hear back from you."

I could hear the disappointment in her voice, which made me feel worse. She had been increasingly concerned about the All-In Killer's apparent interest in me. That threat was keeping her on edge; I didn't like to admit it, but it also had its effect on me. I wondered if she had heard about the latest killing in Colorado; it was a subject I purposely avoided bringing up.

"Sorry," I said. "I guess I was too preoccupied to notice your texts."

Lisbet invariably texts instead of calls so as to not disturb me while I'm working. On this occasion I wish she had been less thoughtful and just called me, because now I was remembering other broken promises as well.

"And too preoccupied," I added, "to remember that I was supposed to bring home takeout for the two of us."

I waited a moment for her to forgive me, but the silence told me I might be waiting a long time.

"For what it's worth," I said, "I haven't eaten dinner."

"Is that supposed to make me feel better?" Lisbet said. "The last thing I want to hear is that you haven't been taking care of yourself. That only makes me more concerned. Please tell me you fed the dogs."

"Droolius Caesar and Miss Furbulous have eaten and promenaded, not to mention perambulated."

The hoped-for laugh from her end didn't materialize.

"How do I make this up to you?" I asked.

"You don't need to perform some kind of penance, Michael. I'm glad you're okay."

"Do you still want me to come over?"

"I'm tired," she said. "Let's do it another night."

"Tomorrow?" I asked.

"I have—things—I need to attend to. Let's plan something later in the week."

I wanted to ask, "What things?" But I wasn't in any position to make inquiries. With my overfull workload, I also didn't want to make any more promises I might have to break. Still, it was clear something was off. The two of us make it a point to be with each other four or five nights every week. I'd thought our relationship was long past having to "plan something."

"Suit yourself," I said, pretending to be unconcerned.

There was a moment of silence, and then each of us said "goodbye" without the usual endearments. The sterile sendoff left a pit in my stomach that I couldn't blame on hunger. I wasn't used to Lisbet being so distant. There was a part of me that wanted to call her right back to discuss what was going on, but for most of us with XY chromosomes, posturing is more important than common sense. If Lisbet wanted to talk, I told myself, she had my number.

It felt like a long ride home. The dogs were quick to pick up on my mood and grew restive. They tried to jolly me up with noses that tickled and nudged, and I pretended all was well. The dogs knew better than to believe my act, though.

When we pulled into the driveway, my home looked dark and uninviting. If not for the dogs, I think I would have sat there and stewed a long time. I opened the doors, and the dogs went around sniffing the front yard. Their movements set off a motion detector, which caught me in its light. I raised a hand to stave off its beam, and then noticed a second light being turned on next door.

Seth Mann stepped outside, and both dogs forgot their sniffing and made a dash for their uncle Seth. I followed behind them.

"Working late?" Seth called.

"Afraid so."

"Would you like a nightcap? Or maybe you'd prefer guayusa tea?"

I let my shudder speak for me. A few months before, I had been under the weather and Seth had brewed me up some of his special tea that he said was chock full of antioxidants, not to mention caffeine. He told me that guayusa tea is derived from the leaves of holly trees that grow in the Amazon rainforest. Seth served his concoction in a large wooden gourd carved with designs. While my best friend might be a hell of a shaman, he's no barista. I choked down a few sips before forever giving up on his tea.

"If you're sure," I said, offering up a Scottish brogue, "I could do with a wee dram."

Seth opened the door, and the dogs raced inside. When Emily was first brought home from the shelter, Seth helped me carry her inside. Since their first meeting, he's been spoiling her, just as he always does with Sirius.

I took my usual seat, and Sirius went to his hemp doggie bed. Emily now had her own bed as well, and proudly claimed it.

"Have the dogs eaten?" he asked.

"They have," I said.

That didn't stop Seth from giving each of them a carrot. They happily accepted, and started chowing down his offering. When I try to pass them carrots, they typically turn up their noses.

"What about you?" he asked.

"I snacked. But I'll take one of those carrots if you don't mind."

Seth tossed a carrot my way. I did a Bugs Bunny while he made our drinks.

When he delivered my bourbon, Seth raised his glass and I followed suit. "Take everything in moderation," he said, "including moderation."

We clinked glasses. For as many years as we've been drinking together, to the best of my knowledge Seth has somehow managed to never repeat a toast.

Both of us took a drink. I was longer at the trough than he was, and my "ah" was more pronounced.

"Rough day or tough day?" asked Seth.

I wondered if there was a difference but answered, "Both." Then I went in for another sip and decided to not mention Lisbet's and my tiff.

"I heard from the FBI this morning," I said. "The All-In Killer struck again."

"Where?"

"There's the rub," I said. "The victim was murdered in southwestern Colorado, but his body parts were moved. From what I was told, sacks with the victim's remains were left in four equidistant spots about a foot from one another."

Seth's eyebrows came together. "That sounds rather peculiar," he said. "Was there a reason behind that particular distribution?"

"It's possible the killer did it to drive law enforcement batty," I said. "Or maybe it was meant as a sick joke. The murderer situated the sacks so that the remains ended up in Utah, Colorado, Arizona, and New Mexico."

Seth whistled. "You're telling me the remains were left at the Four Corners?"

"They were left in what should have been the Four Corners," I said, "had modern surveying technology been available a century ago. As it is, the geographically correct site is a deserted piece of land, or it was until those remains were placed there. I'm told the murderer was able to draw what looked like a law enforcement convention from all over the Southwest."

"Sick bastard," he said.

"And that was only my appetizer," I said. "I haven't even had a chance to look at the FBI file they sent me because the chief assigned me to the death of a woman who was bitten multiple times by a rattlesnake."

Seth nodded in recognition. "The media has been all over that. Their stories make it sound as if a rattlesnake invasion is besieging LA. Her death is being played up as *Beauty and the Beast* without the Disney ending."

"Did any of the reporting insinuate there was anything suspicious about Carrie Holder's death?"

"Not that I heard," said Seth, and then turned his head so as to read my eyes. "Was there anything suspicious?"

I shrugged. "An actuarial might say that the numbers themselves are suspicious. Very few people die from snakebites."

"I'm sure that same actuarial would have a formula showing that such a numerical anomaly fits within the parameters of probability."

Before becoming a shaman, Seth had been a CPA. It's not the usual career path, but he does know his numbers.

"You had me at *numerical anomaly*," I said.

"There is that," he said, "but what I find even more convincing is the picture the victim took of a rattlesnake sunning in her own backyard."

"You saw the picture?"

He nodded. "You didn't?"

"I heard about it from one of her coworkers. She told me Carrie sent the picture to her friends at work."

"They showed the picture on the news," said Seth. "The rattlesnake was a big one, at least five feet long. Some snake expert identified it as a western diamondback."

"Maybe I should put out an APB on it," I said.

"Her death was tragic," he said, "but in a way it was somewhat ironic given that she worked for the Church of the Gate."

"What do you mean?"

"Symbolism is important to the church, and some of those symbols include snakes. One of their icons is a modified ankh, wherein the top loop of the cross shows a snake eating its own tail—an ouroboros. The ancient Egyptians and Greeks incorporated the ouroboros in their mystical traditions. It was supposed to represent infinity. The Church of the Gate uses it and the ankh as a symbol of eternal life. They use other snake imagery, too. I imagine you've seen those huge wrought-iron gates in front of their property on Gower Street?"

The world headquarters for the Church of the Gate was now in Hollywood on an old movie studio lot they had renamed Ark Studios. Bolstered by its successful television broadcasts, the church had bought the fifty-acre lot in the complex where their services were already being filmed. Since its purchase, new buildings had gone up, as had the imposing gates. The gates to heaven, some called them. In classic branding, the gates had come to be associated with the church and were featured on billboards around LA with such messages as *Do You Have a Key to*

Open the Gate? The latest teaser billboard had the message *Join Us to See What Is Behind the Gate.* I intended to do just that.

"Those gates are hard to miss," I said.

"I wasn't referring to the gates so much as their designs. In shamanism, snakes symbolize many things."

"Totems? Spirit guides?"

"Those and more," Seth said. "The shedding of a snake's skin is seen as a rebirth of sorts, much like the phoenix rising from the ashes in Greek mythology. But there are other parallels as well. The shamanistic tradition has its own version of the ouroboros."

"If I saw a snake swallowing its tail, I wouldn't be thinking about eternal life as much as I would the snake's having some serious indigestion."

"Imagine the circle as life, death, and renewal. If you look at it that way, the ouroboros is infinity."

"Somehow I missed that snake symbolism in catechism class."

"The Judeo-Christian tradition isn't as favorably disposed to serpents," Seth said. "Snakes are thought of as the personification of evil, such as the cunning and deceptive serpent who entered the Garden of Eden."

"When I saw Carrie Holder's body," I said, "I couldn't help but remember that story."

"If you had been born into another culture," Seth said, "you might not have your bias. In Mayan mythology there was a Vision Serpent, and the Australian Aborigines have a Rainbow Serpent. Here in the New World the Hopis have long had a snake dance; they dance with live snakes in their mouths. And in the Buddhist and Hindu traditions, there's *naga.* Lord Shiva is often depicted with a naga encircled in three loops around his neck, symbolizing the past, present, and future. The Church of the Gate incorporated that symbolism—there are multiheaded nagas on its gates. In temples of old, such nagas were supposed to act as guardians."

"You hear that, Sirius?" I said. "I might replace you with a three-headed naga."

My partner opened one eye at the sound of his name, stretched out on his bed, and then closed the eye.

"He doesn't look too worried about that prospect," Seth said.

"I think he's feeling his age. He's been sleeping a lot more during the day. And the last two nights I woke up to find him absent from his usual spot next to my bed. He and Emily seem to have reversed roles. She's the one who's been taking up the real estate next to me."

"Do you think what's going on is some kind of doggie politics?"

"I'm not sure what to read into it. The two of them get along great. And I don't think it's a matter of them vying for the place of honor. It's more like Emily's assuming Sirius's spot because it's vacant. But why he's sleeping by himself, I don't know."

"He's probably sick of your snoring."

"That must be it."

Each of us took another pull on our drinks.

"Ready for a refill?"

I shook my head. "One will do me," I said. "I'm actually going to try and read through the FBI file before turning in."

Seth, taking notice of my tiredness, cocked his head. "There's something to be said about starting afresh in the morning."

"Tomorrow, Sister Carrie gets all my attention."

"Sister Carrie?" he said.

"That's how she was known at the Church of the Gate. Her job title was penitent, which I find somewhat ironic being that she lived in a multimillion-dollar home in Bel Air that was owned by the church. I guess they don't make penitents like they used to."

Seth was more interested in her name than in my observation. "Theodore Dreiser wrote a book called *Sister Carrie*. It's considered an American classic."

"No wonder I haven't read it," I said.

"It's a story about a beautiful country girl who moves to the big city," he said. "She becomes a kept woman, and then marries but is unfaithful. Even though she becomes an actress and a star, Sister Carrie never seems to find what she was looking for."

"Interesting," I said. "Carrie Holder was a beautiful actress as well. I haven't seen any of her performances, but I'm told she was the headliner in the Church of the Gate's weekly television production."

"Was she a country girl like Dreiser's Sister Carrie?"

"Anything but," I said. "She was a born-and-bred LA woman."

I finished my drink and got to my feet. "Take your glass?" I asked.

"Haven't hit bottom yet."

"I wish I could say the same thing."

My shaman friend is all too perceptive and heard something in my lament. I forced a smile, then offered an explanation that didn't involve my relationship with Lisbet.

"The Feds threatened to withhold the latest All-In Killer file unless I play ball with them. I had to agree to visit Haines later this week. I'm hoping you can look after the dogs."

"You know I'm always happy to dog sit," he said, "even though I have mixed emotions about enabling your visits to San Quentin."

Seth believes Haines is a contagion upon my soul, and that any interaction with him threatens my spiritual well-being. From what I understand, he thinks there's a part of me that has still not escaped the fire Sirius and I had to forge through after we'd captured Haines. I'd like to say his theory is mumbo jumbo, but at the same time I know that the fire still reaches for me. My physical scars remind me of that, as do my dreams. Denial keeps me going, although I'm aware enough to know that my symptoms are textbook PTSD.

"I appreciate your concern for me," I said, "even more than I do your dog care."

I patted my good friend on his shoulder, and the dogs and I took our leave of the comforting refuge of Seth's house.

CHAPTER FIVE

EYE OF NEWT, TOE OF FROG

Instead of getting comfortable on the sofa, I took a seat on a stool at the kitchen counter. I wanted to stay alert while poring through the FBI files. The dogs settled on both sides of the stool. They were probably hoping I'd include them in a midnight snack.

Ben Corning had been busy during the day sending me additional files and updates to the investigation. His information came with a price tag in the form of a not-so-subtle note asking me if I'd set a date and time to go and see Ellis Haines. When you make a deal with the devil, the payment always comes due.

The FBI files didn't come unencumbered; to open them I had to proceed beyond a warning screen that looked similar to the one that threatened action against film piracy. I made ready with my yellow legal pads, proof positive that I wasn't a millennial. A younger person would have used the digital highlighter option to tag areas of interest; I needed my paper notes. I also needed my reading glasses.

There were two main files, along with all the updates to those files. Even though there was only one homicide, two separate teams were working the case because the Feds were processing two crime scenes. Jim "Rocky" Packer had died in southwestern Colorado, but bits and pieces of him had ended up in the Four Corners. The fifty-three-year-old white male was an amateur geologist, or, as he preferred to be called, a rock hound. He'd died at the entrance of an abandoned mine, killed when several pounds of binary high explosive were set off by a high-velocity bullet. Shrapnel in the form of small nails and glass had been positioned next to the combination of ammonium nitrate and aluminum powder. The explosion had riddled Packer's body with shrapnel and he had bled out at the scene.

I looked at the crime scene photos: skin, blood, and bone were spread over a rocky area outside the cave entrance. There is little dignity in death; unfortunately for Packer, what was left of him made him look like a Smurf. His body and its scattered remains were covered with blue powder, the residue from the explosive. Shooting enthusiasts employ binary explosive targets to signal when the mark is hit. Much like theatrical flash powder, it ignites in colors, the most popular of which are blue and red. The reactive targets can easily be purchased in sporting goods stores and gun shops. They're safe when used judiciously, but the All-In Killer had far exceeded the recommended amount of powder. Acting as a hidden sniper, the killer must have fired a high-velocity bullet that essentially set off a long-distance bomb right in front of Rocky Packer.

Packer's death was in the cards—so to speak. He was the fifth victim in the All-In Killer's warped card game. The first known victim had been a duck hunter who was shot; I had come to learn that in poker parlance, aces are referred to as bullets, and twos are called ducks. Because of that, being dealt the hole cards ace-two is known as hunting season, something the All-In Killer had declared to the world. His homicidal spree had targeted individuals fitting the pattern of playing cards. Deaths associated with a king-three (a hand often called king crab), queen-four (the prince maker), and jack-five (which turned out to be linked to the Jackson 5 song "ABC") had followed. The next homicide should have had something to do with a ten-six hand, often referred to as sweet sixteen, but the killer had instead given us a pocket pair of tens, a hand Texas Hold 'Em players call TNT. Hence the explosive powder.

Why had the killer diverged from the high-low card pattern? Was it a one-time deviation, or was there a new pattern in play? It was possible the killer had decided upon a wild-card strategy in order to defy predictability and throw off law enforcement. It was also possible that the apparent randomness was disguising something else.

Whatever the answer, the homicides were still proceeding in a westerly direction. All roads seemed to be heading to Los Angeles. To me.

With a black sharpie, I wrote the letters TNT on one of the legal pads. The murder of Rocky Packer had been meticulously planned, as had the disposition of his remains. I started taking notes on everything staged at the Four Corners scene. In the center of the four sacks of remains was the black leather pouch Corning had mentioned.

It was like some sick treasure map, I thought, with X marking the spot.

Corning had dangled the gris-gris bag's eleven items at me. What he hadn't mentioned was the design etched into the leather, an S-shaped symbol with an arrow running through it. According to the Feds, the elongated S was the meteorological symbol for a dust storm or sandstorm.

On the face of it, the symbol was a wink to Haines, aka the Weatherman. It also seemed to be a taunt aimed at law enforcement, a gibe that they were walking around blind in the midst of a storm. The difficulty in interpreting any of the killer's potential clues was that it was all too easy to read multiple meanings into them. It was also all too easy to miss the actual meaning of a clue.

I began listing the items in the pouch, starting with an index-card-sized birth announcement with large blue letters declaring, *It's a Boy!*

The FBI provided a potential explanation: that the use of blue and pink binary high explosives was popular in gender-reveal parties. When the target was struck, the powder detonated to reveal the sex of the baby. The report referenced occasions when the gender reveal hadn't gone quite as planned, including a recent wildfire caused by the explosion of a reactive target. In that instance, the baby announced had been a boy.

Fires always get my attention. Once burned, twice shy. I wondered if the birth announcement was meant as a warning to me. The killer knew I would be studying everything left at the crime scene. My gut feeling, though, was that it was just another dose of sick humor—not so much a birth announcement as a death announcement of the almost unrecognizable blue remains of Rocky Packer.

The other items in the gris-gris bag weren't as ambiguous. I studied a picture of a replica LAPD detective's badge. At the bottom of the badge a piece of white adhesive tape had been applied, the numbers 9842 written on it in a precise hand.

The numbers on my badge.

And circling the middle of the badge was a black mourning band, the kind used to signify a line-of-duty death within the department.

The second detective reference in the bag of tricks was a cartoon image of Flattop Jones, a recurring criminal character in the comic strip *Dick Tracy*—a hired killer, in fact, who'd been paid by crime lords to assassinate the plainclothes detective. On the back of Flattop's picture was the message: *Love My Police Department.* The letters were too precise to have been written with a free hand. According to the FBI, the killer had traced a template so as to stymie handwriting analysis.

I'd certainly gotten the message by then, but I was surprised to discover that two other items also referenced me. There was a plastic bag containing salt-and-pepper hair that looked to be the same color as mine. There was also rock salt in the bag—apparently, salt was commonly put in a gris-gris bag to ward off evil, in much the same way as people throw a pinch of salt over their left shoulder to keep the devil at bay.

As disturbing as it was to be targeted in the killer's messaging, what bothered me even more was the next item. Instead of a plastic bag, the killer had used a restaurant doggie bag to serve it up. There was an image of a smiling dog on the bag, and inside was a dog bone.

Sirius was also in the killer's crosshairs.

The threat only escalated. The next photograph appeared to show the desiccated webbed toe of a frog, although confirmation was pending laboratory analysis. Still, the FBI believed the amphibian's remains were linked to a scene in Shakespeare's *Macbeth* where the three ugly witches hover over a boiling cauldron, casting their spell.

My body felt hot all over, as though I were standing over a cauldron myself.

The witches' words were highlighted in the report: *Eye of newt, toe of frog, wool of bat, tongue of dog.*

"God damn you to hell," I said.

Sirius looked up; my anger put him on alert.

"It's all right," I told him, stroking his head. "It's all right."

But it wasn't. Love me, love my dog. The All-In Killer was using psychological warfare to get to me, and it was working.

I chewed on my index finger and took some deep breaths. It's one thing to bring evil into your own life; it's another when innocents are targeted merely for being part of your world. I was glad none of the items in the bag seemed to be directed at Lisbet. One of her misgivings about our relationship was that I kept her at arm's length. I argued she was wrong about that, but the truth was that she was more right than wrong. There are things in my world I don't want to burden her with. The All-In Killer was one of them.

My hands were shaking; I think it was out of anger, but I can't swear it wasn't fear. I leaned down again, this time stroking both dogs. It took a few minutes of that before I felt settled enough to read the rest of the quote from *Macbeth*:

For a charm of powerful trouble, like a hell-broth boil and bubble.

I read the words and did my own boiling and bubbling in a cauldron of hell-broth.

When I was able to continue reading, I discovered that the killer had me on quite a scavenger hunt. A piece of petrified wood had been left in the bag, as had a green lodestone. According to the FBI, a rhyme associated with gris-gris bags was that their contents should include "sticks and stones and roots and bones," a rhyme reminiscent of the chant of Shakespeare's witches.

The killer's bag had all those things. The Feds said that green lodestones were thought to increase the power of the magic. As for the petrified wood . . . the Petrified Forest National Park was located in northeastern Arizona, not far from the Four Corners. The killer might have been identifying his route. Or it could have been a commentary on how something living could transition over millions of years to stone; the forest had petrified through permineralization. In the report, the phrase "like getting blood from a stone" was referenced.

Analyzing the mind of a warped killer was not an easy exercise. It was also not for the faint of heart.

The last three items in the pouch were a hummingbird's nest, a plastic bag containing residue believed to be gunpowder, and three as-yet-unidentified brown-and-black beans. The nest was about the size of a thumb. The report said that pieces of bird's nests were often included in charm bags, as was gunpowder. It didn't take much imagination to work out potential messages: the bird had flown from the nest and wasn't to be found; and the gunpowder in a bullet had led to the death of Rocky Packer.

Eleven disparate items: a birth announcement, an LAPD detective badge, Flattop Jones and his message of law enforcement love, salt-and-pepper hair and salt, a doggie bag with a dog bone, a frog's foot (or at least a desiccated toe or two), a piece of petrified wood, a green lodestone, a bird's nest, a plastic bag with gunpowder, and three unidentified beans.

Everything, I thought, but a partridge in a pear tree.

On one page I made a list of the eleven items, and then devoted a separate page to each of them so that I could write down my thoughts.

All the items came with possible explanations save for the beans. I looked at the pictures again. They resembled pinto beans in color, and were similar in size.

Aloud, I said, "Maybe they're Jack's beans. Maybe we should plant them and then climb the giant beanstalk."

Sirius raised his head and gave me a tail thump. He must have thought that what I was suggesting sounded like fun. Or more likely he was trying to reassure me: the pack had my back.

"'Fee-fi-fo-fum,'" I said to him. "'I smell the blood of an Englishman.'"

Sirius sat up; Emily followed suit. The two of them leaned in against each of my legs. Being part of a dog sandwich was certainly the highlight of my day.

I made a few more notes, but my anger—and my denial—could only take me so far. The computer screen was becoming blurry. I needed sleep.

"Bedtime," I told the dogs.

Sleep is not something most dogs have to be enticed into. The three of us made our way to my bedroom. Sirius took up his spot in the carpeting next to my bed, while Emily went to her nearby dog bed.

The All-In Killer's threats didn't go unheeded. Normally I keep my Glock hanging in my shoulder holster in the closet. Tonight, it was under my pillow. Cold metal is not usually a comfort to me, but I fell asleep with my hand on its hard surface. It allowed me to sleep, but also proved to be my passport to hell.

I awoke in flames. My partner was bleeding out, and I was burning. As my skin sizzled, I screamed. The only thing keeping me sane, and able to stave off complete and total panic, was Sirius. His survival depended on my keeping my head.

The Santa Ana Strangler was my dance partner. We were dancing to the flames, and to the directional guidance of my gun. The two of us carried Sirius, looking for a way out from the fire.

Smoke clawed at our eyes and choked our lungs. There was no escaping it. The Strangler tried to appeal to my reason. He didn't know that it had been burned away.

"The dog's dead," Haines said. "We have to leave him behind."

"You don't leave a fallen comrade," I said, lifting my gun so that it was leveled at him.

Haines nodded, blinking away the smoke, trying to blink away his death. My trigger finger tightened.

"Sirius," I called. "Sirius!"

Or was I calling something else? I might have been saying, "Lazarus! Lazarus!"

My partner seemed to hear. He stirred ever so slightly in my arms. He saved me, this time from being a murderer.

"Sirius," I said, finding relief in the flames.

I awoke from the fire walk with my partner's name on my lips. In fairy tales, Snow White and Sleeping Beauty are awakened by the kiss of a prince. My escape from the fire has always been at the paws of an insistent dog. It's the only way out I have ever known. But on this occasion my spell was not broken by Sirius, but by Emily.

My scar-faced princess was licking my own scarred face, bringing relief to my burning cheeks and pulling me back from the brink. With a weak, unwieldy hand, I reached for her beautiful oversized head with its chewed-away ears.

"Thank you, sweetie," I said. "Thank you."

My throat was raw. It had been raw for weeks after the fire, damaged by the smoke and flames and my screaming. Years had passed since I'd escaped the fire, but I was still burning. I wondered if I would burn for the rest of my days.

Emily continued to comfort me. My fire dreams were much less frequent now, but this one had come on with a vengeance, a harsh reminder that my PTSD was still with me. The sheets were soaked with my sweat.

I was reaching for the glass of water I keep at my bedside when I heard a noise out in the living room, a whoosh of sorts, and a slamming, which caused me to grab my gun. But then I released my grip on it. The false alarm was Sirius. He came running into the room and hurled himself onto my bed. Normally he stays clear of my mattress, but not now. He was the mother hen reacting to my distress, licking me, prodding me with his muzzle, pawing at my chest as if trying to revive my heart.

"It's all right," I said, "it's all right."

The words felt much truer now than when I'd been so shaken by the threats in the gris-gris bag directed at my partner. The only reason Sirius had come to the attention of the All-In Killer was because the two of us had captured Ellis Haines. We had been paying for that ever since.

Sirius kept fussing over me, as did Emily. My partner was acting guilty, as if he knew he'd let me down by not being here. I wished I could ask him why he'd ventured from his usual spot next to me. By my count, this was at least the third night in a row I'd awakened and found him absent. Maybe he'd been attending to the call of nature, or maybe his age was catching up to him and his hearing was failing. It was possible the noise I'd heard was him coming through the doggie door in the kitchen, although to my ear it had sounded as if it came from the living room.

"I'm okay," I told him.

It was the same lie I always offered, but it got Sirius to stop his worrying. Musical chairs commenced, with my partner taking up his usual position on the floor below me, and Emily moving over to her doggie bed.

Now that I had escaped the fire, it was almost as if I was freed of an entrapping spell. Relief flooded over me, and I relaxed back into sleep. Between consciousness and the realm of Morpheus, I began to see with what Seth would call my third eye. I'm not sure if the visions that always follow my fire dreams emerge from my subconscious, or if they're whispered by some unseen oracle. A gateway opened. Or maybe it was a rabbit hole.

Fire had followed me. A large, cast-iron cauldron was set atop blazing firewood. Women's voices—and their cackling— could be heard over the cauldron's boiling and the hissing flames.

"Green venom," said one.

That brought on complicit laughter, and the chorus of "It isss so, it isss so."

White sparks shot from the flames. They were impossibly bright, but then the shock of white was explained by rumbling sounds. Thunder had followed the lightning.

"The storm is clossse," said a different voice.

"It isss so, it isss so," said the others.

As the sound and lightshow of the oracle blazed and thundered, I found my troubled sleep.

CHAPTER SIX

THE FAKE SNAKE

I awoke less than human, feeling more like a husk than flesh and blood. It was as if some huge spider had sucked my life fluids dry. I felt so drained and exposed that I considered putting on one of my old compression garments. After the fire, I'd worn them almost as a substitute for the layer of skin I'd mostly lost. For too long a time it had felt as if I were a network of scar tissue being held together only by those garments.

The scars were no longer as visible, but the unseen scars are usually the worst. In the aftermath of my fiery dream, it took three glasses of water and four ibuprofens to get me walking around. Coffee followed that, and I forced down some cereal with lots of milk.

As I did my cud-like chewing, I thought about the strange vision that had descended upon me after my fire dream. The logical part of me said that reliving the fire allowed my subconscious mind to respond to worries, fears, and pressing thoughts. The questioning part wondered why it was conjuring up witches.

The crones at the cauldron had spoken of green venom, which seemed a likely byproduct of my rattlesnake investigation. The venom's color might have stemmed from the green lodestone in the gris-gris bag. Or the color might have been significant for another reason—to signify jealousy, or envy, or the environmental movement. And when someone turns green, other than Kermit the Frog or the Hulk, it means they're sick.

Thunder and lightning had also been a prominent part of my vision. An S had been carved into the gris-gris bag, signifying a dust storm or sandstorm. "Stormy Weather," I thought. Ellis Haines had sung that song during his trial, belting it out with a surreal sultriness until the judge had ordered him removed from the courtroom.

To this day, his recital was a YouTube favorite, but I didn't think my oracle was directing me to Ellis Haines. There was more this sense of a storm bearing down on me. Instead of feeling as if I were caught up in that storm, I decided to work. The revelation from my vision would come to me in its own time, or it wouldn't.

I looked through email and texts. Sister Hannah from the Church of the Gate had written to say that "the returned prophet Elijah" had agreed to an audience with me at 12:30. I was asked to be prompt, and told that my time would be limited, as Elijah had "many other pressing commitments."

You want to get on a cop's bad side? Just mention your pressing commitments and imply that talking with the police is not high among them. It also didn't help my mood being told Elijah was a prophet. I'm always more at home with those who are seeking answers than with those who say they have them.

The timing and location of my appointment was good, though, for it would afford me the opportunity to see to business, as well as make a stop along the way to see an old friend.

I made calls to Detectives Duarte and Grier. Both men were still in the process of looking at security tapes and trying to run down Carrie Holder's most recent visitors. The detectives seemed to have lost their attitude from the day before, probably because I wasn't putting much of a fire under them. Proceeding with a low-key investigation made sense, at least pending the coroner's determination about whether there was anything suspicious about Sister Carrie's death.

Since my awakening, Sirius had stayed close to me, almost as if responding to an unspoken command to heel. I wondered if his keeping to my side was guilt at having been absent the night before. Most animal behaviorists would have thought the notion silly, as they believe dogs live in the moment and aren't capable of such a complex emotion as guilt.

"The experts say your brain doesn't work that way," I told him.

Sirius rested what looked to be an apologetic head on my knee. "You're right," I told him, scratching behind an ear. "What do the experts know? But if anyone should feel guilty here, it's me."

For the last few days I hadn't run the dogs through their paces. Computer software engineers like to say, "Garbage in, garbage out." If the code isn't written well, there won't be a good outcome. It's the same with a dog handler. I needed to work with my charges.

I rummaged through a closet that contained items from my days at Metropolitan K-9, found what I was looking for, and smuggled it outside in a bag. Both dogs followed me to the front lawn, curious about what was in my mystery bag.

After telling them to sit and stay with their backs to me, I positioned my fake snake. Some handlers use electronic shock collars for aversion therapy, but I never felt right about being a shock jock, and have always trained my charges through force-free aversion therapy and impulse-control exercises.

I called to the dogs, and they turned their eyes to the object in the grass that I was circling around. Then I said, "Sirius, *Hier.*" My partner knows my commands and signals, and is alert to them. As he approached the fake snake I yelled, *"Lass es,"* German for *leave it.* That stopped him in his tracks. Then I yelled, "Back up." He performed the moonwalk better than Michael Jackson ever had.

Emily watched with interest, especially when I rewarded Sirius with a bite of jerky treat. We repeated the training multiple times. For Sirius, it was a refresher course on snake aversion therapy. After that, we worked on impulse control. I produced a few of his favorite toys, and in the midst of our play I would tell him, *"Lass es fallen,"* the command to drop it.

Then it was my partner's turn to watch, and Emily's turn to learn. Through trial and error, she began to understand the commands. Reinforcement and praise work wonders. Add jerky treats to that combination, and you have the potential for canine genius. Some working dogs only get fed after successfully performing the tasks put to them. I am not that draconian, but I do believe in reinforcing good behavior with savory rewards.

When I was satisfied with that morning's training, I announced, "Let's go for a ride."

It wasn't a command but an invitation, and the dogs responded with wagging tails.

The morning's training with the dogs had benefitted me more than it had them, helping me to put the fire and witches and green venom behind me. Still, my miasma didn't totally lift. On those nights Lisbet and I are apart, she invariably calls the next morning. The absence of such a call today seemed significant. I wanted to call her but didn't know if she wanted to hear from me, and

I was afraid to find out for sure. I vacillated between calling her and not calling her right up until the moment I pulled up to the church, at which point I decided my arbitrary time clock had run out. It was the chicken's way out, although I pretended otherwise.

More than a month had passed since my last visit with Patrick Garrity, the priest known as Father Pat by his flock at the Church of the Blessed Sacrament on Sunset Avenue. These days it's rare for a priest to stay so many years in one parish. I was lucky that Father Pat had been a young priest with good ears on the occasion of our first meeting. If he hadn't heard the cries of the newborn abandoned in the church's back lot, I wouldn't have survived that cold January morning.

In the years since, Father Pat has stayed a part of my life. He believes that God brought the two of us together. It was long overdue for the prodigal son to return to the scene of the crime.

Our parking spot had a view of the blacktop where students from the Blessed Sacrament school were enjoying recess. The sight of playing children entranced Emily, and she didn't seem to mind that Sirius was the only one allowed to go with me onto church grounds. Dogs are discouraged from being on the property, but Sirius gets a pass because he's an official K-9 officer, or at least that's the cover story. Father Pat was happier with that pretext than with my claim that a papal dispensation for my partner was "in process."

Sirius knows his way to the rectory office, and decided to go ahead of me so as to see what he could cadge. From the hallway I heard Father Pat welcoming my partner, and arrived just as Sirius was being rewarded with a treat.

"I hope that's not a communion wafer," I said.

Father Pat opened his arms and I bent down and gave him a hug. He is as small in stature as he is big in heart.

"And here I was worried about our school budget," he said. "I should have remembered how the birds in the sky do not sow or reap, and yet the Lord provides. Thank you, Michael, for your generous hundred-dollar contribution."

Father Pat doesn't mind my irreverence, for it comes with a price tag. I either mind my p's and q's, or I assist the church's coffers.

"And you wonder why I don't visit more often," I said.

Father Pat didn't charge me for that line. Thank the Lord for small favors.

I declined an offer of coffee or tea, and both of us sat down. Father Pat is a worrier, and I tried to give off the aura that all was well, but he saw right through me. The man wears thick glasses, but I've still never been able to pull one over on him.

"You look tired," he said, "and troubled."

With basso not profundo, I sang the words "Nobody knows," but even I knew it was a lame avoidance. At least my abbreviated spiritual didn't merit another fine.

"I was working late on a case," I said. "I'm investigating the death of a young woman who was bitten by a rattlesnake."

Father Pat made the sign of the cross and under his breath said, "Poor soul." Then he added, "I heard about her unfortunate death."

"Were you aware she was on the staff at the Church of the Gate?"

"I heard something about that," he said.

"Do you have any dealings with your neighbor church?"

"We're not exactly neighbors," he said. "There's a divide between us of three miles or more."

"And not only a geographical divide?"

Father Pat shrugged. "We're not a New Age church, and don't aspire to that. They seem content with keeping their gates closed, metaphorically and physically."

"What do you mean?"

"Most gates open," he said. "Their large gates do not."

I made a little noise of surprise. "They're a façade?"

"Not a façade so much as a statement. The gates were never designed to open or close."

"Strange," I said.

"They serve the purpose for which they were designed: to be noticed. For thousands of years monumental gates and archways have signified power. And the gate as a religious metaphor is part of virtually every faith."

I thought about that and decided to be contrary. "Does that include images of the gates of hell?"

"As a cautionary tale, yes," he said. "If Dante is right, the sign atop those gates warns, 'Abandon all hope, ye who enter here.'" He gave a little shudder before adding, "I prefer the counterpoint of the image of Saint Peter at the pearly gates."

Sirius lifted a paw and tapped the priest's knee. "And so, evidently, does Sirius," he said.

"I think Sirius is appealing to the gatekeeper of the treats," I said.

"Then I must not be negligent in my duties," he said, reaching into a drawer and pulling out another snack for Sirius.

"After my visit here," I said, "I'll be going to visit your competition."

"'Competition'? I wasn't aware that a rivalry between our two houses of worship existed. This isn't a case of USC versus UCLA."

"That's for sure," I said. "That's always a hot ticket."

I was surprised to not be fined another Benjamin. "Los Angeles is not the spiritual desert that so many think it is," the priest said. "In fact, it could arguably be called one of the great religious cities of the world."

"You're serious?"

Nodding, he said, "Our City of Angels has quite a religious history. And don't think the Church of the Gate's Elijah is the first so-called messianic figure to come to town. Back in the nineteen twenties, Aimee Semple McPherson was a rock star before there were rock stars. Her Angelus Temple in Echo Park was one of the first megachurches and drew millions of visitors. Movers and shakers and Hollywood stars attended her services."

That was the same crowd now associated with the Church of the Gate.

"Last night I became acquainted with another LA-area church," I said. "Ever hear of the Church of Sss-sss-synanon?"

My sibilance got a rueful shake of Father Pat's head. "Unfortunately," he said, "LA has also been fertile ground for cults, such as the Church of Synanon. The Children of God also started in Los Angeles."

"Doesn't ring a bell," I said.

Father Pat's expression looked pained, though I wasn't sure if he was bothered by my ignorance or by the information he was about to impart. "Its founder was David Berg. He employed tactics that were described as engaging 'happy hookers for Jesus.'"

"I'm glad I missed that."

"There was worse," said Father Pat. "Before Jim Jones served his followers cyanide in the jungles of Guyana, he operated out of the People's Temple on the corner of Hoover and Alvarado."

The Jonestown Massacre had resulted in one of the largest mass suicides/murders in history—more than 900 individuals. The tragic deaths brought about the expression "drinking the Kool-Aid," even though the sugary grape mix Jones used to mask the cyanide wasn't in fact Kool-Aid.

"Before that," said Father Pat, "LA had to deal with the murderous cult of the Manson Family. And forty years before that, Los Angeles was home to the Blackburn Cult, named after its leader, May Otis Blackburn."

"That's another one that's new to me."

"Blackburn's followers thought she had supernatural powers, and she went so far as to tell two of her grieving parishioners that their newly dead teenage daughter might live again if certain practices were followed. It's said the girl's corpse was wrapped up in a shroud full of spices and buried under the floor of the family home. Next to her body authorities found seven dogs that had been sacrificed as offerings to God."

I would have offered up a favorite curse word, but seeing as that would set me back too much money, I made a few sounds of utter disgust.

"And who thought that was a good idea?" I asked.

"Blackburn's followers, evidently," he said. "She referred to herself as a queen and high priestess. Her supporters believed it."

"Some of Elijah's followers think he's a prophet."

When Father Pat didn't react, I added, "His church seems to have established a huge foothold in a short amount of time. Why do you think that is?"

"I'm sure his background as a filmmaker has helped him find an audience," he said.

Most people knew that Eli Green had made documentaries long before he claimed to have had a calling to serve God and became Elijah.

"Not the usual career path for a prophet," I said.

"I suppose that all depends on how you spell the word," said Father Pat.

"P-R-O-F-I-T?"

"That, many suspect, was the reason he started his church."

"If that's the case, he certainly succeeded. The dead woman lived in a Bel Air home owned by the church. I doubt a vow of poverty was ever high on Elijah's list of priorities."

"That makes me wonder what his priorities are."
"Great minds think alike," I said.

CHAPTER SEVEN

ALL IN THE FAMILY

A skeptic and a man of faith had their usual wide-ranging discussion. At the end of my conversation with Father Pat, I don't think I was any less skeptical, but I felt better for our time together, despite walking away lighter in the wallet by two hundred dollars. Then again, that's less than I'm usually fined.

As we hugged one another goodbye, Father Pat said, "I noticed you avoided talking about Lisbet."

Busted, I thought. In the midst of so many topics, I had imagined he wouldn't recognize that omission.

"We're having a little rough patch," I admitted.

"I'll pray for the two of you," he said.

It is humbling to know you are in someone else's prayers. Even doubters appreciate that kind of reassurance. I waved my thanks, and Sirius and I made our way to the car, where we found Emily waiting patiently for us. I decided to reward that patience by taking her for a little walk. It hadn't been that long ago when she'd been left for dead on the streets of LA. Now she was taking her time sniffing those streets. I didn't rush her. As far as I was concerned, she had priority over my meeting with a supposed prophet.

"Guess what," I told her. "Pit bulls are now being used as K-9 officers throughout the country. In fact, I just read about two K-9 pitties who were rescues."

I hoped the trend would continue. Of the more than one million dogs euthanized in the US every year, almost half are pit bulls.

When we returned to the car, I searched out the right tune for the drive. Talking about Carrie Holder and the serpent in her garden had prompted Father Pat to comment, "Paradise lost."

I wasn't sure if he'd been referring to my deceased LA woman, or the Garden of Eden, or both, but it was reason enough to crank up Coldplay's "Paradise." There seemed to be a synchronicity between the lyrics and what was going on in my life, from a stormy night to a young woman's trying to find an elusive paradise.

Though it was a short drive along Sunset Boulevard to Gower, I decided upon a grand finale. Forty years before Coldplay's take, Joni Mitchell had sung her cautionary anthem of paradise lost. I called up "Big Yellow Taxi," and joined Joni in singing the song's refrain: "They paved paradise and put up a parking lot."

The huge and imposing wrought-iron gates loomed at the edge of the Church of the Gate's property. Now that I knew those gates wouldn't open, they looked different to me. The nearby entrance hadn't changed much since its movie studio days, save for the signage that identified the property and its production facilities as Ark Studios. At the time the church had bought the studio lot it had seemed like an odd purchase, but what some had thought was an expensive folly had proved to be an astute business move. The church now had its own dedicated facilities in which to produce its weekly broadcast, as well as a location that brought the Hollywood community to them. As most of their membership were "electronic churchgoers," the Church of the Gate liked to tout itself as the first e-church. Their dogma, such as it was, stressed "principals for living" espoused by the charismatic—some would even say messianic—Elijah.

As I drove up to the security gate, I turned off the music, but the irony of Joni's singing wasn't lost to me. The Church of the Gate promised a path to paradise, but the structure closest to me was one of the studio's massive parking lots.

With a wave of his hand, the security guard in the booth motioned me forward. Both dogs stuck their muzzles out to make their introductions, but he ignored them.

Unsmiling, he asked, "Your name, sir?"

I gave it, and he consulted his list. Once he found me, I was provided with a visitor's badge on a lanyard and advised as to where best to park. I was also told that it was against the rules for dogs to be walked anywhere on the grounds.

The entry gate lifted, and I drove through.

There had been a time when movie studios dominated the space along Gower and Sunset. Even during my lifetime in LA, the business had changed drastically. Huge studio lots now functioned much the way Ark Studios did—as a multi-use facility, offering up its space and production capabilities to a variety of renters. Judging from the notices and ads I'd seen, it was host to a constant stream of film screenings, rehearsals, and productions, as well as being home to the world headquarters of the Church of the Gate. One of the large soundstages on-site had been permanently set aside for church programming. Their weekly service was broadcast to audiences from 175 countries. Not far from that soundstage a new church had been built, but it was only available for special events and ceremonies. Detractors said the church served more as a set than as a house of worship. The real church was said to be in the soundstage. Incorporated into that space was a store selling Church of the Gate merchandise, including books, DVDs, and Elijah's self-help and inspirational audios.

Finding God, and enlightenment, was a big business. To help people do that, a food court had been built, with tenants like Starbucks and Subway.

I found a parking spot, then turned my attention to the dogs. "Everyone doing all right?" I asked.

My inquiry was met with wagging tails. I reached back, offering a hand to each of my companions. There is no better mood changer than dogs delighted to be in your company, and I spent a minute or two soaking that in before taking my leave of them.

The parking lot was filled mostly with cars, but there were also a few tour buses. Nearby, a group was just starting its tour. I decided to tag along. A smiling young woman who couldn't have been older than twenty-five was leading the tour. She wore a beige pencil skirt, a white blouse, and a blue blazer. Her name tag said *Sister Paula*. The new face of penitents, I thought.

"Many visitors are surprised that there's not a huge house of worship on the property," she said. "The reason is that what was built on these grounds isn't a church. It's a consecrated temple, open only for certain sacred rituals. As many of you know, before the Church of the Gate found its permanent home here, it utilized various spaces throughout Southern California, and beyond, to conduct services. Our founder, Elijah, still believes it's important to reach a growing and diverse audience. That's why some people refer to us as the first pop-up church."

That got some laughs from the dozen or so people taking the tour.

Sister Paula continued: "Elijah likes to point out that the earliest Christian services were not held in churches, but in homes." She pointed to a building in the distance. "Later, we'll get a better look at the temple, but as I explained, its interior won't be part of our tour."

A woman in the group asked, "Does the temple have a name?"

Sister Paula smiled. "Not officially," she said, "but it's commonly called the Wedding Chapel because some in our flock have had the privilege of being married there."

Even from a distance I could see that the so-called Wedding Chapel wasn't small. When I think of a chapel, Sidney Poitier and the movie *Lilies of the Field* comes to mind. This chapel was considerably larger than the one Poitier built for the nuns in the film. Poitier won an Oscar for his role as handyman Homer Smith, and his spiritual rendition of "Amen" has touched a lot of hearts over the years.

Amen, I remembered, *amen, amen, amen, amen, sing it over.* In my mind I did.

"We'll be proceeding now to a tour of the gardens," Sister Paula said, "and then from there to—"

If I wanted to avoid being late for my meeting, I didn't have time to smell the roses. I split off from the group, following signage that pointed the way to the administrative center, which turned out to be a modern-looking three-story building that seemed to have been repurposed and updated from a soundstage. As I made my approach, I was eyeballed by an armed guard who stood just inside its entrance. Just past the guard was a security gauntlet similar to those found in airports.

"Afternoon," said the guard. It sounded more like a statement than a greeting. I gave a little nod of agreement.

The guard was a muscled white man wearing a too-tight nylon jacket labeled *Security*. I would have bet dollars to cents that his prior work experience was as a club bouncer.

"What's the purpose of your visit?" he asked.

I pulled out my wallet, flashed my badge, and said, "I'm LAPD, here to conduct an interview. FYI, I'm carrying."

Neither my badge nor pronouncement reassured the guard. It seemed to do the opposite. He put his hand atop his holster, and with his free hand waved for assistance. A man carrying a clipboard appeared. He was also armed, but instead of wearing a nylon jacket, he had on a blue blazer. I guessed that meant he was the security supervisor. His name tag read *Sergeant Collins*.

"He says he's LAPD," said the guard.

Because I was still holding up my badge, I shook it in the direction of their faces and said, "Hello?"

My badge didn't seem to have the "open sesame" effect I was hoping for.

"He also says he's armed," said the guard.

"He is," I said.

Sergeant Collins asked, "Name?"

"Michael Gideon," I said.

He studied his clipboard, then nodded to the guard that I was on the list.

"You're here to see Sister Hannah?" he asked.

"I'm actually here to see Elijah."

"We'll need you to proceed through security," Sergeant Collins said. "At this time, you'll need to remove your belt and shoes, and empty your pockets. We'll also need you to put your firearm in the basket."

The point of doing all that after I had already announced that I was carrying a firearm eluded me, but with a shrug and a sigh I did as asked. I had a legal right to not relinquish my gun from my possession, but decided not to argue that point. I emptied my pockets and removed my shoulder holster, placing everything into a basket. A conveyer belt transported the basket, while I was directed to step through a metal detector where a female guard monitored my passage. After not setting off any alarms, I was met on the other side by the sergeant.

"Thank you, Detective," he said. "If you don't mind, we'll hold onto your firearm until you return from your meeting."

"I do mind," I said. "I'm on duty, and disarming myself would be a dereliction of that duty."

Without asking permission, I reached for my gun and holster and put them on.

Sergeant Collins didn't look happy. "I can assure you that your weapon will be secured in a safe."

"I can assure you it won't," I said, drawing my line in the sand. "I'm here on police business."

It was a stupid pissing match, but most are. Still, the supervisor did his best to save face.

"If you don't give us your firearm," he said, "you'll need to be escorted everywhere on this property by Officer Cronin." He nodded in the direction of my bouncer friend.

"Fine by me."

The rent-a-cop came and stood by my side, doing a lot of heavy breathing in and out of his mouth. The two of us weren't allowed to proceed until I officially signed in and was presented with yet another visitor's badge.

"This way," Officer Cronin said.

I followed him over to an elevator, which he had to activate with a security key. We rode in silence, if you didn't count his breathing, to the third floor, then walked down a deserted hallway to a reception area. Sitting behind the desk was an older woman who appeared to have taken fashion notes from Dana Carvey's Church Lady. She wore cat's-eye horn-rimmed glasses and a somber-colored sweater dress. Her name tag said *Darlene*, without a *Sister* preceding it. Her outfit, and her age, made me think she wasn't one of the penitents.

Officer Cronin announced me. "His name is Gideon and he's a cop. Tell Sister Hannah that I'll be accompanying him to their meeting because he refused to give up his gun."

"I'm armed and dangerous," I told Darlene.

Her expression was quintessential Church Lady, offering me an arched skeptical eyebrow. I was a little disappointed she didn't say, "Isn't that special."

Darlene turned her back to us and conducted a brief conversation over the phone. Then she turned back around and faced me. "Sister Hannah is ready to see you now, Detective Gideon. She is waiting for you in the conference room. If you'll go down this hallway, it's the third door on the right."

"Thank you," I said.

The guard moved in lockstep with me, but Darlene applied the brakes.

"Officer Cronin," she said, "Sister Hannah said there is no need for you to accompany the detective, and asked that you return to your post."

I coughed into my hand, which mostly managed to cover up my smile. On my own, I proceeded down the hallway. A dark-haired woman who looked to be around thirty greeted me at the entrance of the conference room.

"I'm Sister Hannah," she said with a hint of what's known as the NASCAR accent, and extended her hand.

After we shook, Sister Hannah asked me to have a seat. The conference room was decorated more like what you'd expect from the boardroom of a Fortune 500 company than a church. The centerpiece of the room was a large, single-slab black walnut conference table. I sat down in a leather swivel chair and resisted spinning about. What I couldn't resist was running my hand along the table's beautifully striated and grained wooden surface. The finish was smooth, and the natural colors were striking.

Sister Hannah took a seat across from me, and we took a moment to study the other's face. Many people look away from me so as to not appear overly interested in the scarring on my face that occurred when I walked through the fire with Ellis Haines. Sister Hannah didn't avert her glance, but looked back with dark brown eyes that were naturally highlighted by long eyelashes. She wasn't wearing a name tag, and her clothes were modern and colorful. Her stylish dress was shorter than I would have expected and didn't hide her long, athletic legs, which were further showcased by the high heels she was wearing.

"Brother Elijah and Sister Joan will be joining us shortly," she said.

"Sister Joan is Elijah's wife?" I asked.

She nodded.

"What is her full, secular name?" I asked.

"Amy Green," she said. "She chose the name Joan after Joan of Arc."

"And what is your birth name?" I asked.

"Annamae Buckley."

"Why did you choose the name Hannah?"

"Because that name means *grace* in Hebrew, something to which I aspire."

I aspired to being the kind of person my dogs think I am, but refrained from telling her that. "As far as I know," I said, "Carrie Holder didn't take on a new name."

"No, she didn't. The Church of the Gate does not require its penitents to do so, although most have made that choice."

"When we first talked on the phone," I said, "you mentioned that Sister Carrie had sent a picture to her coworkers and friends of a rattlesnake sunning out in the canyon near her home."

"It was a group text," Hannah confirmed.

"I would appreciate it if you sent me a screenshot with that text and everyone it went out to," I said, and gave her the number of my cell phone.

Hannah did as I asked, and a few seconds later a picture of a large diamondback rattlesnake was staring at me from the screen of my phone. The picture had been sent to eight people, along with Carrie's caption: *Guess what I found in my backyard?* I studied the names of those who had received the picture.

"Are all the recipients of this photo associated with the church?"

"Most," said Sister Hannah, "but not all."

"I'll need the names of your coworkers who were sent the picture."

"I'll be glad to provide that, Detective, although I must admit I don't understand your curiosity since we clearly know the cause of Sister Carrie's death."

"Sister Carrie's body is with the medical examiner-coroner's office," I said. "Until her autopsy is completed and the cause of her demise is definitively determined, it's my job to look into her death."

Sister Hannah didn't look happy, but neither did she offer an objection. She shifted in her seat and raised both hands to her chin, almost as if she were saying grace. An entreaty followed, but not to God.

"I'm hoping you can be—delicate—in your pursuit of answers," she said. "I fear there are many people who are—envious—of the success of Brother Elijah. They would love nothing more than to see his name tarnished. In fact, I'm hoping that the returned prophet doesn't have to be involved in your investigation."

"I'm afraid I'll need to ask him some questions," I said, "but I can assure you that I will not be discussing my investigation with anyone who's not associated with law enforcement."

Sister Hannah reluctantly nodded, then reached for her phone, found the contact she wanted, and called. "We're ready," she said.

If there was a reply, it was very brief. Two minutes later the door opened. An individual who I assumed was Sister Joan entered the room, followed by Elijah. Sister Hannah opened her mouth to make introductions, but Elijah spoke first.

"I am Brother Elijah," he said, "and this is my wife, Sister Joan."

It sounded strange hearing him say "my wife," followed by the word "sister." I was reminded of Faye Dunaway's line in *Chinatown*, when she said in rapid succession, "My sister, my daughter, my sister."

"Michael Gideon," I said.

"A good name," said Elijah. "Gideon led the Israelites to victory over the Midianites, and after that he became a judge renowned for his wisdom."

I nodded but didn't mention that, like everyone else in the room, mine was an assumed name. The only difference was that everyone else knew their birth names; I didn't.

The couple sat down. Elijah was flanked on both sides by the two women, their united front facing me. I had seen pictures of Elijah before. Most public figures never look as good as their publicity shots, and Elijah was no exception. The PR photos emphasized his long, dark locks, arching eyebrows, and piercing eyes. All those features had been enhanced by a good cosmetologist, not to mention cosmetic surgeon. Both he and his wife were pushing fifty, although they were clearly on a Dorian Gray regimen of nips and tucks, artful hair dye, and liberal applications of makeup and bronzer.

"Thank you for seeing me," I said.

Sister Joan broke her silence. She reminded me of another Joan—Joan Crawford—in appearance and bearing. "Both of us were devastated to hear of Sister Carrie's passing," she said. "She was an important member of our family."

"She was a paid employee of the church," I said. "Is that correct?"

Everyone nodded.

"And what was her salary?"

Husband and wife looked at one another. Elijah said, "I'm not certain."

"Ballpark," I said.

"Somewhere in the neighborhood of a hundred and fifty thousand dollars a year," he said. "But that figure doesn't include bonuses she received."

I refrained from whistling, but not from making it clear I thought that was a generous salary. "And free housing, is that right?"

"Not exactly free," said Joan. "She had to oversee church functions held at the residence."

I turned to Elijah and said, "You were the one who hired Carrie, is that correct?"

It was Sister Joan who answered. "We usually go along with the recommendations of our human resources director."

"Are you saying that's the case with Carrie?"

Joan didn't meet my eyes when she answered, "I really don't remember."

I could sense a lot of evasion going on at the table. That's not unusual. People dissemble or lie for any variety of reasons. I decided to push a little harder and insinuate there was a much broader investigation being conducted than there really was.

"Carrie had a bit of a checkered past," I said. "She worked at a strip club, where she was convicted of a misdemeanor. Were you aware of that?"

No one was quick to answer. It was Joan who finally spoke. "We knew about her past," she said. "The doctrine of our church is to forgive those who have transgressed. What impressed us most about Carrie was her theatrical experience. The weekly broadcast of our services is carefully choreographed and produced. Her dancing and singing abilities made her a featured performer."

I turned to Elijah. "Before starting your ministry, you were a filmmaker. Is that correct?"

"We both were," he said, gesturing to his wife. "Joan was with me from the first. The two of us did it all. In our productions, we were chief cooks and bottle washers."

"Yet I understand you struggled as a filmmaker."

"No one making documentaries expects to get rich."

I decided to reference something I had read about Elijah and the Church of the Gate. "Your friends quoted you as saying, 'Anyone who wants to make a fortune should start their own religion.'"

"If I ever did say that," Elijah said, "I'm sure it was spoken tongue in cheek."

It was an artful nondenial.

"Tell me about your relationship with Carrie," I said.

Mine was an open-ended question that could be interpreted any number of ways. What I didn't expect was for it to stump Elijah. His lower lip began to tremble, and it appeared as if he was fighting back tears and emotions.

Joan spoke for him. "As I said, Carrie was family."

I wanted to hear about that family, and to that end said, "We're actively looking at security tapes at the Bel Air home where Carrie lived, and are formulating a list of anyone who visited during the last week."

Joan turned her eyes to Hannah, who offered a small shake of her head. I interpreted the message.

"Although there are no security cameras at Carrie's home," I said, "all the neighbors have them, and we're gathering that footage for review."

Elijah sighed, and then rubbed his neck with his right hand.

"'What a tangled web we weave,'" he said, "'when first we practice to deceive.'"

He wiped a tear away from his face and turned his head right, then left, doing his best to offer a reassuring smile to the women sitting next to him.

"I'm sure you'll find footage of me making one or two visits to Carrie's house," he said.

"You had a personal relationship with her?"

He nodded.

"Detective Gideon assured me that he would be discreet in his investigation," said Hannah, reaching out a hand and placing it on Elijah's back.

"We'll count on your discretion, then," said Joan. "There are no sordid details here. I was aware of my husband's relationship with Carrie, just as I have been aware of his other relationships throughout the years. We keep no secrets from one another. His polyamorous lifestyle is an accepted part of the dynamics of our extended family."

Elijah nodded. His eyes were wet and red, but not enough for his makeup to run.

"Is there anything else I should know?" I asked.

No one admitted to anything. Jesus said the truth will set us free. What he didn't mention was how nothing is quite as elusive as getting to that truth.

CHAPTER EIGHT

CASTOR BEANS AND CURIOUS INCIDENTS

My interview with Elijah, Joan, and Hannah lasted the better part of an hour, and when I returned to the SUV, I decided to go over my notes while they were still fresh in my mind. There were few passersby to observe my review session, which was just as well, as Sirius and Emily acted as my sounding boards. No human offers as sympathetic an ear as does a dog, especially when you spice up your conversation with periodic doggie treats.

"I employed the tried-and-true method of my late father," I said, displaying my notepad and tapping where I had written the initials JG. Both dogs stared where I tapped. "When I use this notation, it signifies the name Jack Gideon and the interviewing technique he taught me when I was just a pup."

I had been fourteen or fifteen at the time, in the throes of my first love. When my father asked me about the object of my affection, I declared, "She's perfect in every way." Instead of challenging my declaration, my father merely said, "If you want to learn about her flaws, go tell her friends what you just told me."

At the time, I didn't do as he suggested, but his words always stayed with me. Eventually I began to employ them in interviews and interrogations.

"Humans don't like to speak ill of the dead," I told the dogs, "at least not initially. After letting everyone in the conference room portray Sister Carrie as a saint, I made a point of recapitulating their tributes right back to them."

The attention span of my audience was beginning to wane, so I reached for the snack bag. Their attentiveness was rekindled as I handed out some dried pieces of apple.

"That's when I began to hear that her character wasn't without flaws. Joan confessed that Carrie had an *artistic* temperament and sometimes chafed under her direction. In fact, Joan admitted that sometimes she had to ask Carrie to take her performances down a notch or two. Let me quote exactly what she said: 'There were a few rehearsals where I had to remind Sister Carrie that she wasn't performing the Dance of the Seven Veils.'"

I tapped that entry in my notepad. The dogs seemed to think that meant I was going to give them a treat; either that or their drools were a tactic to get a treat. It worked in their favor, and they inhaled my offering. I took a pause from oratory and made some notes. There was a method to my madness, or at least I liked to think there was. By repeating what had been said during the interview, I was able to recall my gut feelings at the time. After I finished my jots, I began talking again.

"When she mentioned the Dance of the Seven Veils," I said, "I was envisioning something exotic, erotic, and beguiling. Like when Salome performed her dance in front of Herod, and it so captivated the king that he promised her anything she wanted. Was Carrie's dancing enticing like that? Did it cross a line?"

I wrote down some more notes. Carrie had been a stripper. I wondered if there was any possibility that Elijah had seen her perform in that capacity prior to her employment at the church.

"The JG method is good about revealing undercurrents," I said. "When I was doing my premature canonizing, Hannah informed me that as much as Carrie loved performing, she was often late for rehearsals."

I consulted my notes—and my feelings. Hannah's words had been gentle enough, but at the same time disapproving of what sounded like a double standard on Elijah's part.

"Does the dog rule tell us anything?" I asked. It wasn't my father who taught me that stratagem, but Sherlock Holmes. He referred to it as the "curious incident of the dog in the night."

"Holmes noticed that the dog in question didn't bark while the victim was being murdered. From that, he deduced that the murderer was known to the dog."

If I was expecting my captive audience to cheer on the inspiration provided by one of their own, that didn't happen. I did get some tail wagging, though, when I passed each of them a treat.

"It's important to be looking for curious incidents when you talk to suspects," I said. "When I asked what Carrie's primary work duties were, I was told that in addition to performing at the weekly shows—I mean services—she also hosted fellowships at her home. Carrie played the role of hostess, usually with Elijah at her side.

"It was a very select *flock* that came to these fellowships," I added. "That was Elijah's word—flock. And when I think of a flock, what comes to mind is a fleecing."

That was the extent of my notes. I flipped through the pages, but nothing else—either said or unsaid—jumped at me.

"On the face of it," I said, "everyone was cooperating with me. They answered my questions, but in a cautious manner. Does that constitute a curious incident? People like to paint themselves in a good light, so that doesn't necessarily make them guilty."

Nor did it necessarily make them innocent. I didn't get a chance to tell the dogs that, because my phone began to ring. The display told me Ben Corning was calling.

I answered by saying, "I'd love for you to tell me you've had a huge breakthrough."

"Not as much as I'd love to be able to tell you that," he said, "but that's not the case. I'm calling with an update. Forensics has determined that the beans left in the gris-gris bag are castor beans."

"Castor beans?"

Corning didn't have a response, which I interpreted as a curious incident.

"What's your brain trust have to say about that?" I asked. "Wasn't castor oil that stuff with an awful taste that our grandparents were forced to swallow when they were kids? I seem to remember it was supposed to be a cure-all for anything that ailed you."

"I wouldn't know about that," said Corning. "I do know that our brain trust, as you called them, reported that castor beans are still used for medicinal and pharmaceutical purposes, but that's not what caught their attention. Nowadays, castor beans have a much more notorious connotation. They're used to create ricin."

I had heard of ricin but was short on specifics. "That's some kind of poison, right?"

"It's a toxin that's extracted from the pulp of castor beans. One castor bean can produce enough purified toxin to kill a thousand people, depending on the delivery system, be it powder, a mist, or a pellet."

"Tell me it's hard to manufacture."

"I wish I could," he said.

I looked for any bright spot in the darkness, and found a straw to grasp at. "The killer has been targeting one person at a time."

"We hope that continues, especially if he's considering using ricin as a means to that end."

That wasn't encouraging. "From the first, we've been playing catch-up with this joker," I said. "What's the plan for getting ahead of the curve?"

"Our behavioral analysis team believe a new card pattern was established with this latest death, and that there will be a nine-nine association with the next victim. Unfortunately, the nine-nine card combination is rife with Texas Hold 'Em nicknames."

"Let's hear them," I said.

Corning sighed before responding. "Some poker players call it Agent Ninety-Nine, because Agent Ninety-Nine was a female secret agent in *Get Smart*. On the TV show, she was played by Barbara Feldon; in the movie, it was Anne Hathaway. That leaves us with potential victims named Barbara and Anne."

"What else?" I asked.

"Another nickname is the German Virgin," he said.

I thought about that for a moment, and then said with equal parts German and disgust, "*Nein, nein.*" No, no.

"*Ja,*" said Corning. "There's also the nickname *neener neener*. And we haven't even talked about the number nine itself. In card circles there are those who refer to it as a nine-millimeter, a niner, and a pothook."

I started thinking about all the possibilities available for selecting a target, or dispatching a victim.

"The killer is offering up a rigged game," I said. "There are so many variables that it would be next to impossible to try and predict where, when, and who will be the next target."

"That's pretty much what we concluded," said Corning. "We'll continue to make an effort to extrapolate likely victims, but our primary focus will be the examination of the crime scenes. We want to be sure that we haven't overlooked anything. To that end, we'll need your help."

I knew where this was going, even though I pretended ignorance.

"I'm so busy that I've only had time to give a cursory look at everything you sent. When I get up to speed . . ."

He interrupted me. "We need you to engage Haines on this most recent killing, and we need you to do it A-sap."

"I'm jammed up."

"This isn't a request," he said. "I got my orders from up high, and now I'm passing them along to you."

"Haines is going to take a hell of a lot more than he gives. That's who he is."

"Have you made arrangements to see him yet?"

I didn't answer, which was answer enough.

"Haines and the killer seem to have devised some kind of system to communicate," Corning said, "even though we haven't been able to figure out what that is. It could only help our efforts if you got Haines talking about the murders. Maybe he'll let something slip."

My world seemed to be growing smaller, and the threats in it larger. Sighing, I promised, "I'll set up the meeting."

"For tomorrow?"

"I'll do my best," I said.

The words didn't match my true thoughts. They weren't even close.

Because Seth had suggested I look at the symbolic gateways of the Church of the Gate, I decided to take the dogs on a walk. I conveniently forgot the warning given at the gate about dogs not being allowed on the property, nor did I pay any heed to the signs reiterating the dog prohibition.

The three of us closed in on the looming gates, which dwarfed everything around them. They were there to be noticed. There was signage on both sides of the wrought iron referencing other famous gates. According to what I read, the Buland Darwaza in India, also known as the Gate of Victory, had been built in 1572 and was the tallest gateway in the world.

"No mention of the Black Gate of Mordor," I said.

Tolkien's *The Lord of the Rings* was a favorite book of mine, as well as a favorite movie series. Aragorn had rallied his troops in front of those insidious and foreboding gates. I had seen the film so many times the line Viggo Mortenson cries out was emblazoned in my memory.

"'A day may come when the courage of men fails, when we forsake our friends and break all bonds of fellowship, but it is *not* this day.'"

The dogs did not seem to be as inspired as had the soldiers of Gondor and Rohan. They were probably considering the source, which was definitely not Aragorn.

Seth had talked about the Hindi and Buddhist influences on the gate, and how multiheaded snakes could be seen amidst the wrought iron. Now that I was looking for them, the naga seemed to be everywhere. Most of the snakes appeared to be giant cobras with spread hoods.

Poisonous snakes, I thought. Was that just another coincidence?

My musing was interrupted by a utility cart being pushed pedal to the metal along the pathway. The driver was the guard who had initially stopped me at the entrance of the administrative building. Judging from Officer Cronin's scowl, he was still smarting from our encounter. I should have known that he was likely monitoring my movements through security cameras.

His golf cart came to an abrupt stop only feet from where we were standing. As he exited the cart he tried to pull off the swagger of a hard-ass, but that wasn't easy given his mode of transportation.

"This is private property," he said, "and just because you're a cop doesn't mean you can violate the rules."

"Which rules are those?" I asked.

"No dogs allowed," he said. "You've passed multiple signs alerting you to that fact. And I confirmed that you were told that when you entered the property."

"These aren't civilian dogs," I said, "but LAPD K-9 officers." That was half true.

"You have proof of that?" he said.

His aggressive tone of voice, and the intimidating posture of his body, put Sirius on alert. My usually affable partner growled. When he goes from Dr. Jekyll to Mr. Hyde, you had better take notice.

"You can ascertain the bona fides of the dog voicing his displeasure with you by running the name Sirius through a search engine," I said. "You'll find Sirius is a recipient of the K-9 Liberty Award, the highest distinction the department offers. And while you're checking on that, you can also look up California Penal Code six hundred, which states that anyone interfering with or obstructing a police dog in its duties can be imprisoned for up to a year and fined up to a thousand dollars. That's for a minor offense. A major offense means a bigger fine and more jail time."

Officer Cronin backed off. I think that had more to do with Sirius's growling than with my quoting the penal code.

"Next time," he said, "you need to report the presence of these—officers—before you take them around the property."

"Will do," I said.

As Officer Cronin was positioning his big body back into the golf cart, I asked, "How long have you worked here?"

He didn't look happy about continuing our conversation, but reluctantly answered my question: "About a year."

"Then you knew Sister Carrie?"

He nodded. "She actually helped me get my job here."

That interested me, as did his body language, which told me that he regretted having volunteered that. I made a guess as to why that was.

"You probably knew one another from the club where she danced," I said. "You worked there as a bouncer, right?"

Officer Cronin looked around, as if afraid someone might overhear what we were saying, before giving me a tentative nod.

"Carrie was arrested at that club," I said. "I know she pled to a misdemeanor."

"There was a misunderstanding," he said.

"That often seems to be the case," I said.

He wasn't sure if I was being sarcastic or sympathetic. I wasn't sure either.

Officer Cronin decided clarification was in order. "The way I heard it, vice, or the ABC, made a mountain out of a molehill. They said Carrie knowingly served alcohol to two underage guys. The thing was, Carrie knew these guys from drama classes, and she said they'd lied to her about their ages."

"So she wasn't pleading down from a prostitution charge?"

Officer Cronin shook his head. "No way," he said. "Carrie wasn't like that. She was dancing to pay for college."

"You know about her and Elijah?" I asked.

He looked away, not wanting to meet my eyes. "I don't know anything for sure."

"How long ago did you work with Carrie at the club?"

"It was a couple of years back."

"Carrie have any problems at work other than when she was arrested?"

Another shake of the head. "She liked to dance."

"She enjoyed stripping?"

"That's not what I said. Most of the girls at the club worked one hustle or another. You could tell Carrie was a real dancer, not someone doing the bump and grind for dollars. She moved to the music."

"Did Elijah frequent the club?"

The question made Officer Cronin even jumpier than he already was. "If he did, I never saw him."

Then he said, "I got to go."

He made a U-turn with his electric cart and rode away. It didn't have quite the effect of the roar of an engine, patching out and leaving a trail of burning rubber.

CHAPTER NINE

KILLER DAFFODILS

As the dogs and I walked back to the car, I heard the *ping* of a text message. I was quick on the draw in grabbing for the phone. My hope was that Lisbet had opened our lines of communication, but the phone's display showed the text had been sent by Detective Andrea Charles of the Las Vegas Metropolitan Police Department. Her message was brief: *Might have something. Call when u can.*

I settled the dogs inside the car before making that call. Andrea was working with me trying to tie Ellis Haines to murders that we suspected he had committed in Las Vegas. Haines ostensibly went there to play poker, but my belief was that Southern California hadn't been his only killing grounds.

Detective Charles and I were still working our leads off the books because we hadn't wanted Haines to catch wind of what we were doing. Somehow, he had. The last I'd visited Haines he had gone ballistic on me, acting as if I'd been plotting his murder. In some ways, I had been. Nevada is a capital punishment state, and with Haines trying to appeal his California conviction, I wanted to make sure he had no wiggle room to ever rejoin society.

As might be expected, Haines hadn't taken kindly to the Nevada investigation. What complicated the situation was the presence of the All-In Killer. With this admirer—or disciple, or perhaps even collaborator—on the outside, Haines had a new weapon at his disposal. It made no sense for Haines to help the Feds in their investigation. Why would he do anything to derail the efforts of someone targeting me? For Haines, it was a case of the enemy of my enemy is my friend. I'd tried explaining that to the FBI without success.

"Mine is not to question why," I muttered, "mine is but to do or die."

Then I added something that wasn't in Tennyson's poem: "Not."

Andrea picked up on the first ring and offered the greeting, "Hollywood."

Whenever we talk, I try not to feel old. Andrea's detective badge was still shiny, and she hung around in youthful circles I'd long ago put in my rearview mirror. That didn't mean this codger didn't try to keep up.

"'Hollywood'?" I said, then threw one of the phrases she'd taught me right back at her: "Aw naw."

She laughed, probably because of my ineptness at incorporating African-American slang into my speech. Andrea had told me that when you called someone "Hollywood," it meant that they thought they were all that. As for "aw naw," that was a newer term for *no way.*

"So, I've been making lots of inquiries about Bad Weather," Andrea said, using her nickname for Haines. "He's screepy."

Scary and creepy. "Tell me something I don't know," I said.

"Carol Shipley's friends, coworkers, and neighbors only have vague memories of our creep," she said.

Belatedly, we had linked Haines to Shipley, a woman stabbed to death in what was originally believed to have been a robbery. Most people survive knife wounds; Shipley's cuts had been more like surgical incisions designed to dispatch her with maximum efficiency. The killer had known what he was doing.

But there was no evidence to connect Haines to the scene. Our best witness was a cocktail waitress who remembered Haines and Shipley being in one another's company on several karaoke nights. The waitress had remembered Haines's singing—and his selections. His song of choice had been Radiohead's "Creep." Her ID of Haines seemed solid; she had chosen his picture out of a six-pack, a photo lineup of six possible suspects.

"He's usually been good about blending into the background," I said, "the affable, anonymous stranger."

Piercing his cloak of invisibility had been tough sledding for us.

"I think we caught a break yesterday," she said. "Two of Carol's friends also identified photos of Haines, and independent of one another they said that she had introduced him by the name Dell."

"'Dell'?"

"I'm thinking Carol never knew his real name. And I'm sure along with his false identity came all sorts of other frontin'."

"I think we can bank on that," I said. "A pseudonym makes sense. Ellis isn't a common first name. But he would have wanted a name that sounded something like his own so that it would be second nature for him to respond to it. El and Dell rhyme."

"Let's not forget *hell*," she said, which got a laugh of endorsement from me.

"You didn't happen to get lucky on either of them remembering what surname Dell used?"

"Nothing so far."

"Someone might yet surprise us," I said. "You're doing great. Let's build this one brick at a time."

"You think we should still keep this on the down low?" she asked.

"For your own sake," I said, "I do. Haines knows I've enlisted help, but I'm hoping that's as far as it goes. For now, I want your profile staying low to no."

"I'll try," she said, "but I don't think we'll be able to keep the investigation under wraps for much longer, especially with me asking the lab to review the Shipley crime scene evidence."

"You can decide who needs to know," I said, "and impress upon them that mum's the word."

"Will do," she said. "Have you had a chance to study Haines's phone records during the times he was in Las Vegas?"

"I have," I said. "Without exception, every time he visited Sin City his cell phone use was almost nonexistent. I found that revealing."

Detective Charles was spared the story of Sherlock Holmes and his "curious incident." After all, the dogs had already heard it. I cut to the chase.

"That says to me that Haines used a burner phone whenever he came to town," I said.

"Why would he be doing that if he wasn't up to no good?"

"Why indeed?" I said.

"We're going to get this MF."

"Amen," I said. I liked her adamancy. "Let's keep gathering nails for his coffin."

"Uh-huh," she said.

"Even before you texted me," I said, "I was going to call you. It's likely that tomorrow I'll be having a face-to-face with Haines. Anything you want me to ask him?"

"I thought you'd closed down that shop."

"I had," I said. "The Feds reopened it through good old blackmail. They threatened to take me out of the All-In Killer loop if I didn't talk to Haines."

"Shit," she said. "Don't they know we're supposed to be playing on the same team?"

"I reminded them of that, but it didn't seem to help. I think the FBI's motto is 'What's yours is ours, but what's mine is mine.'"

"That sounds like my last boyfriend."

"In case you hadn't heard," I said, "the All-In Killer struck again the day before yesterday. I've been sworn to secrecy, so I can't give you details other than to say it was ugly."

"There's a case of that going around," she said.

"I won't be asking any Las Vegas questions of Haines," I said. "I think that activated his radar last time."

"Don't worry," she said. "I'll stay in stealth mode."

"You do that," I said. "And happy hunting."

"You too," she said, and then added, "Call me after your meeting with Bad Weather."

I promised her that I would.

The sun was high in the sky. It was one of those June days that seemed reluctant to end. I was glad darkness wouldn't descend until after eight o'clock. The way things were going, I would need every minute of light that the day offered me.

I was on the schedule to volunteer at Angie's Rescues. As tempting as it was to reschedule, I didn't want to no-show at the last minute. Besides, staying busy kept me from ruminating, or at least that was the plan.

Lisbet still hadn't called or left a message, and her silence was preying on my mind. I decided to bite the bullet.

"Call Lisbet on cell," I announced to my phone.

My electronic genie complied, and Lisbet's phone rang four times before her recording began playing. When the beep sounded and I was supposed to leave a message, I was at a loss as to what I should say. After a moment's silence, I disconnected the call. My excuse was that I didn't want to bother her if she was busy.

I didn't play any music on the drive. I probably should have, if only to mask my sighs. The dogs seemed to take my cue and were more restless than usual. At the moment, none of us had a good outlet for our angst. My sex excels at denial, but even I knew something was amiss on the home front.

When we arrived at the shelter, Sirius was shaking with excitement. Emily was shaking as well, but I was pretty sure for a different reason. She had been a rescue at the same shelter before we opened our home to her. I didn't know all the details of her early life, but I knew enough of them. Emily had suffered unspeakable abuse, but had somehow never lost the sweetness at her core. With each passing day, she was becoming the dog she was always meant to be.

I told Sirius to relax, and spent a little time reassuring Emily. Gradually her anxiety lessened, and when she appeared to be sufficiently comforted, we left her in the car. It didn't take long for Sirius to find Angie, a big hound mix. The two dogs had the run of the facility and bounded off together.

After signing in at the front desk, I checked the duty log. Next to my name was a sticky note asking me to go and see Heather. Before I could ask where she was, the desk attendant volunteered, "Heather is in the quarantine area with one of the new dogs."

I waved my thanks. Dogs and cats that were new to the shelter each had their own special area. I found Heather Moreland squatting down inside a kennel, talking to what looked to be an older salt-and-pepper wiry-haired terrier mix. A handwritten placard on the door identified the dog as Cricket.

Heather looked up at me and smiled. Every time I saw Heather, the smile seemed to come more easily to her. Like Emily, she had not only survived circumstances that might have killed the less resilient, but had thrived. The no-kill shelter she had established was the ultimate story of her having made lemonade from lemons.

"I'm hoping you'll have better luck than I've been having with Cricket," she said. "Even though Dr. Misko has her on anti-anxiety meds, they don't seem to be helping as much as we'd like. She's been hiding in the corner and hasn't been interested in food and drink. I think she misses her brother and her dad."

"Where are they?"

"C-R-O-C-K-E-T died," Heather said, spelling the dog's name, "and her human is in the hospital. Cricket got lucky, although it was touch-and-go. That luck won't last, though, if she decides not to live."

"What happened to all of them?"

"I don't know what happened to Cricket's human, other than that he's old. Dr. Misko suspects that Cricket and C-R-O-C-K-E-T probably ingested some kind of poison. The dogs were brought in by a neighbor who saw them having seizures in their yard. He then found that Cricket's human, a Mr. Carter, collapsed inside the house."

While Heather talked, she continued to gently rub Cricket's fur. The dog was staring at me. It seemed to me that Cricket was hoping that I might change into the human she so wanted to see.

"Is there a Mrs. Carter?" I asked.

"I was told she died a few years ago. For Cricket's sake, if nothing else, I'm hoping Mr. Carter survives. It's so hard to find homes for older dogs."

"You want me to take over for you?"

"That would be great."

I opened the door. "Hello, Cricket," I said. "I know I'm a poor substitute for Heather, and especially for your dad, but if you ask my dogs, they'll tell you I'm pretty good in the scratching department."

As Heather stood, I took a knee and let Cricket sniff my extended hand. After I passed the smell test, I began to gently massage her old joints.

"You've got the touch," said Heather.

"I wish that was enough." I spoke with the kind of dulcet tones that only manifested themselves in the presence of dogs.

"Cricket's house is in Sherman Oaks," said Heather.

There was a hopeful tone in her voice that was meant for me and not Cricket. I didn't want to adopt another dog, and was afraid that was what Heather was hinting at. Luckily, that wasn't the case.

"Since you and Cricket are neighbors," she said, "I'm wondering if you could have a talk with Mr. Carter's next-door neighbor, a man named Schmitt, and also take a walk through the neighborhood. It would be in lieu of working here this afternoon, of course."

"I'm glad to do the walk and talk," I said, "but why?"

"Mr. Schmitt said that Cricket and her brother haven't been the only dogs in the neighborhood to fall ill. According to him, at least two other dogs on their street became violently sick. I suspect something is in bloom, or the dogs have found a food source that's poisonous."

"That sounds likely," I said, "but I don't know what good I would be since I don't know which plants are poisonous and which aren't."

"If you could use your phone to snap some photos of the neighborhood plants and send them to me, I can identify the likely suspects. Most people have no idea that their landscaping can be a murderers' row for their dogs."

"Do you have a particular suspect in mind?"

"There are all sorts of potential culprits out there," she said. "Certain crocuses, tulips, azalea, oleander, larkspur, sago palms, belladonna . . . even daffodils."

"Not daffodils," I said. "Say it ain't so."

"You like daffodils?" she said, sounding surprised.

My joke hadn't been helped by the soothing tone of speech that I'd adopted in Cricket's presence. "I don't even know what daffodils look like," I admitted.

"They're usually trumpets of yellow," Heather said. "But like I said, don't worry about identifying any of the plants. Just snap some pictures as you walk along the street. I can't imagine an old man and his old dogs ventured too far from their home."

"I'll take your pictures," I promised, "but before doing that I'll spend some time with Cricket."

CHAPTER TEN

PRETTY LITTLE FLOWERS

The short time I spent with Cricket seemed to get her a little way out of the darkness, but she was still a long way from adjusting to life without her pack. I hoped her human would survive. Without him in the picture, I didn't think she would have the will to live.

Heather sent over a relief caretaker to be with Cricket, so I went in search of Sirius. I'd been forwarded Walt Schmitt's telephone number and address, and had a general familiarity with the neighborhood in which he lived. Cricket's street was about two miles west of my home, and not too far from the border with Encino.

"Playtime's over," I announced to Sirius.

He and Angie were recreating in the small park-like setting off the pathway leading to what was referred to as the playground. Both dogs came over to me. I extended a hand to Angie, and she took a long sniff. With her extraordinary sense of smell, I wondered what information she divined. Our meet and greet was a short one. Without even a backward look, Angie took off for parts unknown. Heather had made sure the property was fenced to rein in her charges—especially Angie, who always wanted to go where her nose led her.

Sirius and I rejoined Emily in the car. Before driving away, I phoned Walt Schmitt. After identifying myself and my connection with Heather, I told him that I would soon be in his neighborhood and asked if he could spare a few minutes to talk.

"That's fine," he said, "except I'm out of the house right now. I should be back home in about an hour. That work with you?"

I told him that it would work just fine, and that I would see him then.

One of my guilty pleasures was taping all the vet shows on television and binge-watching them when time permits. A continuing motif when it came to dog ailments was that they often ate what they shouldn't, everything from fishing lures to pantyhose. Biting off more than they should chew sometimes proved life-threatening, with the biggest offenders being puppies, who were known to gnaw on and ingest whatever they could. Cricket and Crocket certainly didn't fit that profile, nor were terriers known to be the canine vacuum cleaners that some breeds are.

I tried to remember what I could from my television veterinary education. When dogs eat poisonous plants, the symptoms can manifest in lots of ways—vomiting, diarrhea, seizures, high temperatures, and comas and/or death. Heather had mentioned Cricket's having suffered seizures. Judging from the shaved patches on her body, it seemed likely that Dr. Misko had used IVs to flush out the toxins.

When my wife, Jenny, and I had first moved to Sherman Oaks, the area had been considered a nice middle-class burb. Buying our house had been a stretch, even with both our salaries, but our leap of faith had gotten us what was supposed to be the home of our dreams. If Jenny had lived, she would have been shocked to see today's house prices. The only thing that makes Sherman Oaks prices look reasonable is what it costs to buy in West LA.

The neighborhood is known for its "birdhouse" ranch homes that were built by William Mellenthin, as well as other builders who imitated the look. A semi-custom Mellenthin birdhouse has a pitched roof with a prominently built-in dovecote or cupola, diamond-paned windows, and high-beamed ceilings. The Mellenthin homes have withstood the test of time, with their exterior look carefully preserved throughout the area.

From its inception, Sherman Oaks was designed with lots of cul-de-sacs. Cricket's home was on one of them. As I drove along, I could see roughly half the homes on the street consisted of well-kept birdhouses.

I parked on the street. Even if Walt Schmitt's ETA was accurate, there was still half an hour before he'd return. In his absence, I decided to walk around and do a looksee, as well as take the pictures that Heather had requested.

The dogs and I got out of the car in front of the home where Cricket lived. Mack Carter, I had confirmed, was still in the ICU at St. Joseph Medical Center in Burbank. The Carter home wasn't as well kept as most of the residences on the cul-de-sac. It was ranch style, but not a birdhouse. A pine tree out front had caused the front walkway to lift and crack in a number of spots. There was a layer of pine needles covering the small lawn, which seemed to be equally divided between grass and weeds, but I wasn't one to judge; my own lawn has pretty much that same ratio.

The house was in need of TLC. I suspected its deferred maintenance extended back to the death of Mrs. Carter. Speaking from personal experience, I know that without "honey do" lists most men are blind to what needs upkeeping. The front of the house had long ago been painted a robin's-egg blue with white window trim, but now those colors were faded and chipping, and the fascia was showing the black discoloration of dry rot. Waiting for God seemed to be the old man's plan.

It was possible that the interior of the house was also suffering from long neglect. Mold might have made Carter and his dogs sick, but that didn't explain why other dogs on the cul-de-sac had become ill. With Sirius and Emily on leashes, we walked through the front yard. I multitasked with my phone, using it to both snap pictures and identify the foliage I was seeing. It probably would have been easier had I downloaded a plant-identification app, but Google served in place of Carl Linnaeus. I didn't stop to smell the roses—there weren't any at the Carter house anyway—but I did get a primer on botany.

The dogs didn't seem particularly excited by any of the plants they encountered, nor did they exhibit any desire to chew on any of them. We came across two potential datura plants whose white flowers bore some resemblance to what was pictured on my phone, but what I was seeing could also could have been some kind of lily. According to Wikipedia, datura, or jimsonweed, was a powerful hallucinogen and deliriant. The article also warned that eating it could be fatal.

There was a weathered gate with rusted hinges at the side of the house. Beyond the gate was a weed-infested gravel pathway that might have once served as a dog run. I tried to work open the gate, but it was fused shut. With the backyard temporarily denied us, the dogs and I walked back to the sidewalk, and then continued along with our garden tour of the street. The next house down had a front yard that mostly consisted of beds with colored pea gravel, but at the side of the yard I saw some familiar flowers of yellow, pink, and red. Lantana is a common sight in Southern California, despite its being potentially fatal to dogs. It seemed that wherever we turned there were potential dangers for unsuspecting animals. It was a jungle out there.

"'Lions, and tigers, and bears,'" I said. Sirius and Emily looked up, and I added, "'Oh my.'"

The landscaping in the home two doors down from the Carters' looked to have been designed to discourage canine visitors. There was a fence that extended along the front of the property, with the additional barrier of thorny natal plums. At the base of those plants was a white powder that looked like baking soda, and all through the shrubbery there was the pervasive smell of vinegar. I'd encountered baking soda and vinegar before. They were supposed to be a deterrent to animals, but Sirius must not have gotten that memo. He raised his leg and took aim at one of the natal plums.

The three of us came to the end of the cul-de-sac and then continued along on the other side of the street. We walked by two residences before encountering another home where dogs were clearly *canis non grata*. Along the edge of a dry creek that traveled the length of the front yard were several signs. One of them looked like a scarred scratching post and read, *Beware of Attack Cat!* On the other side of the creek was a second sign that read, *All Visitors Must Be Approved by My Cat!*

As I scanned the yard looking for toxic plants, I suddenly became aware of the movement of curtains from inside the living room. An older woman, her arms akimbo, glowered at the three of us. I waved at her. She didn't return the wave, but my attempt to be friendly didn't go unnoticed.

"I think Marjorie is giving you what she calls *catitude*," said a voice from the next yard.

I turned to the cat woman's neighbor, a tall woman wearing cotton coveralls. She lifted her sun hat, ran her hand through her short gray hair, and looked at me with unconcealed curiosity. In one hand she was carrying a gardening basket; in the other she held hand pruners.

"'Catitude'?" I asked. "I've always been more of a believer in latitude."

The dogs and I approached the woman. Sirius had noticed her pruners and was taking a cautionary approach, while looking to me for his cues.

"I'm Patricia Gaspar," she said, "captain of our neighborhood watch. Who are you?"

I'd noticed that at least half the homes on the cul-de-sac had neighborhood watch signs in their windows warning potential bad guys that they were being monitored.

"I guess you could say I'm with the neighborhood watch as well," I said, showing her my wallet badge. "Detective Michael Gideon, LAPD."

"Are you here responding to the complaint that I took up with Captain Hill?"

I knew Hill by reputation. He was one of the captains at the Van Nuys Community Police Station. "What complaint is that?" I asked.

"There was a young, suspicious-looking Hispanic male who was circulating flyers along our street," she said. "I suspected him of casing the neighborhood."

"Is that so?"

"I questioned him," she said, "but he didn't even speak English. That, or he didn't want to speak English."

That, I thought, or he couldn't get a word in edgewise. I suspected Patricia Gaspar was a regular caller to Captain Hill and the Van Nuys Community Police Station.

"What kind of flyers was he passing out?" I asked.

"They were for a paving company."

"Was it a legitimate business?"

"I called the number and talked to someone who said they worked at that business, but I don't know how legitimate they are. And that doesn't mean their laborer wasn't casing the neighborhood anyway. Besides, what he was doing was illegal."

"What was his crime?"

"He was putting leaflets into mailboxes. As you know, it is against the law for anyone to put anything in a mailbox other than a US Postal Service employee."

I wanted to quote from Ebenezer Scrooge and ask whether there were still workhouses, but instead asked, "Did you contact the US Postal Service?"

"I did," she said. "They promised to communicate with the paving company and tell them to cease and desist."

"Let's hope they didn't send a letter," I said. "It might have gotten lost in the mail."

Gaspar did not appear to be amused.

"I observed you taking pictures while you were walking your dogs, Detective Gideon," she said. "What is your interest in our neighborhood?"

By her imperious attitude, she seemed to think that being captain of her neighborhood watch meant that she outranked me. I was tempted to disabuse her of that notion, but decided to answer her question.

"From what I understand," I said, "there's been a spate of sick dogs in this neighborhood. One of those dogs died and another is very ill. I'm here trying to determine what might have poisoned the dogs, and to that end I was documenting potentially toxic plants."

"That doesn't sound like police business," she said.

"I'm here on my own time doing a favor for a friend of mine who runs a local shelter."

"And which shelter is that?"

I didn't feel like answering directly. "The shelter that's housing a sick dog named Cricket. Unfortunately, Cricket's brother didn't survive."

Ms. Gaspar didn't commiserate. "If those dogs ate something they shouldn't have, I'm not surprised. On too many occasions they've ventured out on their own and soiled the neighborhood."

"I imagine you talked to Mr. Carter about that," I said.

"Oh, I did. Mr. Carter seems to think that because he's lived in this neighborhood for more than fifty years, he's exempt from following rules."

"How long have you lived on this block?" I asked.

"My late husband and I moved here almost eight years ago."

I wondered if dying had been a relief for the late Mr. Gaspar.

"If you need to look at my yard," she said, waving her pruners in the direction of her house, "make sure you keep your animals on the pathway. And don't let your male dog lift his leg like he did at the Oakleys'."

"Troublemaker," I told Sirius.

My partner knew from my tone that he wasn't being taken to task. Sirius was on alert, still mindful of the pruners the woman was holding. The two of us had done countless training sessions on disarming the bad guys, and the sharp pruners in Gaspar's hands registered as a potential weapon.

"It's okay," I told him.

Sirius relaxed a little but stayed close to my side as we made our way up the walkway. Under the dictionary definition of *perfectly groomed*, there should have been a picture of Patricia Gaspar's front yard and its profusion of carefully cultivated colors and scents. The oleander hedges on both sides of her property were awash in blooms. Gaspar seemed to think that my interest in her landscaping was an invitation to lecture.

"I like the ornamental trees," she said. "What you're looking at there is an ornamental plum, and over there are an ornamental pear and apple."

I was more interested in her flower beds. Even for a nongardener like me, the abundance of colorful flowers couldn't help but be appreciated. I wasn't the only admirer. Hummingbirds were seeking out the nectar in the flowers. Several of them were vying to feed, and none believed in holding patterns. The sky was abuzz with dueling aces and dive-bombing. Mrs. Gaspar took notice of the fly-by activity going on around us.

"I never thought I'd have to wear armor in my own yard," she said. "I had hoped to be able to work my garden in peace by hanging up a feeder."

Her eyes went to a hummingbird feeder hanging from one of her ornamental trees.

"It's empty," I said.

"I'll have to remedy that," she said.

I turned my head back to her garden beds. "I don't know too much about flowers," I said. "What do you have planted here?"

She was pleased to educate me. "Over there are foxgloves, along with columbine and daylilies. Then lupine and hollyhocks and poppies."

The memory of green-skinned Margaret Hamilton portraying the Wicked Witch of the West came to mind. Standing over her crystal ball, the witch had cast her spell while muttering, "Poppies, poppies."

I snapped some pictures of the flowers, and then spoke into my phone and called upon Google to retrieve an article I'd been reading that included pictures of poisonous plants common to Southern California.

"I was afraid of that," I said. "Those very attractive trumpet-like blossoms on your foxgloves are poisonous, as are the leaves and seeds of your lupine. The *poppies* aren't good for *puppies*, either, but at least they're not potentially fatal."

The neighborhood watch captain didn't look pleased at my pronouncement, or maybe it was my alliteration. "That is why an ounce of prevention is worth a pound of cure," she said. "Responsible pet owners don't need to worry about their animals encountering poisonous plants. By not allowing pets to roam the streets, there's no fear of them getting poisoned. As you can see, my planter beds are well away from the sidewalk."

"I'm not suggesting it's your problem," I said. "I'm just looking for potential causes as to why the dogs on this street have fallen ill."

"If those dogs got into something they shouldn't have, it's the fault of their owners. Dogs should not be trespassing in yards other than their own."

"Was that a problem with Mr. Carter's dogs?"

"On multiple occasions I found his dogs digging up my yard. And I wasn't the only one. If you ask Marjorie, she'll tell you that those dogs were neighborhood menaces. And the Oakleys"—she pointed to the home with the baking soda and vinegar—"would tell you the same."

A Ford F-150 truck passed by and turned into a driveway just beyond where I'd parked. Walt Schmitt was home, and I was glad for an excuse to get away.

"Thank you for your time," I said. "I need to go talk with Mr. Schmitt."

She nodded. "I'll be here gardening should you have any more questions, or need to take any more pictures."

I kept the dogs on a tight leash as we made our way down the front walkway. We crossed the street—I hoped Mrs. Gaspar wouldn't report me for jaywalking—and managed to catch Schmitt just as he was about to enter his house.

"I'm Michael Gideon," I said. "We talked on the phone earlier."

Schmitt turned away from his door. From inside the house loud barking could be heard, prompting Schmitt to yell, "Shut up, Barney." The two of us shook hands. Schmitt looked to be around fifty. His denim shirt was untucked, and his jeans looked worn through work, and not as a fashion statement.

"Nice to meet you," he said. "Sorry I ran a little later than I thought."

"No problem," I said. "It allowed me the opportunity to walk the neighborhood."

Schmitt looked across the street to where Patricia Gaspar was working in her garden, as well as not so surreptitiously observing our every movement. "Yeah," he said, "I guess you already met *mi capitán*."

"She seems to be a stickler for the rules."

"I'll say." And then he must have decided that he'd sounded too enthusiastic. "But to her credit, she's willing to do the organizing that no one else in the neighborhood has the time or inclination to do. And she does make great cookies, even if they do come with a price."

"What do you mean?"

"I'm just saying that when she drops off cookies, they usually come with a request to do something or other."

"There's nothing more expensive than something free," I said.

"You're right about that."

"Anyway," I said, "I'm here to try and figure out what happened to Cricket and Crocket. From what I was told, they weren't the only dogs on this street affected by some mysterious illness."

Schmitt nodded, and jerked his thumb in the direction of his own house. "One of them was mine," he said. "That noise machine inside the house is Barney. He's mostly Lab, which means he's an eating machine. About a week ago, he dug a hole under the gate and got out. He wasn't gone long, but when he did come home, he was sick as could be. We were going to take him to the vet, but then he made a recovery. Barney's a big boy and eats anything that's not nailed down, so we figured he must have gotten into some garbage or eaten something he shouldn't have."

"Crocket wasn't so lucky."

"Yeah, damn shame."

"You mind running me through what happened when you noticed the two sick dogs next door?"

"No problem," he said. "The day before yesterday I wanted to get an early start on the workday, so I left our house a little before seven in the morning. That's when I saw Cricket having these seizures on their lawn. I ran over to see what was wrong with her, and that's when I saw Crocket lying on the ground and not moving. There was no sign of Old Man Carter, so I ran up to the front door and began banging on the door and shouting his name. When Mack didn't answer, I tried the door and found it unlocked. I stuck my head inside and shouted for Mack, but I didn't hear any response. Since he's hard of hearing, I stepped inside the house, and that's when I found him sprawled on the floor. I called nine-one-one. After that, I called my wife, Evie, to come over. She's a nurse, and I knew she'd know what to do. While she was working on Mack, she told me to get some blankets, wrap up the dogs, and rush them over to the animal care clinic where Barney goes."

"Is that where Dr. Misko treated them?" I asked.

He nodded. "There was nothing she could do for Crocket, but she did manage to save Cricket."

In addition to having her own practice, Dr. Misko is also the on-call vet for Angie's Rescues.

"Any idea how Cricket and Crocket ended up in the front yard?" I asked.

Schmitt shrugged and said, "My guess is that Mack let them out. He usually gets around with a cane, but there are days he's not up to walking them, so he lets them out front and tells them to 'go sniff.' Usually they do their business and come back into the house, but not always. Now and again they'd get selective hearing and wander the neighborhood. Whenever Evie and I would hear Mack calling for them to come home, we'd go out and help him corral them. Both of us work, though, so we're not always around."

"Why didn't he just let them out back to sniff?"

He looked a little guilty. "There are some holes in the fencing," he said. "I've been meaning to help him patch them, but haven't gotten to it."

"On those occasions when Cricket and Crocket decided to take themselves on walks, where would they go?"

"As far as I know, they never strayed from this street. It was just a matter of going for a little stroll."

"Tell me about the other dog who got sick," I said.

Schmitt waved his hand toward a nearby house and said, "Matilda lives two doors down at Sara and Gary Lazarus's house. She got sick maybe two days after Barney did."

"Same symptoms as the other dogs?"

"It sounded like it."

"Did she get out as well?"

He shook his head. "When Sara came home, she found Matilda in respiratory distress in their backyard. Sara took her to the emergency animal hospital on Van Nuys. It was touch and go, she said."

"What was the vet's prognosis?"

"He said it looked like she'd ingested something toxic, but there could be several likely culprits."

"Thanks for talking to me," I said. "I think I'll proceed over to the Lazarus house and see if they're up for answering some questions."

"I'm pretty sure only the sitter and kids will be there," he said. "Gary and Sara usually don't get home before six."

I checked the time and saw that it was quarter past five.

"If you want," he said, "I can give you their contact information."

"I'd appreciate that," I said.

"My cell phone's in the truck," he said, and went to retrieve it.

The dogs and I waited for him in the front yard. During his short absence, Sirius and Emily tugged at their leashes to go exploring, but I reined them in and made sure they stayed close to me. Protective parents do things like that.

CHAPTER ELEVEN

NEENER NEENER

On the outskirts of Winslow, Arizona
527 miles from Los Angeles

The killer didn't stop at the Corner Park, but he did slow down to look at the Glenn Frey tribute statue on the northwest corner of Second Street and Kingsley. Frey was dead, but his statue made him look forever young. At Frey's side was his guitar. Nearby was a red flatbed Ford.

"'Take it easy,'" the killer said, "'take it easy.'"

Those words were forever associated with city of Winslow because of the Eagles song. The phrase was posted on several storefront signs in the small city.

It was a quiet night in Winslow, Arizona, but then most nights were. Everything shut down early. Even the Turquoise Room Restaurant at the La Posada Hotel didn't seat after 8:30. The killer's appetite would need to be satisfied another way.

There had been a time when Winslow was a busy railroad stop, as well as one of the hubs along the Mother Road, Route 66. It was still considered a Route 66 photo op, and the railroad still made occasional stops there, but the opening of Interstate 40 had diverted travelers onto a different course. Evenings like this, Winslow almost appeared to be a ghost town.

The killer's destination was five miles south of Winslow. There was no one driving along Arizona State Route 99, but that wasn't too surprising. Everyone seemed to be in agreement that the road was a pretty poor excuse for a highway. A few days earlier, the killer had made a trial run of the area after sundown, and another reconnaissance two hours ago. It was important to choreograph potential scenarios, just as it was necessary to know the lay of the land.

The evening's destination was the McHood Park Campground. For the budget minded, it was hard to beat. The campground didn't charge for its campsites. But tonight, that would prove to be a case of someone being penny-wise and pound-foolish. From what the killer had been able to observe earlier in the day, the campground was only about half full. There had been seven RVs parked there; it appeared no one was tenting it.

The June night was warm, the temperature in the mid-eighties. There was a steady breeze, though, with some strong wind gusts. Those winds had likely driven most of the campers inside their RVs. The campground had what was called a host, an individual who lived on-site in his camper, but he was a lax babysitter. The odds were good that he was already asleep.

On the wings of the Eagles, the car closed in on the campground. The killer turned down the entrance road, but made a U-turn at the halfway point, then parked the vehicle on the side of the road so that it was positioned in the direction of SR 99.

That would make for an easy getaway. It also meant hoofing it to the campground, but it was a good night for a walk.

The road to the campsites was mostly paved, but the sliver moon was parsimonious with its light. The breeze stirred up the trees along the road, masking any footfalls. As the killer had expected, there were no campfires blazing, and no late grilling going on. Lights could be seen peeking through closed curtains on most of the RVs. One of the campers had an outside lantern set up on a table, along with a radio tuned to a baseball game.

A distant voice announced, "With the runner in scoring position, the D-backs have the heart of their order coming up."

The killer stayed in the shadows, working toward the sounds coming from the radio. It must have been a close game; the crowd was still into it. Their noise made a perfect cover for movement, as well as the sound of fitting a suppressor onto the barrel of a nine-millimeter.

When all was ready, the killer moved in close. "Batter up."

Even through the wind, the man sitting in his camp chair must have heard the whisper. As he turned his head toward the sound, two shots were fired, muffled by the suppressor, the wind, and the announcer's voice coming from the radio. The man's last gasps went unheard.

"Hernandez swings," said the broadcaster. "It's a long drive to left field. Jackson's settling under it. Waiting on third base is Thompson. He's tagging up."

The killer didn't wait on the outcome of the play.

Later, when Winslow was far in the rearview mirror, there was one last task to attend to. By that time, it was likely the body had been discovered.

"Nine-one-one," said the dispatcher. "What is your emergency?"

It wasn't the killer who spoke. It was a recording of the late Stephen Hawking using his voice synthesizer. The message, of course, wasn't meant for the emergency services dispatcher, but for one particular individual.

"Neener neener," Hawking said.

CHAPTER TWELVE

SNAKE, RATTLE, AND ROLL

When you awaken in hell, be it real or imagined, your day hasn't begun well. Ever since getting out of bed that morning, I had been fighting the aftereffects of my fire dream and doing my best to look like I was still among the living. It was mostly cussedness that had carried me through the long day. It was probably a good thing that work had kept me running. It hadn't left me time to ruminate.

As I made the dogs their dinner, I told them, "'The sun will come out tomorrow.'" If Annie believed that, then maybe I could as well. Not hearing from Lisbet had hung a dark cloud over me all day. It didn't look as if we were getting together this evening. I wondered if that was a portent of things to come. Despite her silence, I was hoping that we were still *we*.

Vestigial pride got thrown out the window. I called Lisbet's number, hung in there for four rings, then heard her request to leave a message. This time I wasn't silent.

"Hey," I said. "I hope you're not still mad over my spacing out yesterday. Anyway, call me. Even if we can't get together tonight, it will be good to hear your voice."

I paused a moment, wondering if I'd said enough, wondering if I'd said too much. I wanted to close on a good note, and to conclude with something more than *goodbye*.

"Miss you," I said, and ended the call. Pent-up air came out in a big sigh, but the pit in my stomach remained.

My antidote to angst has always been to work. I turned on my laptop and decided to read up on Eli Green, starting with IMDb—the Internet Movie Database. Green and his wife, Amy, had created six documentaries. None of those films had ever found a mainstream audience, and had played mostly at small film festivals around the country. They'd gotten a second life once Elijah's Church of the Gate had become established. The films had covered a number of subjects, ranging from women who served during the Vietnam War *(Forgotten Healers)*, to the Iowa State Fair *(Hawkeye Heaven)*, to what went into putting on small-town parades *(Main Street Memories)*.

I was curious about Elijah's life before he became a self-proclaimed prophet, and by web surfing I was able to flesh out his biography. Half of what I read seemed more like PR than journalism, and I wondered if the pieces had been commissioned directly or indirectly by the church. At the same time, I found articles painting Elijah as the "triumph of style over substance," and his church the "unholy union of Hollywood and religion." One writer called its teachings "scripture by sound bites."

Elijah claimed he was born "in America's heartland." While that wasn't untrue, it did sound better than the reality—that he was raised in the wealthy Chicago suburb of Lake Forest. Many of the critical articles credited Amy Green—aka Sister Joan—with being the true creative force behind their documentaries, and subsequently behind the Church of the Gate.

"She's an incredible director and producer," said one unnamed source. "Every week the church puts on a great show."

I decided to put that to the test, and downloaded a recent broadcast of one of the Church of the Gate's services. What I saw wasn't anything like a Catholic Mass. There was no reading of the Nicene Creed or Apostles' Creed or Lord's Prayer, nor any scripture readings or psalms. The liturgy was absent. There was a homily of sorts, but not one based on readings from the Scripture.

At the center of the service was Elijah, but he acted more ringmaster than Old Testament prophet. His message was "finding your way by following your heart." Among others, he quoted from the Beatles ("Love is all you need"), Khalil Gibran ("Your daily life is your religion. When you enter into it, take with you your all"), and Einstein ("A ship is always safe at shore, but that is not what it's built for").

Like any good performer, Elijah commanded the stage, and his enthusiastic audience was clearly enamored of him. There were close-ups of his parishioners, and the variety of humanity displayed on camera suggested he had a diverse appeal. There was lots of exhorting, and head nodding, and cheering. Some were even moved to tears. The camera paused on one young woman who was wiping away tears, and I was surprised to recognize it was Sister Hannah. For a moment I wondered if she was a plant, put in the audience to elicit enthusiasm from those around her, but then decided that was unlikely. Her emotion appeared heartfelt. When we'd first talked, she had referenced the "returned prophet Elijah." Maybe she really believed that.

The service was as much a variety show as it was a ministry. Perhaps that's why it appealed to so many viewers. Carrie Holder, I soon learned, was as talented a performer as people had said she was. When you first meet a person who is already dead, that tends to color your impressions; it's like looking through a glass darkly. Now I was seeing my LA woman in a new light.

Women who can sing and emote like Carrie Holder have a siren quality whether they like it or not. Over the course of the show she sang three songs, all of them spirituals like "Joshua Fought the Battle of Jericho." Her ability to emote somehow made her face radiant, showcasing an inner light. I wasn't the only one taken by her singing. The audience offered loud ovations. Of even more interest to me were the camera angles that occasionally revealed a transfixed Elijah.

After her third song, she didn't reappear, but Carrie stayed in my thoughts and I found myself singing, "'And the walls came a-tumbling down.'"

The song was a reminder of the task in front of me. I needed to do as Joshua had done and get some walls to fall, so I went back to looking for anything that might be of interest to my investigation. Elijah had talked about his "divine calling" to one reporter, and said that he couldn't deny the work God commanded him to do. For him and his wife, that meant abandoning plans to work on a short film they had tentatively titled *Shake, Rattle and Roll*. I was familiar with the song of the same name, a single that was arguably the first big hit of rock and roll. That was enough for me to find out what I could about the aborted documentary. After several false starts, I stumbled upon a reference Elijah made to him and his wife working on a film in Middlesboro, Kentucky, before they left for California to start their church.

Wondering what had brought Eli and Amy Green to Kentucky, I did a search on Middlesboro. I wasn't interested in what the chamber of commerce had to say about the city and its population of 10,000 people. The filmmakers had been drawn to the town for some particular reason. At first, I thought it might be Middlesboro's connection to music. The city claimed to be the home of ragtime music, but that wasn't the shake, rattle, and roll sound associated with Bill Haley & His Comets.

Geographically, Middlesboro was located only a mile from the Cumberland Gap. Daniel Boone was credited with blazing his Wilderness Road through the Cumberland Gap, but I was pretty sure the Greens wouldn't have been doing a documentary on an American frontiersman.

It's not easy to find something when you don't know what you're looking for, but I got lucky. As soon as I started to read about a Pentecostal church in Middlesboro made famous because of its snake handling, I was certain that was what had brought the Greens to town.

"Not shake, rattle, and roll," I told the dogs. "*Snake*, rattle, and roll."

I knew next to nothing about snake handling, also called serpent handling, even though it has existed in this country for more than a century. For a time, the practice was essentially a secret society confined to Pentecostal churches in Appalachia. Few outsiders were allowed to witness preachers lifting up poisonous serpents in hand, actions they believed honored the Lord. The preachers cited the words of Mark 16:18: *With their hands, they will take up serpents.* Practitioners believed themselves anointed by God, and said their handling snakes was an act of obedience to the Lord. This extreme devotion was not without its consequences, with at least one hundred individuals having died from handling poisonous snakes.

Despite serpent handling being illegal in many states, its practice continued. What had changed more than anything was the advent of social media. The internet had taken the cloistered practices of backwoods preachers and put them out to the world. Several snake-handling pastors had even become celebrities of sorts through television shows and social media. Unfortunately, the limelight had proved short-lived for some of its biggest names and practitioners. Obituaries went hand in hand with snake handling.

I watched footage of these preachers at work. Some dared to do even more than take up poisonous snakes; several also challenged fate by handling fire and drinking poison. They did this, they said, in accordance with scripture. They did this, they said, for God.

The Holy Spirit called not only the pastors to these deeds, but often their flock. One young woman looked to be in a trance as she held multiple venomous snakes—what almost looked to be a hydra—aloft. The spectacle was hard to look at, but even harder to look away from.

"'Shake, rattle, and roll,'" I whispered. "'You'll never do nothing to save your doggone soul.'"

The vibration of my cell phone gave me an excuse to stop watching the spectacle of the snakes. I was sure Lisbet was finally calling me back, but I was wrong. Ben Corning was the caller. I thought about not picking up so as to spare myself from talking about meeting with Haines the next day, but curiosity got me to bite.

"I thought the FBI worked banker's hours," I said, looking at the time. I was surprised to see it was half past nine.

"Yeah," he said, sounding very tired, sounding as if he were reconsidering his vocational path. "Like all bureaucrats, we close shop at five o'clock every day. Most criminals are happy to cooperate with that timeframe."

I gave him a laugh. He sounded like he needed that. Then I said, "What's up?" My hope was that if I hurried our conversation along, he might not ask me about Haines.

"That gris-gris bag has been keeping our lab people busy," he said. "It's probably nothing, but one of the items in the bag was incorrectly identified. What we thought was a dried-up frog's toe, or more accurately, several of its toes, are actually toad's toes."

I repeated the alliteration: "Toad's toes."

"From a Sonoran Desert toad," he added.

There was some alarm going off in my head, but it was in the bad reception area between my conscious mind and subconscious. Shakespeare's witches had spoken of "toe of frog." Why had the killer given us toes of toad as a substitution?

"Bait and switch of amphibians," I said. "If your investigators are right about the killer referencing the bard's rhyme of frog and dog, how is it that we instead got toad and dog?"

"We're thinking it's possible that the killer believed it was a frog's foot."

"No," I said. "There's some message here."

"We've been looking into that as well."

"And?"

"Thus far, we haven't found any explanation we like."

"Tell me about what your people didn't like."

"There are plenty of racist and sexual connotations to the word *toad*, but none seemed a good match. We also looked at secondary and tertiary definitions of *toad*, but they seemed to be nonstarters."

"What about acronyms?" I asked.

"There are two," he said. "Take Off and Die, and Temporary Obsolete Abandoned or Derelict."

"The first sounds interesting," I said.

"It's mostly an acronym used by surfers just as they're setting off to catch a huge wave."

"No," I said.

"That was the impression from our end as well. And after turning our wheels, we decided that any more speculation would just be a waste of time."

"You're probably right."

I was positioning myself to make a quick exit from the call, but Corning wasn't about to let me get away that easily. He needed that pound of flesh.

"One more thing," he said. "My boss asked me to confirm that you'll be talking with the Weatherman tomorrow."

I didn't answer right away. After a two-second wait, an anxious-sounding Corning asked, "You there, Gideon?"

"Yeah and yeah," I said.

"You're going to see him tomorrow?"

"You already heard me, right?"

I managed to put some righteous indignation into my words, but the truth was that it wasn't the Feds who needed to be convinced about my intentions to see Haines; it was me. Just the thought of the meeting made me feel ill.

"Good, good," he said. "Do you need anything from our end?"

"Thoughts and prayers?" I said, not sparing the sarcasm. In these times of senseless mass shootings, no words seemed so fatuous or inadequate.

"Done," he said. "We want Haines talking about the All-In Killer. Any chance you can make a recording for us?"

"We'll see. I'm not even certain he'll agree to talk to me."

Actually, I was, but the hopeful tone in my voice seemed to panic Corning. "We're counting on you to be persuasive."

The longer the two of us talked, the more it became apparent that the FBI wasn't getting anywhere in their All-In Killer investigation. Corning was selling me, and I was supposed to sell Haines.

I was anything but reassured.

I called Lisbet again. Even if she was angry with me, it wasn't like her to not respond to my calls. This was the longest we had gone in our relationship without talking to one another. The silence had me so worried and frustrated that I actually found my hands shaking. When she picked up on the first ring, my relief was enormous. At the same time, I could feel the rise of heat building up from my chest to my head.

"I was just going to call you," she said.

"I'd sure as hell hope so," I said.

I regretted the words as soon as I said them. But I didn't take them back.

"Maybe now you have a little idea of what I was feeling last night," she said.

"So, your silence has been payback?"

"No," she said.

"What would you call it?"

"I refuse to be treated like one of your suspects," she said.

I backtracked half a step. "The longer I didn't hear from you, the more worried I became."

There was heat in my voice, but she also heard the note of concern. "I'm sorry I didn't get back to you sooner, but since early this morning I've been on the go. It's been a hellacious day, and I'm still feeling numb."

"What happened?" I asked.

"A newborn boy was abandoned," she said. "He didn't make it."

I exhaled and said, "I'm sorry."

My words felt inadequate. It was an abandoned newborn that had first brought Lisbet and me together. Baby Moses hadn't survived. Death had brought us together again with Baby Rose. In both instances I had been the investigator, while Lisbet was the one who had made sure the babies were given names and proper burials. For years, she has been tending to the throwaway newborns of Southern California. I know how traumatic each and every death is for her. We'd been fortunate that this was the first death in more than a year.

"This one really hit me hard," she said.

"Is there anything I can do?"

"No," she said.

I didn't like the immediacy, and seeming firmness, of her answer. I wanted to be a shoulder for her to lean on, or weep into, but she clearly didn't want that.

"You're shutting me out," I said.

"I need time to think," she said. "There are matters I need to work out."

"What are you telling me?"

"I need a break from us."

My heart was pounding. Her words scared me. There were a hundred things I wanted to say, but I only managed to say the one thing I didn't want to.

"Okay," I said. "Call me when you figure things out."

If I hoped to provoke her, it didn't work. A moment passed, and there was no response. Her silence seemed like the ultimate rebuke to me, so I clicked off.

CHAPTER THIRTEEN

SAYING MY PIECE

Even before talking to Lisbet, I had been fighting the dismals. In the aftermath of our call, my sense of gloom and doom felt overwhelming. The mere act of breathing seemed a chore, and I was at a loss as to what to do. Everything seemed pointless.

The dogs immediately sensed something was wrong. They came over and tried to give me their version of a group hug. I told them everything was fine. They knew I was lying, but that didn't discourage them from staying near to me.

Promises and the sense of duty that had always guided me kept me from going into full retreat mode. God help them, but some people were still counting on me. I called Seth. When he answered, I could hear the hum of background conversation, and I guessed he was in some restaurant or cocktail lounge.

"I'm sorry to interrupt you," I told him, "but I had mentioned that I'd probably need you to dog sit this week. If at all possible, I'm hoping you can watch them tomorrow."

The conversation didn't go as I had planned. It was supposed to be matter-of-fact, professional but friendly. Short and sweet. I had no intention of alluding to any personal problems. Seth was just supposed to agree to my request.

"What's wrong?" he asked.

His question wasn't part of my script. I decided to bluff, and quickly learned there's a reason I don't play poker. "Nothing," I said.

Seth believed my lie about as much as the dogs had.

"If you want me to watch the dogs," he said, "you're going to have to do better than that."

"Why is it that everyone seems to think I'm a great target for extortion?" I asked.

Instead of bothering to answer, Seth just waited me out. It took two seconds, and a long sigh, for the clam to open.

"I think Lisbet just broke up with me," I said.

"Expect my knock on the door in half an hour," he said.

The idea of Seth putting an early end to what I suspected was a date didn't sit well with me.

"There's no need for you to cut your evening short," I said. "You're overreacting."

"I am not overreacting," he said, "but I'm about to. Either you agree to my visit or I call nine-one-one and tell them that I'm afraid for your safety."

A few months back Seth had made a similar call that might very well have saved my life, but these were quite different circumstances, or at least I wanted to think so.

"This is ridiculous," I said.

Seth didn't argue. Once again, he just waited.

"Fine," I said.

It was almost half an hour to the minute when he knocked on the door. The dogs acted ferocious until they saw it was their uncle

Seth standing there, and then the lovefest began. All of us made our way out to the family room.

"Drink?" I asked.

"A beer sounds good."

I went and got both of us an Angel City Pilsner. Seth took the easy chair; I settled on the recliner. For once, Seth didn't offer a toast. Both of us tilted back our beers. Normally I enjoy everything made by Angel City Brewery, but this time my throat was so tight it was hard to even swallow the beer, let alone enjoy it. My discomfort must have been apparent, because I found Seth and the two dogs staring at me.

"What is this?" I asked. "An intervention?"

"I'd like to hear about you and Lisbet," said Seth.

"I think I've pretty much exhausted that subject."

"You told me she broke up with you. You didn't offer anything other than that."

"Isn't that enough?"

"What did she say, and why did she say it?"

"She said she needed a break from us."

"And what prompted her to say that?"

I shrugged my shoulders. "How would I know? We didn't talk all day, and when she finally returned my call, I wasn't in the best of humor. I guess we had a few words. What I didn't know was that she had been dealing with a baby that was dumped."

Seth nodded. "I heard about that."

"I guess I'm the only one who didn't."

"So, what you're saying is that Lisbet asked for some alone time, and you took that as a rejection of both you and your relationship?"

"It wasn't just that," I said. "Recently she's been acting distant. And that's not my imagination talking."

"And you've taken that personally?"

"Is there any other way to take it?"

"In a word, yes. There could be any number of external factors influencing her. You're assuming that you are the root cause of Lisbet's needing some time to herself. That might not be the case."

"I'm not going to engage in wishful thinking," I said.

"Is it just wishful thinking you're going to avoid," he asked, "or is it any kind of thinking at all?"

I glared at Seth. He stared right back. Unfortunately, the dogs interpreted my look as being meant for them, and they turned away. That made me feel like a bully. I directed my attention to the bottle of beer and tried to take another swallow. It hadn't gotten any easier.

"Maybe this whole thing is just as well," I said.

"Is it?"

"The All-In Killer keeps getting closer," I said. "If Lisbet and I aren't seeing each other, she won't be in danger of being targeted, or suffering collateral damage."

"Has that scenario been playing in your mind?"

I nodded. "I'm being targeted by a killer. By extension, that puts Lisbet in danger."

"You said that Lisbet was withdrawing from you," said Seth. "Since you admit to being worried about her safety, I'm wondering if it isn't you who's been withdrawing from her."

"There might be some small truth to that," I said, "but I'm a cop. I haven't imagined her behavior. Things have come to a bit of a head lately, but even before that she was acting preoccupied. Usually I'm the one who does the shutting out, but there's been a role reversal. There's something not right there."

"I'm sure your observations are valid, but why jump to conclusions? And why think the worst?"

"Because it's easier to pull the bandage from the scab in one motion and not in stops and starts."

"That's not a good analogy," said Seth, "especially when applied to relationships."

"You've never even been married," I said. "That doesn't exactly make you the last word when it comes to couples counseling."

"That's true," said Seth. "But you seem awfully intent on blaming the messenger, instead of listening to what he—that is, I—has to say."

"If that's the case," I said, "then I'm sorry."

It was only half an apology, but Seth was gracious enough to accept it.

"What time will you be bringing the dogs by tomorrow?" he asked.

"Probably midmorning," I said. "I'll text you with the time after I book the flight."

"I suppose it will do no good for me to tell you that with all the tumult going on in your life, this is probably the worst time possible for you to see Haines."

"I appreciate your concern," I said, "but I promised the Feds. They're hoping he'll help them get a handle on the All-In Killer."

"But you don't believe that?"

"If Haines offers anything up, he'll do it on his own terms, and for his own purposes. For him, it's a game, but his is the perspective of the cat playing with the mouse. If you ask the mouse, it's not a game."

"Do you feel like the mouse?"

"I feel like someone who doesn't want to be played," I said.

Both of us retreated to our beers. Finally, I said, "I'm sorry that I'm not better company. Every day it feels like the pressure ratchets up that much more."

"Considering your circumstances," he said, "I think it would be impossible not to feel that way."

The dogs left Seth's side and came over to me. They must have decided the intervention was over. I scratched them on their favorite places.

"I need to ask you a just-in-case favor," I said.

"Shoot," he said.

"If something happens to me," I said, "I'm hoping you'll agree to take care of the dogs."

I almost succeeded in saying my piece without my voice cracking. Almost.

CHAPTER FOURTEEN

DOGGIE BALLS

While Seth nursed his beer, he asked about my cases, and my life. I didn't feel like talking, but he wouldn't let me retreat into silence, which proved a good thing. Our time together put me in a better state of mind, and when he finally took his leave, I felt better for having had his company.

At the front door he paused and offered a last bit of advice. "Both you and Lisbet have been under enormous pressure of late," he said. "Neither of you should feel as if there is a stopwatch ticking to get everything resolved right away. During my lifetime I've come to know the truth of the saying 'act in haste, repent in leisure.' I would advise you not to act precipitously."

"I don't even know what *precipitously* is," I said, "so I should be safe."

He gave me a smile, probably more as encouragement at my attempt to engage than from appreciation of my one-liner. "Be well," he told me.

When I closed the door and stepped back inside the house, the dogs stood there as if expecting some form of direction. "Don't look at me," I said. "At this moment, I have no idea what to do. Just breathing seems like a stretch."

Since I was clearly no fun, the dogs went and settled on the sofa. Some people find solace in booze, but when I'm out of sorts the last thing I feel like doing is drinking. The one beer I'd tried to down was still half full. It was also warm, so I went and poured the remainder into the sink, and then cleaned some dishes. Usually I find that one of the best times to think about my cases is while washing dishes, but despite my scrub-a-dub-dubbing, I didn't gain any new revelations or insights.

When I finished with the dishes, it was too early to go to bed and too late to be productive. I wanted escapism but lacked the energy to find it. My ringing cell phone grabbed all my attention and got my pulse racing. Be Lisbet, I prayed, but the name on the display wasn't the one I so wanted to see. Ben Corning was calling again. Seeing that, my stomach tensed. No one calls after ten o'clock at night with good news.

"There's been another one," he said.

"Shit," I said.

"Shit," Corning agreed.

"When did it happen?"

"Earlier today."

"The killings have accelerated," I said.

"We noticed," said Corning.

Before, months had gone by between the All-In Killer's homicides; of late, it had been mere days.

"Tell me about the victim."

"Seventy-four-year-old white male. He and his wife were camping in their fifth-wheel. She said he was outside listening to a ballgame."

"What's the nine-nine tie-in?"

"The homicide happened in Winslow, Arizona, in a spot that's on State Route Ninety-Nine, but I guess that wasn't good enough."

"Meaning?"

"The victim was also shot with a nine-millimeter. And here's the kicker: We're pretty sure the killer decided to be really cute by calling in the crime. A nine-one-one call was made about an hour ago, where the caller played a recording of Stephen Hawking saying, 'Neener neener.'"

"Stephen Hawking?"

"He was a famous physicist."

"I know that. How is it that there was a recording of Stephen Hawking saying, 'Neener neener'?"

"It appears to be a recording taken from an episode of the television show *The Big Bang Theory*."

"Where Hawking used the phrase 'neener neener'?"

"That's right. On the show he called up the character Sheldon Cooper and gloated over having bested him."

I thought about that. Corning must have thought I didn't understand the reference, so he added, "The Sheldon character is this physicist . . ."

"I've seen the show." It would have been hard not to, since episodes of it seem to be replayed 24/7.

"Sorry," he said. "I wouldn't have called this late except that I know you're seeing Haines tomorrow, and we thought it was important to tell you about the homicide. We'll be sending you the preliminary file in the morning. We're hoping you'll be able to use that information to get Haines's input on this homicide, as well as the Four Corners shitstorm."

"Will do," I said, and then did my best to change the subject. "Has anyone on your end had any chance to think about what might be in store with the eight-eight combo?"

"We've only done the most preliminary of analyses," he said. "Once again, we've decided there are too many possibilities for us to be able to mount a credible deterrent."

"Tell me what's in the cards anyway."

Corning took a deep breath. When we'd talked a few hours earlier, he had sounded tired. Now he was clearly exhausted.

"There *is* an Arizona State Route Eight-Eight," he said.

The killer had been there, done that. "I'm more interested in the poker nicknames."

"The pocket pair eight-eight is frequently called snowmen."

In my mind it wasn't hard to envision how a pair of eights could look like snowmen. "What else?"

"Time travel," he said.

"I don't get it."

"In the movie *Back to the Future*, the character needs to reach a speed of eighty-eight miles an hour in order to travel through time."

"Next," I said.

"Piano keys."

I wasn't a musician, but I knew there were eighty-eight keys on a piano.

"Anything else?"

He gave me two. "Pretzels," he said, "and fat ladies."

I wanted to offer up the old sports cliché that it's never over until the fat lady sings, but I couldn't even manage gallows humor.

"You're right," I agreed. "There's no way to play defense."

Corning didn't immediately answer, which made me suspicious he was holding something back.

"What?" I said.

"It's probably nothing to be concerned about," he said, "but there's another common nickname for a pair of eights."

"I'm listening."

"They're called dog balls, or doggie balls."

"Son of a bitch," I said.

I tried to convince myself that Sirius wasn't under immediate threat. The latest homicide had occurred more than 500 miles from Los Angeles. If the homicides held true to form, the killer wouldn't travel all the way to LA for his next victim. For the moment Sirius was safe, or at least that's what I wanted to believe.

I'd told Seth that because of the imminent threat of the All-In Killer, it was a good thing that my relationship with Lisbet was on hiatus. If our being apart meant Lisbet was safer in the interim, it was for the best. Maybe it was also time to find a safe haven for the dogs. Heather Moreland would probably let me house them at Angie's Rescues, but just the thought of doing that troubled me. Emily had finally found her pack. Putting her back into temporary foster care wouldn't be fair to her. And I didn't even want to imagine how my longtime partner would react. Still, that didn't mean I shouldn't consider another temporary home for them. It was my job to look after my charges.

To try and get some needed sleep, I took an over-the-counter antihistamine. The pill, combined with my exhaustion, knocked me out, or at least it did for a time. But in the middle of the night I awakened in a panic, with no idea how long I had been sleeping. My heart was pounding. I was sure something was terribly wrong.

Sirius wasn't at my side. In his absence, my mind went to the worst. My partner had become a target because of me. The killer had somehow lured him away.

"Sirius!" I yelled.

I threw aside the covers and jumped out of bed. My cries alarmed Emily, and she began barking wildly. I ran naked to the living room, calling Sirius's name. Nothing. My fright overcame my reason. I had failed my partner.

The front door was ajar. An intruder must have opened it and lured Sirius outside. I threw the door open and screamed, "Sirius!"

There was no movement on the street. I stepped out onto the porch, looking for my partner. The area was deserted.

"Sirius!" I cried again. "Sirius!"

Emily responded to my madness, matching her calls with mine. That's when my partner bounded into view, and my see-saw ride went from the depths to the heights. We met on the front lawn, where I dropped to my knees, and Sirius ran into my arms. The overwhelming guilt that I was feeling suddenly lifted, and it felt like a straitjacket falling away from my chest.

Sirius was as conflicted as I was. Even while he was whimpering, his tail whipped back and forth. I buried my face in his fur, and that's when I heard the sounds of uncontrollable crying.

It took me a moment to realize that the crazy naked guy on the lawn was weeping. My dogs didn't know what to do to help me, and I didn't either.

CHAPTER FIFTEEN

AIN'T NO SUNSHINE

At Jenny's funeral, I remember being numb to what was going on around me. Somehow, I managed to hold in the waterworks. It has always been my way to mute any public emoting, and when I did allow myself to grieve, it was done behind closed doors. That's not to say that I coped well in the aftermath of my wife's death. It was all I could do to go through the motions of being among the living.

The other shoe dropped a year later, when Sirius and I almost died chasing Haines into what turned out to be an inferno. My burns required a long convalescence, but they might have been the least of what I needed to recover from. Even with those difficult circumstances, I didn't have a breakdown like I'd experienced the night before. I'm sure a shrink would have been able to offer a detailed explanation for my emotional collapse. My own self-diagnosis was that I was a mess.

As dawn broke, I was working on my second cup of coffee and hoping the caffeine would kick in. Sirius hadn't left my side since the night before. Maybe he was sensing something that even I didn't know.

"You're acting like you're on suicide watch," I told him.

"Don't worry. I'm not a danger to myself. Only to others."

I wished that wasn't true, but increasingly that's what it felt like to me.

"So, where the hell were you last night?"

I looked to Sirius as if expecting him to offer an explanation, and he looked away. Most people think their dogs are smart. Sirius, I'm convinced, is a canine genius. He's even smarter than many humans I know, maybe myself included. This wasn't the first time he'd opened a locked door. He'd saved my life at least once doing just that. Opening locked doors, even car doors, was puppy play for the Houdini of dogs.

"Did you hear something last night that made you go out to investigate?" I asked.

Sirius does not like coyotes. He bristles at their yips, and yells out challenges. It was possible he'd let himself out of the house and chased off the perceived threat.

"You might think you're the big, bad wolf," I said, "but you're asking for trouble when you take on a pack."

Sirius offered me his paw. Sometimes he does that unsolicited. We shook, even if I wasn't sure what we were shaking on.

There was gray in Sirius's muzzle; there was now some gray in my hair. That was something that hadn't been there at the onset of our partnership.

"Let's not grow old gracefully," I said.

Once again, Sirius offered his paw. This time I knew what I was shaking about. Emily came over and joined us. She was still trying to get a handle on the command to shake.

"Shake," I said to her.

Emily lifted her paw, and we shook. It was a morning of re-assurances, but I sensed the dogs were out of sorts for the same reason that I was.

"'Ain't no sunshine when she's gone,'" I said.

I didn't try and sing the words; Bill Withers had done that as no one else ever could. But I was feeling the words to his song deep in my soul. I wondered if I should call Lisbet; I wondered if I should give her the time and space she'd asked for. Neither choice seemed like the right thing to do, but I wasn't sure there was a right thing to do.

"'It's not warm when she's away,'" I told the dogs.

I finished my second cup of coffee and considered pouring myself a third. As promised—or threatened—Ben Corning had already sent the Winslow homicide file that morning. I had yet to look at it, or print it out. I had also put off booking my airline flight. By waiting, I suppose I was hoping that something would come up to prevent my going to San Quentin. Maybe if I was lucky all the flights would be sold out.

Using my phone, I called up that day's flights to the Bay Area—and found plenty of available seats. With great reluctance, I booked an early afternoon flight.

Instead of calling Seth, I decided to forward him my flight information along with a brief message. That was the chicken's way out. It was possible he'd heard my screams the night before, and that wasn't anything I wanted to discuss with him. He might even have witnessed his naked neighbor having a nervous break-down, which was a topic I would just as soon avoid in this life-time. I told Seth that if it was all right with him, I would drop off the dogs in his backyard later that morning, as I needed to make a stop prior to my flight. Less than a minute later, he responded.

Looking forward to my play date with the dogs, he wrote.

There was no emoji in his text showing a naked guy, which I considered a positive sign.

Before driving to Burbank, I made sure that Mack Carter was well enough to receive a visitor. Carter had been moved out of the ICU and was recovering in Neurology. Like any big hospital, it wasn't easy navigating the St. Joseph Medical Center, and when I managed to find my way through the maze, I wasn't even rewarded with a piece of cheese at the end. Carter was being housed in a semi-private room. As I stepped through the open door, I addressed the older man in the bed nearest to me.

"Mack Carter?" I asked.

As the man shook his head, I heard a weak voice coming from behind a curtain that divided the room: "I'm over here."

Because I wasn't in Oz, or at least I didn't think I was, I decided I could pay attention to the man behind the curtain.

Mack Carter looked like I felt. The side of his head was bandaged, and sunken eyes looked out from white, pasty skin. No one looks good in a hospital gown, and Carter was no exception. His thin arms and crepey skin resembled chicken flesh, save that his had bruising from the invasion of needles into his old veins.

"Good morning, Mr. Carter," I said. "My name is Michael Gideon, and I'm a detective with the Los Angeles Police Department. Yesterday I spent some time with your dog Cricket."

Hearing the dog's name made Carter suddenly alert. "How is she?" he asked.

"She's doing much better," I said, "but she really misses you. While I was with her, she made it clear that I was a poor substitute for you."

Tears started falling down his cheeks. "With Crocket now gone," he said, his voice tired and beaten down, "she's about all I have in this world."

"No children?" I asked.

He shook his head. "Over forty years ago we lost our Susan in a car accident. And two years ago, my Karen died. We were married over sixty years."

"I am sorry," I said.

His lament was deep; I knew his pain because it was my own. "I always thought my women would outlive me," he said. "I wish they had."

Carter's eyes welled up with more tears.

"Would you like me to get you a towel or some tissues?" I asked.

He shook his head, and wiped his eyes with his fingers. I didn't want to delve into the personal. If I did, we'd both be at the tissues. It was easier just to be in cop mode.

"Please sit down," he said.

I pulled up a chair and did as he asked. "Your neighbor Walt Schmitt had Cricket treated by the same vet who sees the animals at a private shelter where I volunteer," I said. "After meeting Cricket, I was asked if I had time to walk your neighborhood to see if I could identify what might have made the dogs on your street sick. As you probably know, Cricket and Crocket weren't the only dogs to become ill."

Carter tentatively nodded. "I seem to remember something about that. But it's all—fuzzy. They tell me I took a fall and got a concussion, but I don't even remember that."

"What do you remember?"

His lips moved as if they wanted to release a thought, but after a few seconds of trying he shook his head. "The last few days are"—he struggled to finish the sentence—"foggy."

I tried to ease his frustration and get him back on familiar ground. "Cricket seems like a very sweet dog," I said.

A smile, the first I'd seen, broke through on his face. "The sweetest," he said. "She's always been a daddy's girl, whereas Crocket was crazy about Karen."

"That's how my wife was with our dog," I said. "Nowadays he has to make do with me."

Carter took a moment to consider what I'd said. "What happened to your wife?" he asked.

So much for my plan to keep our conversation professional. "Like you," I said, "I also lost my wife."

That surprised him. "But you're so young," he said.

Earlier that morning I'd felt a thousand years old, give or take a century. "It happened five years ago," I said.

I wasn't looking for sympathy, but Carter offered it. "It must have been terrible losing your wife at such a young age."

"I guess there's no good age, is there?"

He nodded in agreement, and again I tried to move away from the potentially maudlin.

"I talked to some of your neighbors," I said. "From what I understand, your dogs were sometimes out on their own."

Carter winced a little. "That's true," he said, "but it wasn't very often. When my arthritis acts up, it's hard to walk. That's why I'd sometimes stand on the stoop and let them out on the front lawn. Usually they come right back inside when I call, but now and again they got it into their heads to take a stroll. They never went far, though. Cricket would follow the leader, and Crocket would follow his nose, but they never left the street and they always came back to me."

His chin began trembling.

"Did you let them out on the day you fell?"

He shook his head. "I'm not sure."

"Walt Schmitt saw Cricket having seizures in your front yard, but said he found you inside the house with the front door closed. Why do you think that was?"

"I'm not sure," he said. "I always kept watch on the dogs when I let them out."

"Perhaps you had to go back into the house for something?"

He shook his head and sighed. "I just don't know."

"Maybe it will come to you," I said. "You've lived in the neighborhood a long time, haven't you, Mr. Carter?"

"More than half a century," he said.

"I'll bet you've seen some changes."

"Oh, yes," he said. "When Karen and I bought the house, living in Sherman Oaks felt like we were out in the country."

"How do you get along with your neighbors?" I asked.

"Fine," he said, but with what I detected was a little defensiveness. "Walt and Evie are very kind. Since Karen died, they've often checked on me to see how I'm doing."

"During my walk I was stopped by Patricia Gaspar," I said.

Carter didn't look surprised. "She's the neighborhood watch captain," he said.

"That's what she told me. She seemed rather"—it took me a moment to come up with the right word—"controlling."

"Karen once called her the Queen of Mean," he said in a conspiratorial voice. "We both laughed at that."

"Some people are difficult."

"She's not always unkind," Carter said. "She got me set up with my meal deliveries."

"That was good of her," I said. "What can you tell me about the cat lady on the street? She glared at me and my dogs when we walked by her place."

"You mean Marjorie Jensen?" he asked. "I've always found her to be more bark than bite. Or whatever the cat equivalent of that is."

"More hiss than fit?" I suggested.

He gave a little nod of approval. "I told her that she didn't need to worry about my dogs, but that it was my dogs who needed to be worried about her cats."

"Have there been any run-ins between your dogs and her cats?"

"Nothing other than some barking. I think her cats might have had a few dust-ups with other dogs in the neighborhood, but as far as I know they've never been hurt."

"What can you tell me about the house with the fencing, baking soda, and vinegar?" I asked.

"I don't know that couple very well," he said. "They like to keep to themselves."

"I'm guessing they don't have a dog," I said.

Carter nodded.

"When I walked your neighborhood," I said, "I found a lot of plants, weeds, and shrubs that are potentially poisonous to dogs."

He looked alarmed and said, "I had no idea."

"You're not alone. I'm actually surprised more dogs don't get sick, especially as many of the poisonous plants on your street are common throughout Southern California. The only positive is that most dogs aren't in the habit of grazing. That said, did you ever notice Cricket and Crocket eating any of the neighborhood plants, or getting into something they shouldn't have?"

Carter's eyes narrowed as he strained to remember. "I don't think so," he said. "But then they must have, right?"

"It looks that way," I said, rising from my seat. To my eyes and ears, Carter had grown increasingly weary during our talk. "I'm sure you must be very tired, so I had better take my leave."

"Will you be seeing Cricket?" he asked.

"Not today," I said, "but I'll try to spend some time with her during the next day or two. I don't want you to worry, though. There are a lot of good people at the shelter looking out for her."

"For her sake," he said, "I want to get out of here as soon possible."

"She needs you healthy, so that means you have to do your best to get well."

He gave a determined nod. If anything would get him up and about, it was his dog.

"Karen picked them out, you know. And she named them. 'Cricket and Crocket,' she said. I didn't have any choice in the matter."

"We rarely do," I said.

CHAPTER SIXTEEN

JUST A LITTLE DOG

On the drive over to LAX, I kept thinking about Carter and his dogs and Hitchcock's classic film *Rear Window*. It was a favorite of mine, and no matter how many times I've watched it, I always seem to find something new. I'm a sucker for almost any film in which Jimmy Stewart ever acted, but he was never better than in portraying photojournalist Jeff Jefferies. Not to be outdone, Grace Kelly turned in her own best role. The combination was screen magic, but to my thinking, the story of what's going on in the apartment complex that Jefferies's rear window looks out upon is even more compelling than their acting.

Every neighborhood has its stories, and so it was with Jefferies's. With a cast on his leg, the hobbled photojournalist occupied himself by watching the dramas going on outside his window. Among the cast of characters was terrier who lived in a third-story apartment and had his calls of nature accommodated by a basket-and-pulley system.

It was the terrier's nose that proved his undoing. The little dog sniffed out a murder. When his owner discovered the lifeless terrier, her anguish drew the attention of everyone in the complex, including the revelers at a party. Almost so as to not be heard, one of the partygoers made the pronouncement, "Let's go back in. It's just a little dog." The words were never written in the screenplay, but Hitchcock allowed himself the little editorial.

The dismissive words from the movie kept playing in my head. As always, the thought of those words ignited my anger. It was possible the dogs in Mack Carter's neighborhood had just eaten something they shouldn't. Maybe there was some innocent, or at least understandable, explanation. But I needed resolution. There were always bigger issues that couldn't be dealt with or that were beyond me. I needed to make sense of what I could.

For now, though, I had a flight to catch, and a psychopath waiting to be questioned.

For my conference with Haines, I was taken deep into the bowels of the San Quentin penitentiary and left to wait in a conference space that was referred to as the lawyer's room. In the past, Haines had made a spectacle of himself while being brought over for our talks. His performances usually included singing and loud commentary, but today there was no grand entrance. I might not have even noticed his approach if not for the clinking of his chains as he made his way toward our meeting space.

The lawyer's room was about twice the size of a San Quentin cell. At its center was a stainless-steel table bolted into the concrete. Under the table was the so-called hitching post, a metal bar running the length of the table. As Haines entered the room, our eyes met. His were unblinking and predatory. There was something reptilian about them, or maybe I'd been forced to spend too much time thinking about rattlesnakes. If eyes were supposed to be the windows into the soul, then he didn't have a soul.

I did my best to respond in kind.

"Thank you," I told the three correctional officers who had escorted him. During past visits, Haines had referred to them as Manny, Moe, and Jack, or collectively as the Pep Boys, which they were decidedly not. When they prepared to secure his chains to the hitching post I said, "That won't be necessary. And please remove his hand restraints."

"Sure?" asked one of the Pep Boys.

I nodded, and the man shrugged, clearly convinced that mine wasn't a good idea.

After the Pep Boys filed out of the cell and locked the door behind them, Haines made his way over to the food slot and turned his back so that he was facing away from it. Then he placed his hands through the opening. One of the COs unlocked his shackles, removed his chains, and then secured the food slot.

Haines decided to keep me waiting while he massaged his wrists. Then he slowly shuffled over to the table and lowered himself into a seat opposite from me. He decided to let me be the one to break the silence between us.

"As I'm sure you've already surmised," I said, "I'm here on behalf of the Feds. They'd like to get your thoughts on two recent homicides."

"And that is the totality of your interest?" he asked.

"Isn't that enough?"

"The last time we were together you led me to believe that you would not be visiting here ever again."

"That was my hope."

"And yet here you are, and by your own admission you are serving as a delivery boy for the FBI. Is that right?"

I shrugged. "I guess that sums it up."

"How the mighty have fallen. Why did you agree to help them?"

"I'm a prince of a fellow. Just ask anyone."

"That's one—*explanation*," he said, not hiding his skepticism. "But I think it would be more accurate to say the FBI blackmailed you into cooperating with them. Their stick was threatening to freeze you out of their investigation of the individual they call the All-In Killer."

His eyes turned to the folder that I had placed on the table. "Their carrot was to provide you with their field notes, but only if you passed on that same information to me. Clearly the FBI is up a creek without the proverbial paddle, and they're hoping I can get their investigation back on track. Does that adequately sum up everything?"

I didn't answer except to say, "Is it all right if I tape you?"

Haines pretended to consider my request. "I'm not sure I'm comfortable with that idea."

What he wasn't comfortable with was the idea of making our talk any easier than was necessary. He wanted me to jump through hoops, and I was sure he especially liked the idea of my having to take down his dictation.

"Tough," I said.

"Drawing your line in the sand?" he asked. "I doubt your handlers will be pleased if you come back empty-handed."

"I'll take that chance," I said. "I already told them that coming here was a waste of time. I also said that you might refuse to talk with me. If that's your choice, I'm okay with it. If you don't want to talk into the box, then I might as well walk."

We locked eyes for a few seconds, then I reached out to retrieve the folder detailing the TNT homicide investigation. I knew the crime scene photos were calling to Haines in much the same way heroin calls to a junkie. He needed his fix.

He smiled at me, acting as if he were amused. "I guess I should be complimented that the FBI is so interested in hearing my every word. Or perhaps they fear that you couldn't keep up with me. I know my lawyers have had all sorts of qualms regarding your account of our first meeting, especially as your report omitted so many very important details of what occurred between us."

In the midst of the inferno, I had threatened to murder Haines on multiple occasions when he'd tried to walk away from helping me carry Sirius. There was also the matter of Miranda between us. I claimed that I had read him his rights; he knew otherwise. During his first trial I had lied under oath, convincing myself I was acting for the greater good. If I were put on the stand a second time, I wasn't sure I could lie again. That was another reason for my wanting to nail him for one of the Las Vegas homicides I was certain he'd committed.

"I'm assuming that somewhere in your long-winded diatribe," I said, "you just agreed it's okay for me to record you?"

He waved a benevolent hand. "If it means that much to you, Detective Gideon."

I reached for the mini-recorder and spoke into it, identifying the day, time, place, and who I was talking to. Usually I make recordings with my cell phone, but because personal communication devices aren't allowed inside the prison the FBI had cleared the tape recorder with the warden.

"Ellis Haines," I said, "I would like you to go on record and say that you have agreed to answer my questions by your own free will and without duress."

"That is correct," he said, "although we could have a long debate about the very notion of free will, and how I am not sure if I adhere to any of the branches of determinism, be they causal or noncausal."

I stifled a pretend yawn and said, "As fascinating as that discussion might be, what I would prefer hearing from you is that you're okay with my recording these proceedings. Do you have any problems with my doing that?"

"I do not, Detective."

"Then go to it," I said, gesturing to the folder. "When you finish looking at what the FBI has provided you, I'll ask you some questions."

Haines stretched out a languid hand toward the folder; both of us were putting on an act for the other. I knew that Haines was jonesing to see what I had brought, despite his attempt at indifference, and he knew that I needed him to cooperate for my own purposes. As soon as the folder was in his hands, he began quickly flipping through its contents. His hunger was extreme, and it needed to be satisfied posthaste. It was only after he'd turned through all the pages and pictures from the ten-ten and nine-nine murders that he began a more detailed examination from the beginning. After his second go-around, Haines sorted all the crime scene photos before starting to place them down on the table. To me it almost looked as if he were dealing cards. Within moments, the tabletop was completely covered.

The chairs were attached to the table and bolted to the concrete, which made for uncomfortable seating. Since I couldn't lean back in my chair, I lowered my head and closed my eyes. My apparent disinterest spurred Haines to start talking, as I'd hoped it would. More than anyone, Haines needed an audience. Maybe just as importantly, he also wanted to deny me the possibility of napping. Giving succor to the enemy wasn't in his nature.

"TNT," he said. "What a well-*executed* demonstration."

I opened an eye, saw him mugging over his pun, which was enough for me to start scratching my forehead with an extended middle finger. That only made him smile wider. To him, all attention was good attention.

"No doubt about it," he said. "The FBI can check their organized-killer box. Some behavioralists might contend that the method used to kill the victim entailed mutilation, but that argument would be specious. The killer had a carefully thought-out plan for the remains. And while we know that occasionally victims are posed by their killers, in this instance that posing was done with not only imagination, but precision. This was a *man* with a *plan*."

He lifted up one of the photos and looked at it critically. "The report doesn't speculate on the origins of the vinyl sacks holding the body parts. If I had to guess, these bags started out as a larger human-remains pouch. If so, then we were treated to the sight of four small body bags."

"Some treat," I said.

"Body bags," he continued, "are usually only brought out in wars, or natural disasters, or *killer storms* and the like. Perhaps we should put this homicide in that context."

The crime scene photos would have turned most stomachs, but they inspired Haines to quote from a children's rhyme: "'Baa, baa, black sheep, / Have you any wool? / Yes sir, yes sir, / Three bags full.'"

"Four bags," I said.

"A four-bagger," he said. "A home run. That's what this was. And it's five bags if we include the gris-gris bag. You might have your overlords check on the slang for a five-bagger. It wouldn't surprise me if there were a hidden meaning in such. Our black sheep is very clever."

"Murder isn't clever. It's a brutal, abhorrent act."

"I wasn't aware that this was a morality play, Detective," he said. "The FBI wouldn't be chasing its own tail if the killer were not clever. Like any good chess master, the killer is thinking multiple moves ahead, and the taking of pawns is part of the game. The game within the game is adroit. In the TNT homicide, the waters were muddied, which was certainly part of the plan. The kill was in one place, the body parts put on display in another. A jigsaw puzzle with thousands of pieces. Humpty Dumpty couldn't be put together again, as our black sheep was well aware. That's what he was counting upon."

The cop in me had always suspected that Humpty Dumpty was pushed, but I didn't voice that opinion aloud.

Haines went on to another children's rhyme involving smashing and smushing, and in a singsong voice he said:

A peanut sat on a railroad track,
His heart was all a-flutter.
The five-fifteen came along.
Toot toot! Peanut butter!

He gave me a sideways glance. "When I was a boy, that was a favorite rhyme of mine."

"I'm sure it's a favorite among all young psychopaths," I said.

"You wish it were that easy to explain my behavior, don't you, Detective?" he asked. "But you're no psychologist, nor are you much of a sleuth. That's why you and the FBI are hoping I'll throw you some crumbs. You think you're Mr. Big Stuff. But *who do* you think you are?"

I wondered why Haines was quoting from Jean Knight's old song "Mr. Big Stuff." He was taunting me, but I wasn't sure about what. I tried fishing for its source.

"A favorite song of yours?" I asked.

"I always liked its lyrics," he said. And then he repeated, "*'Who do* you think you are?'"

I wondered if that had been one of his karaoke songs but knew better than to ask that question. Detective Charles was in the process of compiling everything that had to do with Haines's karaoke singing in Las Vegas. Our hope was that there might even be some videos of him belting out tunes. It was something we planned on pursuing.

"Eleven items in the charm bag," he mused. "And so many messages directed your way. Even a shout-out for Sirius. I'm glad he wasn't forgotten."

I hoped the anger I felt didn't translate to the flushing of my skin. It was better not to let Haines know which of his provocations worked best. "It sure was a good thing his shots were up-to-date when he chewed on you," I said. "How are your scars from that encounter? I hope they healed up. No one likes visible reminders of failure. I imagine that wouldn't be easy to endure, especially in a place like this."

Haines pretended to be philosophical. "As Gandhi was quick to point out," he said, "you can't imprison a mind. In many ways I am freer inside these walls than I ever was outside them."

Unfortunately, that was probably true. One of the reasons inmates are so manipulative is that they don't have the time constraints that the rest of us have in the outside world. If a con is intent on causing mayhem, he can make that his full-time job. To that end, Haines seemed to be working overtime.

He went back to looking at the photos on the table, then reached for one of them and showed it to me. "Is this your fleece, Detective? If so, it's becoming white as snow. I hope that's not a result of too much stress and worry. And do tell me, how is it that the killer was able to collect a lock of your hair?"

"We don't yet know if it's my hair, unless you would like to confirm that for a certainty."

"How could a cloistered inmate like me have that knowledge?"

"It's obvious that you and the All-In Killer have been communicating."

"Is it?"

I went on to my next question: "Care to offer a theory as to why he left some toad's toes in lieu of a frog's?"

"What do they always say are the three rules of real estate? Location, location, location."

"Explain that to me."

"*Make him understand*, oh lord? Use your *brain*, Detective. The All-In Killer is making his way through the wilderness of the desert. In such a location you are much more likely to encounter toads than frogs."

"Does anything else in the gris-gris bag stand out?"

"Each item makes a statement, although some of the charms are more traditional than others."

Like the hair, I thought, and the bird's nest.

"What about the castor beans?" I asked. "Do you think the killer is threatening to unleash ricin?"

Haines shook his head dismissively. "There's no need to hire a taster, if that's your worry."

"Then why castor beans?"

Haines lifted his hands above his shoulders and shrugged.

"What do you make of the birth announcement?" I asked.

"Alpha and omega," he said. "Along with the birth announcement, there was a death announcement, was there not?"

"What death announcement are you referring to?"

"Isn't that obvious?" he said. "Why, the mourning band on the LAPD badge, of course."

"Which had my badge number written on it."

"Oh, really?" he taunted. "I had no idea what those numbers signified."

"What about the message from Flattop Jones? Does that suggest a contract was taken out?"

"Sometimes a cigar is just a cigar, Detective. Flattop Jones is a character out of the comic pages. His presence shouldn't be taken literally."

"How about figuratively? Why would Flattop say he loves his police department?"

"I believe that's called *sarcasm*, Detective," he said, his tone dismissive.

"The frequency of the murders has greatly accelerated. Months passed between the jack-five homicide and the ten-ten homicide. But now we've had the ten-ten and nine-nine homicides in rapid succession."

"As they say, you ain't seen nothing yet."

"What do you mean?"

"I would guess the eight-eight homicide has already occurred. It is history, or perhaps herstory. Those cards have been dealt, or at least dealt with."

"Where does that leave us?"

"We're on to lucky seven, or in this case, sevens."

"Sevens are lucky?"

"They always have been for me."

CHAPTER SEVENTEEN

THE SMELL TEST

I asked Haines every question on the FBI's list, and lots of my own. Psychopaths like Haines are good at beating the box. Lie detectors detect physiological changes in such areas as heart rate, pulse, blood pressure, and perspiration. Because Haines was able to lie with complete equanimity, it was useless to hook him up to the machine. Luckily for me, I come equipped with my own personal bullshit detector.

While waiting for my flight, I rewound the tape and began listening to our interview. I used a set of earbuds so as to not disturb those around me, and kept the crime scene photos locked in my briefcase. Haines, and those like him, are toxic to normal human beings, and I know from personal experience it's better if people are spared from being touched by their pitch. Cops don't have that option. We serve as buffers to the worst ugliness in this world.

I began taking notes, writing down anything that didn't feel right, or sound right. To Haines, everything was a game, and it was fun to see how close he could get to the flames without being burned. He and the All-In Killer both enjoyed guising clues with misdirection, red herrings, and sensory overload. Because of that, I focused on those areas that Haines had glossed over during our conversation, or somehow downplayed. Wherever he deflected or diverted, I took notice. His inflections also raised flags, as well as when he repeated himself. Had he been monosyllabic, I wouldn't have been able to get much of a read on him, but that wasn't his way. Haines needed to show how clever he was.

On one of my notepad pages I had jotted down those words he had lingered over, or repeated, or finessed in such a way as to stand out; on another page I had tried to reconstruct the body language that accompanied his speech at the time he said it.

One of my first entries was *man* with a *plan*. That was followed up by two words in his "Mr. Big Stuff" song: *who do*. And when he'd talked about the four sacks—or body bags, as he called them—he had seemed energized by the notion of *killer storms*. Then again, he had been a meteorologist and was the infamous Weatherman, a name almost synonymous with the boogieman. But it hadn't sounded like he was giving me a weather report. There was something else there.

I went back to my listening. One sentence struck me as atypical. Instead of speaking to me directly, he'd acted aggrieved at my ignorance and said, "*Make him understand*, oh lord?" And then he'd followed up by saying, "Use your *brain*." What had made him react that way? I'd asked him about the killer's substituting toes of toad for toes of frog, and he'd pushed back with some real estate folderol.

Think. I wrestled with the context of our conversation and the words he'd chosen, and tried to make those words submit to me. The answers were elusive, like a word on the tip of your tongue. I knew there were important connections to be had, but I couldn't break the code.

My phone vibrated, and I checked the caller ID. Ben Corning was calling to get my report.

"My plane is about to leave," I said, which was more or less true.

"How did the session go?" he asked.

"He talked a lot, but I'm not sure how much he said."

"We're sending a special agent to LAX to meet your flight," he said. "We'll gather your tape so that we can get out transcripts of it."

I would have preferred having more time with the tape for myself, but at least the flight would offer me the better part of two hours to listen to the recording.

"Word to the wise," I said. "Haines seems to think an eight-eight murder is already a fait accompli."

"I hope he's wrong."

"That's two of us," I said.

The boarding announcement went out for my flight, but I decided to make a call before strapping in. Andrea Charles picked up on the first ring and asked, "Got a weather report for me?"

"Haines is his own severe weather event," I said. "I didn't get any forecast out of him, or at least I don't think so, although during the course of our conversation he did use the phrase *killer storms*, but not in the context of weather."

"What context was it?"

"The bringing out of body bags," I said.

"Right now, it's a hundred degrees outside," she said, "but I'm feeling a little chill. Was that some kind of warning?"

"It felt more like he was lording it over me for knowing things that I didn't."

"Don't sweat it," she said.

"He did say something that made me think of your karaoke angle," I said. "You might remember that a few months back we talked about you compiling a list of his favorite karaoke songs. I was wondering if you've had a chance to get to that."

"It's on my to-do list," she said. "I've been asking witnesses if they remembered any of his favorites, but I haven't done a write-up of my results. What do you need to know?"

"Are you aware if he ever performed the song 'Mr. Big Stuff'?"

"No one has mentioned that one yet, and I'd kind of be surprised if it was in his performing repertoire."

"Why is that?"

"It's an oldie. It's also a vocal associated with a woman. And the lyrics are definitely from a female's point of view."

To make her point, she sang, "'Who do you think you are?'"

Detective Charles had a good voice. It seemed like everyone involved in this case could sing but me. Even Sirius has a better voice than I do.

"I'm surprised you even know the lyrics," I said. "You weren't born when that song was released. I wasn't even born."

"A classic is a classic. But why was he singing to you?"

"I'm trying to figure that out. He didn't bring up his anger about Las Vegas, but Haines isn't one to forget, nor is he one to take kindly to being backed into a corner. We can't underestimate him just because he's behind bars."

"Got it," she said.

I hoped she did.

"Do you have anything else for me?" she asked.

"On the flight home I'll be reviewing my conversation with Haines. I think he's communicating things to me in such a way as to gloat over not only what's already occurred, but what he thinks is coming. If I'm right, he's establishing future bragging rights for how smart he is."

"Don't let Bad Weather get into your head."

"Easier said than done," I admitted. "He thinks the eight-eight homicide has already occurred."

Detective Charles whistled. "Three homicides in four days."

"I think the killer accelerated the schedule to stay ahead of the investigation. These homicides aren't like spree killings. They're very well organized. With the Feds already stretched thin, another homicide will put them on their heels."

"Did you get Haines to talk about seven-seven?"

"He didn't say much other than that sevens have always been lucky for him."

"Lots of gamblers believe in lucky seven."

"Why is that?"

"I couldn't tell you."

"Haines isn't superstitious as far as I know."

"I haven't uncovered anything to suggest that he is," she agreed.

"If he doesn't believe in lucky numbers, then why did he say that sevens have always been lucky for him?"

"Maybe he won a big pot once with a pair of sevens."

"That's possible."

Detective Charles heard my doubts and asked, "You have another answer?"

"I don't, which is damned annoying."

I had a window seat on the flight back, but took little notice of the view. For once, seeing Haines might have been a good thing for me. There'd been no time to stew about my personal life and what was going on between Lisbet and me. Instead, I felt this urgency to try and work out Haines's hidden meanings. It was a matter of life and death.

Listening closely to someone speaking is a greatly underrated skill, and it's especially hard when you're trying to out-clever that individual during the course of the conversation. The word games were behind me now. I concentrated on the recording and heard myself ask Haines, "Then why castor beans?"

I pressed Pause and thought about how Haines had responded. He'd chosen to answer by lifting his hands up. Most people don't shrug like that. They raise their shoulders, or spread their hands to show their emptiness. It had almost looked like Haines was raising something high in the air.

There were plenty of dots in my notepad. Connecting them was the problem. I listened to Haines reciting "Baa, Baa, Black Sheep," reference Humpty Dumpty, and tell the tale of a peanut on a railroad track. My gut feeling was that he'd been attempting to be cute.

Haines had been his most dismissive when I'd queried Flattop Jones and his message. He'd sounded almost contemptuous of my contract-killer question, relegating Flattop's declaration of love for the police department to "sarcasm." It was almost as if Haines had been annoyed, but not at me. Was it possible he hadn't wanted me to focus on what the All-In Killer had written?

More rewinding, and more note-taking. Haines had seemed to particularly enjoy reciting, "'Who do you think you are?'" He'd repeated the lyrics, but there was something a little off in his intonation. Hearing it twice made it stand out. *Who do* didn't sound like two words, but one. I was hearing *hoodoo*. It was probably nothing, but I still made a note.

And then I heard a voice other than Haines's. The flight attendant was announcing our descent.

The passage of time surprised me. I stowed the tape recorder and looked out the window. More than ten million people live in LA County. From above, the cars moving along the crowded freeways looked like a busy ant colony on the move.

When an ant finds food, it secretes a chemical pheromone for other ants to follow. Once the ant returns to the colony, the other ants have a chemical roadmap to the food source. For them, that's the smell test.

If only I had pheromones to follow, I thought. And then wondered if I did.

CHAPTER EIGHTEEN

WASHING AND DYING

In the last twenty-four hours, he'd come very, very close, but close didn't cut it. Close didn't get you that victory cigar. He needed to seal the deal. Third time was the charm. It had better be. Time was running out.

The watering holes hadn't worked out as planned. Like any predator, he didn't like doing any more work than was necessary. The craftiest predators let their prey come to them. That was the way to get it done. He knew her routines, knew where she lived, worked, shopped, and dined. Her workplace was a nonstarter. It posed too many dangers. But there were other spots that better fit the bill. It was just a matter of getting her to the right watering hole, one without too many eyes in the sky, or too much foot traffic. Success meant getting in and getting out before anyone knew what had happened.

He had staked out her favorite coffee shop, a spot in the Arts District about a mile from her workplace. Usually she parked on a side street. That afforded good hunting ground for an ambush, but she'd switched things up by arriving later than usual, and then parking in the strip mall lot. That might not have been a deal breaker; her being accompanied by a friend was. When it wasn't right, it wasn't right.

The rest of the day she'd avoided her usual spots. That hadn't bothered him much. Everything should have worked out for him the night before. She had a longstanding Wednesday tradition of girls' night out. Hump day meant she and three of her friends always went out for a meal, or drinks, or a movie, or a show. Sometimes they did all four.

Instead of leaving their encounter to chance, he'd targeted her best friend, Jade, informing her by mail that she was a contest winner and the lucky recipient of dinner for four at the Darker Than Night restaurant. The reservation was for that Wednesday night, the letter said, and couldn't be changed. The restaurant offered the sensory experience of dining in the dark. The absence of light was supposed to enhance the senses of taste and smell. Jade and three of her friends had descended upon the restaurant, but the target hadn't. He had waited around for a time, making sure she wasn't a late arrival. Unlike the other diners, he'd smuggled in a night vision scope, along with a special walking stick. He'd left before his entrée arrived, explaining to his server that his date had been forced to cancel. The size of the cash tip he left made that excuse palatable, so to speak.

Because only three days had been set aside for the job, he'd saved the best option for last. Thursday was her laundry day. She always used the washers and dryers located in the basement of what was supposed to be her security building. Thursday night didn't seem to be a popular time for laundry. So far, no one else was using the machines.

He had one load in the wash, and another in the dryer. The clothing had been purchased in an out-of-town thrift shop, and he'd made sure not to get anything in his size.

There was one item in his basket that wasn't being washed or dried. It was a National Hockey League Golden Knights jersey with the number 77. The jersey was covering up a very special double-loop garrote of spring steel. Once it was around the victim's neck, it was a guaranteed death sentence. There was a backup plan, of course. In case she no-showed once again, he knew which apartment she lived in. If necessary, he could pay a visit, but that would expose him to a lot more risk. It was better, much better, to let his victim come to him.

He looked at his watch. Any minute now, he thought.

CHAPTER NINETEEN

WHILE WAITING FOR TEA

Seth wasn't home, so I used a key to his house to retrieve the dogs from the backyard. In the entryway Seth had left a note with the words *I Fed Them!* On the same page he'd drawn a picture of a huge dog bowl, and caricatures of Sirius and Emily chowing down. A second, smaller drawing of a martini glass was at the bottom of the page along with the word *Nightcap?* There was a trail of what appeared to be bubbles rising up the page.

"'I get no kick from champagne,'" I said.

That wasn't exactly true, but that's what Frank had sung in his rendition of "I Get a Kick Out of You."

I studied Seth's drawing, and then carried it with me out to the backyard. Seth had probably produced his creation in under a minute; it would have taken me the better part of the day to produce something half as good.

"Your uncle Seth is one talented guy," I told the dogs, showing them his handiwork.

I was glad the dogs were a lot more interested in me than in the drawing. It was okay with them that I was an artistic failure. One of the reasons dogs are so loved is that they don't set the bar too high for their humans.

Seth's creation came home with us. Parents proudly display their children's artwork; I wanted to put the artwork of my dogs up on the refrigerator. Besides, I wasn't yet sure if a drink tonight was in the cards. Emphasis *cards*. Handing over the recording of Haines to the FBI agent who met me at the airport didn't mean that I was able to put it behind me. I had this sense that there was some imminent deadline that had to be met, and failure to do so would result in severe consequences.

I settled on the sofa with my notes and the FBI's files. Sirius decided to join me on one side, and Emily took the space on the other. The sofa was just large enough to accommodate all three of us, and the proximity of their bodies loosened some of the tightness in my chest and eased my breathing. I put a grateful hand on each dog and scratched them for a few moments before returning to work. They decided it was a good time for a nap. Emily is a snorer, but I welcomed the sound of her repose. For me, it was like reassuring background music.

Once again, I studied my notes, as well as the FBI's reports and crime scene pictures. In the absence of evidence, or at least perceived evidence, I tried to follow my hunches. Instead of attacking the questions head-on, I tried working backward, putting them in the context of different filters and frameworks. My kaleidoscopic detecting didn't get me anywhere.

I used my phone's search engine to ask for a definition of the word *hoodoo*. The first meaning came up as *voodoo, or witchcraft*, prompting me to scroll to secondary and tertiary meanings. My index finger came to a stop at *hoodoo bag*. What I read made me freeze. *Hoodoo bag* was another name for a gris-

gris or charm bag. There was even a fourth interchangeable name: *mojo bag*.

Mojo, I thought. In the hollow of my skull I seemed to hear an echo.

"Mojo," I whispered, trying to breathe life into the flickering spark.

My tinder must have been lacking; the connection that I sensed retreated and then was lost.

Misery loves company, which must have been why my phone suddenly began vibrating. Ben Corning was calling. My antennae, noticeably absent until now, suddenly appeared. I wished they hadn't. I had no doubt as to the purpose of Corning's call.

"The eight-eight homicide turned up," I said.

His sigh was his answer.

"Where and when?" I asked.

"No definitive time of death yet," Corning said, "but within the day. It happened on the outskirts of Flagstaff. The victim was a seventy-three-year-old woman who lived by herself."

"What's the eight-eight connection?"

"She was a piano teacher."

Eighty-eight damn keys, I thought, but all those keys hadn't been able to open my locked mind.

"Her home was only sixty miles from the Winslow homicide," said Corning.

"Our killer had already picked out his victim and knew exactly where he was going."

"That's our thinking."

Flagstaff was about 450 miles from Los Angeles. The killer wasn't lingering between kills, nor stopping for any sightseeing.

"Anything unusual at the crime scene?"

"Our team has just begun processing it," he said.

"Any message left?"

"Nothing that's apparent. But one of the investigators found it unusual that the piano had been wiped entirely clean."

That didn't seem surprising. "Makes sense that he was just wiping clean the crime scene."

"The crime scene was in the next room. It was nowhere near the piano. The victim died of multiple gunshot wounds while in the kitchen."

"In the kitchen," I mused.

"It appears she was in the process of making tea. There were two mugs with teabags in them."

"Your investigators think she was making tea for the killer?"

"That's what it looks like."

"Was there a sign of forced entrance?" I asked.

"There was not. It appears the killer walked into the house."

"And the piano was wiped clean of fingerprints, or any other potential evidence?"

"It was."

"You think the killer was there for a piano lesson, don't you?"

"It's a theory. And it would explain why all the piano keys, and the piano itself, were cleaned so thoroughly."

"Have your people had a chance to canvass the neighborhood?"

"The Flagstaff police have been helping us, but all the houses in the area sit on two acres or more, and they come with a national forest for a backyard. That means even fewer potential eyes than usual."

"I'll bet this wasn't the killer's first piano lesson," I said.

"What makes you think that?"

"Tea makes me think that. And the teacher's opening the door. In the victim's background check, her friends and family need to be asked if she mentioned taking on a new student."

"That's worth pursuing," Corning said.

"One more thing," I said. "Will the Bureau be doing a forensic speech analysis of my talk with Haines?"

While a traditional lie detector read might not work with Haines, there were other available detection tools, including speech analysis. Voice patterns showing laryngeal microtremors often revealed when a speaker was dissembling or attempting to deceive.

"I'm not sure if that kind of an analysis is in the works," he said.

"I'd like to put in a request that it be done," I said. "And when they get around to analyzing the voice patterns, I'd like them to key on the words 'who do.' I think Haines was playing with me on the two occasions he said those words. I believe he was saying it as one word, that being H-O-O-D-O-O."

I finished spelling it and added, "After I followed up on that, I learned a hoodoo bag is the same thing as a gris-gris bag or charm bag or mojo bag."

"And that's supposed to mean something?"

"Haines read the report you people provided where the amulet bag was categorized as a gris-gris or charm bag. He probably thought it was amusing to make an obscure reference to a hoodoo bag without coming right out and saying it. He enjoys being smug."

"And what was he being smug about?"

"I don't know. There's something in my head that has to do with hoodoo, or maybe mojo, but I can't shake it free."

"If the coconut falls, call me."

"I will if it doesn't hit my head."

CHAPTER TWENTY

THE WAITING MONSTER

She thought about putting off doing her laundry until the weekend, but it was always a hassle trying to find an open machine. At the best of times work was demanding, and that was before she had agreed to assume additional duties. Those obligations had meant spending her evenings playing catch-up, not to mention her weekends. She had put her social life on the back burner; her friends were giving her grief about that, but she knew you only got ahead by sacrificing. That meant giving up a lot—but not clean clothes.

"Half an hour for the wash cycle, and a little less than an hour to dry." She checked the time on her phone. If all went well, her laundry would be folded and put away before midnight.

The big question was whether her bedsheets could go another week without being washed. She decided that they could, but then remembered having arrived at that same conclusion the week before. With a small sigh, she trudged into her bedroom and stripped the bed and pillows.

The laundry basket was stored in her bedroom closet. She threw the sheets into it, then went around the apartment adding scattered clothing items that had somehow eluded the confines of the hamper. By the time she set out for the laundry room, her basket was overflowing.

As she stepped out of her apartment, she took inventory. Key, yes. Detergent, plenty. Money for the machines, check. And her phone was in hand. Of late the phone seemed to be ringing nonstop. That reminded her. She looked at the battery and saw her phone was only twenty percent charged. Remember to charge it, she told herself, when I get back to the apartment.

She walked over to the elevator and hit the down button. While waiting for the door to open, she thought about the monster in the basement that lived in the dryer.

"Damn sock monster," she said aloud.

More often than not, that monster claimed one of her stockings.

CHAPTER TWENTY-ONE

CHOPSTICKS

Corning's call had worsened my unease. It felt like I'd been given a bad prognosis with no recourse but to worry. Even without an appetite, I tried to eat. I opened a can of soup, and paced around the kitchen while the microwave heated my dinner. After stomaching half the bowl, I pushed it aside.

The dogs were still snoozing on the sofa when I rejoined them in the living room. I took a seat in my easy chair, opened my laptop, and conducted a search on private piano teachers in the Flagstaff area. There were a lot more individuals teaching piano than I would have expected, especially in a city with a population of under 75,000 people. Maybe the FBI could use their technological whiz kids to try and track down anyone who had done a similar search in the last few months.

When I was a seven-year-old kid, my parents signed me up for piano lessons. Mrs. Gaynor was an older neighbor who had taught piano for many years. I'm not saying I drove her into retirement, but a musical prodigy I wasn't. Nature has endowed me with not one but two tin ears. After a year of lessons, my reper-toire consisted of "Chopsticks," "Twinkle, Twinkle, Little Star," and "Heart and Soul" (which I managed to play with neither). By mutual agreement of teacher, student, and parents, one year of lessons was deemed enough. I always thought it ironic that someone who loves music as much as I do was born without a musical bone in my body.

I hadn't thought about Mrs. Gaynor and my erstwhile piano lessons for a long time. My old teacher, I realized, would have been about the same age as the Flagstaff victim at the time when I began my lessons. My inability to do anything constructive felt crippling. I couldn't even play a dirge. Mrs. Gaynor and I hadn't gotten that far in my lessons.

Out of gallows humor came an idea. It was probably noth-ing, but that didn't stop me from calling Ben Corning.

"Yeah," he said. It was not the usual stiffed and starched protocol of the FBI. He sounded about as deep in the dumps as I was feeling.

"You said the killer left no message," I said. "But his MO is to provide some tie-in with the cards and commentary."

"I didn't rule out the possibility of a message in Flagstaff," he said. "We're still processing the scene. Something might turn up."

"I have this feeling that whatever is there is probably right in front of their eyes."

"We know what we're doing," he said, sounding pissed off.

"I'm thinking it's a purloined-letter kind of thing."

Corning had evidently not had Mrs. Petersen teaching Poe's short story for ninth grade English. "What the hell are you talk-ing about?" he said.

"Listen," I said. "I'm not trying to step on anyone's shoes. But I need you to call whoever is in charge of the scene and have them look at the sheet music that's out."

"'Sheet music'?" Now he didn't sound pissed so much as he sounded annoyed.

"Above the keyboard of the piano there's a music rack," I said. "If your guys are right about the killer sitting down to a lesson, there's probably some sheet music there."

"And you're interested in the playlist?"

"Wouldn't it be like the killer to try and hide something in plain sight?"

Corning didn't answer. I wasn't sure if his silence was the result of skepticism or potential interest. I continued anyway.

"When I was a beginner at piano, I remember there was sheet music for songs like 'Mary Had a Little Lamb,' 'Happy Birthday,' 'Yankee Doodle,' and 'Alouette.'"

"So?"

"So, what if the killer brought his own sheet music?" I asked.

"That's a stretch," he said.

"Yes, it is," I agreed. "But if the All-In Killer is anything like Haines, then he likes nothing better than showing how clever he is."

"Let's say the killer did bring his own sheet music," said Corning. "How would we even be able to distinguish it from whatever might have already been there?"

"Look for something besides 'Chopsticks' or 'Do-Re-Mi.'"

The line was quiet for too long. Finally, Corning spoke. "I'll make the call."

Five minutes passed, and then ten minutes, and then a quarter of an hour. With the passage of time, my glimmer of hope was extinguished. When Corning called back, I answered without much in the way of audible enthusiasm.

That's when he said, "'Riders on the Storm.'"

"What?"

"It was just like you said. All the other sheet music was for beginners, except for 'Riders on the Storm.'"

For a moment I couldn't respond. The neural pathways to my brain overloaded.

"Are you still there?" he asked.

"Let me call you back in five minutes," I said.

CHAPTER TWENTY-TWO

FOR WANT OF A NAIL

Just as the elevator door opened, she said, "Fabric softener." She deliberated for a long moment, one leg in the elevator and one leg out.

"Shit," she said.

The fabric softener wasn't critical. She knew that. But she lived in the static electricity capital of the world. The fabric softener mostly eliminated those zaps. And with the long days she was working, soft-and-scented blouses that didn't electrocute her felt like a necessity.

The jury was still out, though. The elevator made the sound of wanting to close, but the sensor could read the obstruction of her leg.

It was the scent of towels that helped her to decide. At the end of every workday she took a shower, then wrapped herself up in a towel. A shower never quite seemed complete without luxuriating in a towel treated with fabric softener. It was almost like a loving embrace.

She made her way back to her apartment, unlocked the door, and then placed her laundry basket and phone on the coffee table. The fabric softener was in the hall closet, and she went and retrieved it.

Lately, the only snuggling she was getting in her personal life came from being wrapped in a towel. Darned if she was going to go without fabric softener.

She tamped down the laundry basket and found a place for the fabric softener. It was a good-sized basket, and she needed both hands to support it. Getting the door open while holding the basket required using her stomach and hips, but she managed it.

Unnoticed was her absent phone. She had left it behind on the coffee table.

CHAPTER TWENTY-THREE

THE MOURNING BAND

The logjam finally broke, and every clue that had been struggling to emerge from my mind came flooding out.

It's been almost half a century since the Doors played music, but now their chords were invading every corner of my life. Beyond the grave, Jim Morrison was playing, and I was dancing to his tune. There wasn't time to think about the synchronicity of my "LA woman" case—Carrie Holder. Later, I could get back to that, but for now it was just strange happenstance. There were more immediate matters demanding action.

I printed out the lyrics for "Riders on the Storm," and it was like a checklist of most of the items in the mojo bag. In fact, it started with the mojo bag itself. *Mr. Mojo Risin'* was an anagram for *Jim Morrison*, and a pseudonym he liked to use. In the song "L.A. Woman," Morrison was so fond of the prurient anagram that he repeated the words *Mr. Mojo Risin'* over and over.

The FBI had been on the right track regarding the castor beans in the bag. They had worried about the threat of ricin, but that hadn't been the killer's message. The play on words had been *risin'* instead of *ricin*. And there was a reason toad remains had been left instead of frog remains—the lyrics in the song referenced a toad. The doggie bag with the bone had made me imagine a threat to Sirius—throwing me off that way, as well as evoking a reaction, had probably been its intent. Until now I had never imagined that it referenced a line in the song.

The clues were all about the killer on the road. The All-In Killer was riding on Morrison's storm. That storm had even been referenced on the leather mojo bag via the meteorological symbol. Biographers of the Doors and their music claimed the lyrics to the song referenced a well-known spree killer. The All-In Killer had decided to update and incorporate those lyrics. He was the new killer on the road, leaving blood throughout the Southwest.

He was the rider on the storm.

During that day's visit with Haines, he had emphasized the word *storm*. I was certain that wasn't a coincidence.

I thought about another word that Haines had lingered over: *brain*. That had also been lifted from the song's lyrics. I started crossing off items in the mojo bag that could be explained by its words, pausing at the replica LAPD badge with my inked-in number and the mourning band.

All this time I had assumed the badge was a threat directed at me. But was it?

Something was off. If the badge was supposed to be mine, how could I be mourning my own death? The mourning bands were placed on our badges to remember a fallen comrade. I had assumed the badge was a message telling me I was in the killer's crosshairs. It was a logical assumption, but now I wondered if it was the correct one.

The Flattop Jones picture and its message—*Love My Police Department*—also didn't seem to have any direct connection to the song other than the cartoon character also being a killer.

From the first, my interpretation had been personal. Flattop Jones had been hired to kill Dick Tracy. I had just assumed I was the target.

There was an idea that wanted to come out, that just needed a little mental push. I was convinced something was there, but I needed to study the source. Jumping to my feet, I ran over to where I'd left the FBI's folder, and remained standing as I riffled through the pages.

The dogs had been awakened by my movements and were circling around me, wondering what was going on. I studied Flattop's picture and message. And then I saw it.

"Oh," I said.

Until that moment I had missed it, as had the FBI. A stencil had been used to write the words *Love My Police Department*, but my eye had never picked up how the V wasn't a small vee; it was a capital V. *LoVe*. You almost had to be looking for the uppercase letter to even see it. The capital letters told the story: LVMPD.

Las Vegas Metropolitan Police Department.

I pulled out my cell phone and yelled out the command to dial Detective Andrea Charles's cell phone. The call went through, and I listened as it rang.

"Pick up!" I shouted.

There was a second ring.

"Answer! Answer!"

Her phone rang a third time.

"Please, please, please," I said.

The torture continued as her voicemail recording began to play. At its conclusion I shouted, "Andrea, you need to get to somewhere safe, and you need to do it now! I think you're the target!"

The panic in my voice bespoke the urgency of my message. I prayed that it hadn't arrived too late.

CHAPTER TWENTY-FOUR

LOOKING FOR A LIGHT TO FOLLOW

Andrea Charles was not a big woman. She wasn't petite, and certainly not delicate, but neither was she physically intimidating. She liked to claim she was five and a half feet tall, but knew that in actuality she was just a shade under five foot five. As a cop, she had learned to present bigger than she was. On the street, you needed to show that you were in charge. There had been a few dicey situations on the job, but never any life-or-death physical altercations. Still, Andrea had been happy when she had earned her detective's badge. She had survived the streets and done a good job, but thought she was better suited for her current position.

That didn't mean there weren't good things about being an officer, thought Andrea. When she'd had a uniform allowance, there hadn't been the need to do as much laundry.

The elevator door opened, and she started toward the laundry room. From down the hallway she could hear the sounds of machines being used, and hoped that two of the washers were free. At this time of night that usually wasn't a problem.

She entered the laundry room and saw its lone occupant. A man with his back turned to her was sitting in a plastic chair. It looked as if he was playing some kind of game on his phone while waiting for his laundry to be done.

Too late, Andrea realized she'd left her phone in her apartment. She tried to tell herself it was no big deal, but the truth was she always felt more at ease having a phone within reach. As if I can't live without it for ten minutes, she thought. It probably wouldn't even take that long before she was back in her apartment. Luckily for her, there were empty washers. That meant she could start one load of whites and one of colors without having to wait.

The man with the phone hadn't yet turned around. That seemed a little odd to Andrea. She didn't mind being ignored, but most people were at least curious enough to glance your way. It beat the alternative, though. Some guys seemed to think the laundry room was a good place to try and pick up women. To Andrea's thinking, dirty laundry and romance didn't mix.

As she passed by the man on her way to claim a washer, something odd registered. For just an instant, she'd seen the man's eye staring at her from his phone's screen. If she wasn't mistaken, he had been using the reflection like a mirror. That's why he hadn't bothered to turn around. There'd been no need.

Andrea pretended not to have noticed his surveillance; her body language revealed nothing. Lots of guys stared at women, some more obviously than others. The surreptitious peepers thought they were clever; that's probably what this guy was. At the moment, he was trying to give off a preoccupied vibe.

Without looking around, Andrea tried to remember if there was a security camera in the laundry room. She thought there was but couldn't be sure. Unfortunately, there were lots of so-called secure buildings with nonfunctioning cameras—even fake cameras were assumed to be deterrents. Maybe that explained the *Do Not Leave Laundry Unattended* sign posted in the laundry room. Even less reassuring was the sign that said *Management Not Responsible for Lost or Stolen Valuables.*

Andrea found herself facing a washer. The man was now behind her, and she didn't like having her back to him. As she deliberated over what to do, she pretended to look at the instructions on the machine. Flight was no longer an option. The man was between her and the door.

I'm overreacting, Andrea thought. But that wasn't what her body was telling her. Her adrenaline was pumping; blood vessels were contracting and sending blood coursing toward her heart and lungs. Her senses were on alert and seemed to be supercharged. She didn't grow eyes in the back of her head, but with her suddenly heightened sense of hearing it almost felt that way.

The man reached down for something. The motion was almost soundless. Almost. But the whisper of stretched clothing was enough to alert her. Andrea whirled around. A hangman with a garrote noose was lunging at her.

She swung her laundry basket at him and hit him just above his waist, but that only slowed him for an instant. The man came at her again, this time feinting one way and then moving another. The laundry basket was too bulky, and he was too fast. He came at her from the side and rammed her into the washer. Then he used his weight and strength to try and immobilize her.

Andrea screamed, but the sound was abruptly was cut short. An elbow drove into her stomach, emptying her of wind. As the laundry basket fell from her hands, Andrea tried to kick him, but he countered with a foot sweep that dropped her to the ground. Then he tried to press his advantage and slip the garrote over her neck. Just in time, she raised an arm and fended off the wire.

"Help!" she screamed. "Help!"

The only individual responding to her screams was the attacker. He kicked her in the face, and Andrea's head snapped back; for a moment it was as if her internal lights were shut off and there was only blackness. In desperation she reached out and tried to scratch his face, and her neck was again spared the garrote.

Her breathing was ragged, and she didn't use what breath she had to try another scream. The laundry room was noisy; the industrial machines were conspiring against anyone hearing her cries.

The attacker dropped down on her, coming at her head with his knee. She threw herself to the side but didn't come out unscathed. His knee smashed into the side of her neck, then the garrote was around her. Before he could close it tight, before he could strangle her, Andrea struck him on his head with her change jar. The glass shattered and coins spilled out.

"Fuck," he screamed.

Then his hands closed around her neck. He raised her head and slammed it back into the washer. The garrote was forgotten. His fingers pressed into her neck. Andrea tried bucking and squirming but couldn't get him off of her. The world was fading from her sight; blackness was taking her.

There's supposed to be light, Andrea thought. I'm supposed to follow the light.

She didn't hear the sounds, at least not at first. She was gasping and wheezing too loudly to hear much of anything. As her breathing returned to normal, though, she heard the trumpeting of angels, or at least that's what it sounded like to her. It must not have been to the liking of the man who had attacked her. He was nowhere to be seen.

The cavalry continued broadcasting its music. She'd never heard so many sirens sounding off at the same time. Now she knew what a celestial chorus sounded like, but even better.

The crossing of the Jordan would have to wait.

CHAPTER TWENTY-FIVE

LUCK BE A LADY TONIGHT

I entered the hospital room and had to struggle to not lose it. There had been too much misery and too many hospital rooms of late. In my hand was a bouquet of flowers. They seemed incredibly inadequate.

"I am so sorry," I said.

Andrea Charles looked like hell, but her smile managed to be beatific. It offered forgiveness, something I was desperate to receive.

"What do you mean you're sorry?" she said, her voice raspy and raw. "You saved my life."

"Your life wouldn't have needed saving if I hadn't involved you in the first place," I said. "I swear to God I never imagined that your helping me would put your life in danger. When Haines learned I was looking into homicides in Las Vegas, he must have figured I had enlisted help. He must have reacted to the threat and gotten word to the All-In Killer. I underestimated him."

"We both did," she whispered.

"You need to sleep," I said. "The doctor only agreed to let me see you for a minute because your captain intervened on my behalf. I think most of LVMPD is out in the waiting room hoping the doc will have a change of heart and let them see you. They're the real heroes. They got to your building at light speed."

"They got to me only after your call," she said. "I understand you were quite persuasive."

"It was more like I was out of my mind. I thought I'd figured out everything too late. When you didn't pick up my call, I sort of went crazy."

"Anything new on the bad guy?" she whispered.

"They haven't caught him yet, but you don't have to worry. There are a few big guards right outside your door."

"I'm not worried," she said. "I was hoping for a rematch."

Her battle scars and raspy voice forced me to bite my lip so as to hold it together. I looked around for a place to put the bouquet, but the décor seemed to discourage flowers and I didn't have a better option than to leave them on a chair.

"We'll talk tomorrow," I said.

"Are you staying in Vegas overnight?"

I shook my head. "I have two dogs waiting for my return."

"You flew in and now you're flying out?"

"Just call me a jetsetter."

"I wish you hadn't done that, but I'm glad you did. You know how to make a girl feel special, Gideon."

"That's the pain meds talking, Andrea."

"That must be it," she whispered, even as sleep overcame her.

I tiptoed out of the room.

If I could have helped in the manhunt, I would have arranged for Seth to look after the dogs, but I was assured by LVMPD and the FBI that they were going to nail her attacker. The ambush on

Andrea hadn't been haphazard. It was likely her movements had been monitored for some time. There were too many security cameras in Las Vegas for him to have done his stalking unnoticed.

It seemed like much of my day's communicating was occurring between flights. Just before I boarded my plane back to LA, Ben Corning called. He wanted to know about my talk with Andrea, and I detailed our brief conversation. For the first time in days he sounded energized and excited.

"This is the break we needed," he said. "The asshole's not going to be able to get away from us this time."

Corning and the FBI believed it was the All-In Killer who had tried to murder Andrea. There was evidence to support this, including the number 77 hockey jersey left in the laundry room where she had been attacked. That was enough of a link for them. I wished I were as convinced, but there were things that didn't feel right to me. For some reason, this attempt at murder seemed to have a different, less insidious, signature than the All-In Killer homicides, even taking the jersey into account.

I took a cab to McCarran Airport. As it was every night, the Las Vegas Strip was aglow, but the only thing I wanted to do was get out of town. The flight home would take about an hour.

We left on time. The passengers seemed subdued; perhaps it was the hour; perhaps it was the letdown of leaving the bright lights behind; perhaps Lady Luck had been unkind.

Luck, I thought. Andrea was lucky to be alive. When I'd had my epiphany that she was the target, it was the words of Ellis Haines that I'd heard playing in my head. He'd told me that he believed the eight-eight cards had already been played.

"We're on to lucky seven," he'd said, "or in this case, sevens." And I'd asked him, "Sevens are lucky?" To which he had replied, "They always have been for me."

I was pretty sure at that moment he'd been smiling. He'd known Andrea Charles was about to die. Haines had wanted our conversation to haunt me for the rest of my life, no matter how long or short that might be.

The cabin was cold inside the airliner, or at least I tried to tell myself that was the reason for my trembling hands. Not for the first time, I wished I'd shot Haines when I had the chance. I had always thought it would be hard to live with being a murderer, but that was before Haines had come into my life.

After the attack on Andrea, it was doubtful the FBI would ask me to play courier again. They didn't want to look like they were accessories to Haines's machinations, especially now that they had a face and figure to go with the All-In Killer, and believed his apprehension was imminent.

That assurance didn't translate to my hands. The tremors refused to be still.

CHAPTER TWENTY-SIX

IN THE SOUTHERN PART OF FRANCE

The dogs and I took a post-midnight walk. I think I needed the outing even more than they did, although they pretended otherwise. From experience, I know that my PTSD is often triggered when I'm feeling intense pressure, and I was hoping the walk would provide a release valve to stave off a fire dream.

Even though it was late and I was exhausted, I didn't hurry the dogs. Our pace was slow, not even an amble, and I took deep, measured breaths, which seemed to help me unwind. Sirius, in particular, took advantage of the unhurried pace. He stopped to smell the roses. And the grass. And the shrubbery. And the street signs. And the hydrants. Everything and anything we encountered he used as an excuse to sniff, followed up by target practice.

"Were you drinking coffee all night?" I asked. "That's my prostate excuse."

He didn't answer with words, but did stop to mark a neighbor's trash barrel.

His excessive peeing made me wonder if he could have a urinary tract infection. As Sirius was getting older, I was trying to be ever more mindful of his health. My partner was almost eight, but he didn't act his age; in this case, that was a good thing. Recently my vet had surprised me when she'd referred to him as a geriatric dog. When I'd challenged her, she said that dogs over the age of seven were considered geriatric. Like the observation goes, "To me, old age is always fifteen years older than I am."

That was my story and I was sticking to it.

"Maybe we should think about getting a pair of rocking chairs," I said to my partner. "We can sit on the porch and watch cars go by, and every now and again we could discuss the possibility of chasing after one of them."

I ran my hand through Sirius's coat and got a wag of his tail. Then I did the same thing with Emily and she leaned into me, returning the tactile favor.

The neighborhood was quiet. There was no traffic. My mind drifted to another neighborhood not far away. Mack Carter was hoping his doctor would let him go home soon. Whenever that was, I wanted to bring Cricket to his house.

When it comes down to it, I thought, there's nothing quite like the comfort of home. And with that thought, I announced, "It's time we headed back."

I didn't have to pull very hard on their leashes; the dogs seemed to be of the same mind. Still, I wasn't in any rush. The house was empty. If Lisbet had been waiting, I would have made a point of being home already.

Tonight, I'd have to pray for the best, and in the morning, I would call her.

No fire nightmare descended upon me, allowing me my first good night's sleep in a long time. In fact, I awakened feeling more human than zombie, and that was even before downing a big cup of coffee.

Emboldened by caffeine, it seemed like a good time to call Lisbet. Not since I'd first asked her out had I felt this nervous in anticipating our conversation. My palms were wet, and I found myself clearing my throat. When she answered, it was almost in a whisper.

"I can barely hear you," I said.

I could hear the sounds of Lisbet moving to another spot. "Better?" she asked.

"Yes," I said, but I wondered why she'd had to whisper, and then excuse herself to find a quiet place for our conversation.

"Now isn't a good time to talk," she said.

I wondered if there would ever again be a good time to talk, but I didn't say that.

"Should I try you again later today?" I asked.

"I'm going to be tied up," she said, "so I'd better call you."

I swallowed the first two or three remarks that came to mind. My disappointment, I knew, was likely to come out as anger.

"You know the number," I said.

"I'm glad you called," Lisbet whispered, and then clicked off.

I wanted to take heart from her closing words but wished they hadn't been whispered. It made me think she was keeping them from being heard by someone nearby.

"That didn't go as planned," I told the dogs.

They looked up, wondering what was going on. I was wondering the same thing.

"Falling slowly," I said.

That's what it felt like. My world wasn't crumbling all at once, but there was this slow-motion sense of everything falling apart. I thought of the song "Falling Slowly"; a part of me was convinced I was the sinking boat. It's not fun living the lyrics to a sad song, and now that the tune was in my head it wouldn't leave. As it played in an ongoing loop, it felt like the droning of my own dirge.

I had wanted to tell Lisbet that things were better now that the All-In Killer was on the run, and that I wouldn't be as preoccupied as I had been. That's what I wanted to believe, but I couldn't be sure about either one of those propositions. Too often desperate people write checks they can't cash.

One more IOU, I thought, and with it the hope that Lisbet would give me a chance to make good on it. In the meantime, I knew of only one way to confront my malaise.

"No pain, no gain," I said.

It was a favorite cliché of the Iron Maiden, my nickname for the physical therapist who had pushed me to my limits after I'd been burned in my fire walk. She was my own Nurse Ratched, although she worked me for my own good. Rigorous physical therapy is needed if burn patients want to retain a good range of motion in their joints. In all too many sessions, I remembered, I had wondered if the pain was worth it.

"When in doubt, work it out," I told the dogs.

That had been another one of the Iron Maiden's bromides. It was time to work it out. It was time to get busy, if only as a distraction.

"LA woman," I said.

The All-In Killer had declared himself to be one of the riders on the storm at about the same time I had picked up the Carrie Holder case. Sometimes my Doubting Thomas act runs into what feels like the inexplicable, and maybe even just a tad of the indisputable. "Riders on the Storm" was a single on the Doors album *L.A. Woman*. There was nothing connecting Sister Carrie's death to the All-In murders, which had extended throughout the

Southwest. Intellectually, I knew that. Psychologically, I wasn't sure what condition my condition was in.

Carrie Holder had joined the infamous 27 Club. Musicians who turn twenty-seven should beware. Among the musical giants who have died at that age are Janis Joplin, Jimi Hendrix, Amy Winehouse, Kurt Cobain—and Jim Morrison.

I wondered what Carl Gustav Jung would have had to say about that, and was glad my job didn't require me to figure out if there was such a thing as meaningful coincidences. Looking into a death seemed taxing enough.

Detectives Duarte and Grier had known about my San Quentin trip the day before. I had gotten the impression they were fine with my being out of town. The two detectives had seemed to be of the same mind, that Carrie Holder's death was a fluke and not a homicide. I called to see if they'd found anything to change their minds.

Duarte answered, "Jake the Snake here."

"Is that so?"

"Grier's been trying to pin that nickname on me and I kind of like it. You follow professional wrestling?"

"You mean men in tights engaging in make-believe?"

"Greatest sport in the world," said Duarte. "And Jake 'the Snake' Roberts was a classic wrestler. He used to bring live snakes into the ring with him. That's how he beat Andre the Giant. Big as he was, Andre was scared to death of snakes."

I got a word in edgewise—"ophidiophobia"—which is a fancy way of saying fear of snakes. Duarte wasn't interested in vocabulary building or what I had to say. He was on a roll.

"Wrestling fans still love to talk about the match where Jake the Snake took out the Macho Man with an honest-to-God cobra," he said. "You should watch it go down on YouTube. Every year it gets millions of hits."

"You know what they say: No one ever went broke underestimating the intelligence of the American public."

Duarte finally picked up on my disparagement. "People want to be entertained, Gideon."

"'Are you not entertained?'" I said.

I must not have delivered the line as well as Russell Crowe did in *Gladiator*. Duarte said, "That's what professional wrestling is all about."

"I'll take your word on that," I said. "But to the point of this conversation, I'm calling to see what you and Grier—or should I call him Blake the Snake?—have got for me."

"Blake the Snake," said Duarte. "I like that." He laughed before continuing. "We did what you asked us to do. I'm just finishing up a list of people who visited the vic, and a timeline for those visits. We also have statements from the neighbors."

"What did they have to say?"

"Everyone seemed to like her, but it's not like she was bosom buddies with anyone in the neighborhood. They knew her well enough to wave and smile, and to comment on how pretty she was."

"No one had anything negative to say?"

"One or two neighbors said she entertained a lot, but that was more an observation than a ding. They said her gatherings weren't ever very loud, and they never went too late."

"Did you talk to any of her friends?"

"Negative," he said. "We did determine that her longtime best friend visited her at the house twice over the course of the past week, but we never got around to talking to her. We figured we'd wait and see how things panned out."

What he was telling me was that if I had any brains at all, I wouldn't make the detectives spin their wheels unnecessarily until the lab results came in. My inner debate was whether to go along with the detectives, or confirm to them how obtuse I really was.

"Shame I don't speak Parseltongue," I said.

"What?"

Duarte knew his professional wrestling, but not his Harry Potter.

"Snake reference," I said. "I wish I could charm the local rattlesnakes into providing answers."

Duarte surprised me by providing the sound effects that went with the snake charmer song, aka "The Streets of Cairo."

When he finished, I said, "FYI, snake charmers are as real as your wrestlers. They pretend the snakes are charmed by their music, even though snakes can't hear sounds."

"Is that so?"

"It is."

"It's a catchy tune, though, isn't it? You ever stop to think it's the same tune that's used for the lyrics 'They don't wear pants in the southern part of France'?"

"I never made that connection," I said. And I would have been okay if I never had.

"It's a fact."

"I'll need you to send me the files on whatever you've got."

"Your wish is my command, sahib."

CHAPTER TWENTY-SEVEN

MORTALS AND GODS

A few minutes after we talked, Duarte forwarded me what he and Grier had compiled. In the week before she died, Carrie Holder had hosted a number of visitors. Elijah had been to her Bel Air residence on two occasions, and on one of those visits he hadn't left until close to midnight. A woman identified as Taylor Romano had also stopped by on two different occasions, arriving on both evenings at around eleven o'clock. On one night she slept over; on another she left at one in the morning.

I was certain I'd seen the name Taylor Romano before, and looked through my notes. It took me a few minutes to find her; Taylor had been part of the snake photo group text screenshot that Sister Carrie had sent. Most of the others on the group text worked for the Church of the Gate.

Carrie's cell phone records provided me with Taylor Romano's contact information; the two women had enjoyed calling and texting on a frequent basis.

I called Taylor's number. After two rings, the line picked up. I couldn't hear any sounds, but I sensed someone was listening on the other end. It was a tactic I often used when an unfamiliar number surfaced on my screen and I suspected it might be a robocall or unwanted solicitor.

"This is Detective Michael Gideon of LAPD," I said. "I'm trying to reach Taylor Romano. I'd like . . ."

A female voice interrupted me. "Are you calling about Carrie?" she asked.

"I am. Is this Taylor?"

"Yes," she said. "I was wondering if LAPD would ever get around to calling me."

"What made you expect to hear from us?"

"Carrie and I were best friends," she said. "And . . ."

"And?"

I heard an uncertain intake of breath, then a slight clearing of her throat. "And I can't help but think the way she died was weird."

"'Weird' as in 'suspicious'?"

She thought about it before saying, "Let's just say I'm not surprised the police are investigating."

"Can you elaborate on that?"

"I'm not sure if I can," she said.

There was a little defensiveness in her voice, and I got the sense that talking over the phone would be an impediment to Taylor's opening up.

"I'm sure her death was quite a shock to you."

"I still can't believe it," she said.

"I'd love to hear more about Carrie," I said. "Is there any way you can meet with me today so that we can talk about her? How about over a cup of coffee?"

Instead of directly answering, she said, "My work shift starts at two this afternoon."

"Where do you work?"

"Hollywood," she said. "I'm a crew member at the Trader Joe's on North Vine."

"Is that the ground-floor store with all the apartments above it?"

"You know it?"

"I've been in there a couple of times to get my Triple Ginger Snaps fix."

That got a little laugh. "Those are addictive," she said.

"I know there are a couple of coffee places nearby," I said. "If you're okay with meeting up at one o'clock, that should be more than enough time to play Twenty Questions."

"I guess that would be okay," she said, and then named a coffee shop on West Hollywood Boulevard.

"Great," I said. "Two questions now, though: Are you dog friendly, and is the place dog friendly?"

"I love dogs," she said, "and I know they have a few outdoor tables to accommodate the four-legged."

"We'll all see you at one o'clock then," I said.

As the dogs and I approached the coffee shop, we were waved down by a twentysomething woman wearing a Dodgers cap and a Hawaiian shirt. Like so many who live in LA, Taylor was multicultural. She stood up, extended a hand my way, and after we shook, she offered both of her hands to the dogs. They were delighted to make her acquaintance.

"I'll get the coffee while you spoil the dogs," I said, handing her the leashes. "The shepherd is Sirius, and the pittie is named Emily. Both of them love people. I wish I could say the same about me. Now, what would you like?"

"I'd love an iced caramel cloud macchiato," she said.

"Cirrus-ly?" I asked.

Taylor looked at me blankly for a moment, an expression I'm all too familiar with, but then she divined the pun and laughed a little louder than she groaned. The dogs acted as if they were in on the joke, and I left them to be fast friends.

There was a line of the caffeine-needy, but it moved quickly. Within five minutes I returned to the table with the coffees, and two waters for those with fur. Sirius and Emily both had their heads in Taylor's lap. They were probably missing Lisbet as much as I was. Since calling her that morning, I'd done my best not to read anything into her not having yet called me back.

The coffee went on the table, the water cups on the ground. Neither dog seemed in any hurry to get to the water.

"Don't encourage them," I said. "They're notorious affection hounds."

"I think they give better than they get," she said. Her smile was sad, her thoughts on her dead friend. "I'm glad for their TLC."

"I know what you mean." I hoped my smile wasn't as sad as hers.

She left one hand tending to the dogs, and with the other picked up her cloud juice and took an appreciative sip. "Thanks," she said. "I needed this. I'll mostly be working in the box tonight."

"The box?" I asked.

"That's what we call the dairy section. I'll be doing a lot of the stocking."

"Do you like the job?"

She nodded. "I actually do. I hate getting up early, so the hours agree with me. I get off at ten-thirty most nights."

That explained Taylor's recent late-night visits to Carrie's home in Bel Air, I thought.

"Sirius and I used to work second shift," I said. "The only problem with working late is that most of the world is on a different schedule."

"True," she said.

"Did your schedule make it tough to carve out time to see Carrie?"

She shook her head. "Like me, Carrie was a night owl. Usually we'd chill over at her place. I'd go over one or two nights a week."

"When did you first become friends?"

"It must be two, three years ago that we first met. Both of us started volunteering at the Audubon Center at Debs Park at about the same time. Most of the other volunteers were older, so we gravitated toward each other right away."

"You still volunteer there?" I asked.

She shook her head. "I had to give it up when I went back to school part-time."

"What about Carrie?"

"She had to quit about a year ago. I know she felt bad about it at the time. Nature was a real passion of hers. But she couldn't juggle the volunteering with her work hours. The church kept her very busy."

"The life of a penitent," I said.

Taylor made a face. "The life of an entertainer," she said. "That was Carrie's real job. Between singing and acting for the services and hosting gatherings at the house, she was always on the go."

"What can you tell me about the relationship between Carrie and Elijah?"

My question caught her mid-sip and caused her to frown. If she hadn't been drinking an iced caramel cloud macchiato, I might have thought her coffee was bitter.

"Have you met him?" she asked.

I nodded.

"At first, Carrie found him very charismatic like everyone else does."

"Did that change?"

"Their dynamic changed."

I'm not a fan of popular psychological jargon. "What do you mean by that?"

Taylor blew out a little air, causing her lips to slightly reverberate. "I don't know if I even want to talk about it."

"I already talked with Elijah and Sister Joan," I said. "They told me about Elijah and Carrie seeing each other. Everyone was good with that, I was told."

"And you believed them?"

"You have another interpretation?"

"Carrie called church politics the 'palace intrigue.' She and Elijah were a thing for a while, but he seemed a lot more into it than she was. That's what ruffled feathers more than anything else, according to Carrie. Everyone was okay with Elijah calling the shots, but as Carrie's star rose and she became the talent headliner, people got jealous."

"Who in particular?"

"Those entrenched in power."

"Like Sister Joan?"

"I think she was okay with Elijah playing the field, but not getting played by the field. Over time it was like Carrie and Elijah reversed roles. Elijah was the one who became subservient in their relationship. He even told Carrie that he was in love with her."

"But it wasn't reciprocated?"

She shook her head. "Carrie put an end to their physical relationship a month or two ago."

"And how did Elijah respond to that?"

"He became that much more desperate."

"Desperate how?"

"He was supposed to be this larger-than-life figure, not some needy little boy."

"Gods aren't supposed to fall for mortals?"

Her head moved up and down in strong agreement. "That's exactly it. There were people who were all but worshipping Elijah. Everything was going his way, with the church growing like crazy and his show being broadcast around the world. That had always been Joan and Elijah's dream. But now Elijah had another dream."

"And while he was dreaming of Carrie, I'm imagining she had her own dreams, none of which included Elijah."

"You got it. I think the main reason Carrie stayed with the church was that it allowed her to make a lot of contacts in the entertainment industry. In fact, just weeks before her death she signed with CAA and was starting to go out on auditions."

"She didn't hide her ambitions from those at the church?"

"Not in the slightest."

"How did Elijah respond?"

"He did everything he could to keep Carrie happy, and that included making others at the church unhappy. Carrie's roles in the weekly productions kept getting bigger and bigger."

"Did that mean Joan had a smaller say in the programming?"

"Joan was in a bad position. Carrie even felt sorry for her. But there were others who felt undercut by Elijah's favoritism for Carrie."

"Like who?"

"I couldn't tell you any individual names. There were a few people Carrie liked to refer to as the 'true believers.' They believed in the mission of the church, and in Elijah."

"And Carrie threatened to upset that apple cart?"

"The church served Carrie more than Carrie served the church. It was her stage, and what she hoped would be her steppingstone to stardom."

"Did Carrie ever tell you that she used to be a stripper?"

"She mentioned it once or twice. I don't think it was any big thing to her. It was just a means to an end. She was going to school and needed the money."

"Is it possible she met Elijah at the club where she worked?"

Taylor thought for a moment, then shook her head. "I'm pretty sure she didn't meet Elijah until she interviewed for a job at the church."

"When we talked on the phone you told me that you thought Carrie's death was weird."

"The snake thing," she said.

"So, when you say it was weird, what you're telling me is that because it's rare for someone to die from a snakebite, you found it unusual?"

Taylor did something akin to an Indian headshake, and I wondered if part of her multicultural ancestry was East Asian. "I don't know anything for sure," she said, "but Carrie told me that there were some church ceremonies that were closed to her."

"Secret ceremonies?" I tried to keep the skepticism out of my voice, but apparently didn't succeed.

"I know that sounds like something that someone who's paranoid would say," she said, "or like something you'd see in one of those conspiracy films. But she said it was going on for real."

"When someone talks about secret ceremonies," I said, "I always remember the old line about how three may keep a secret if two are dead."

"I'm not disagreeing with you," said Taylor. "Things always come out, which would explain how Carrie heard about some things others were trying to keep secret."

"Did she offer any specifics?" I asked.

"Carrie said she heard that special invitations were given to a select few people to attend these ceremonies. As she understood it, on occasion Elijah did some command performances for the church heavyweights."

"It's not unusual to target the big donors," I said.

"Carrie said it felt like a secret society within the church. I think she was curious about what was going on because she wasn't a part of it."

"Whatever *it* was."

"She was pretty sure the last ceremony must have had something to do with Garden of Eden stuff, because she heard talk of serpents."

That got my attention. "Serpents?"

Taylor nodded. "Carrie said she heard a few whispered references to serpents. And she overheard Joan asking someone if the snakes were ready."

"Did she say who Joan was talking to?"

"Not that I remember."

"But you're certain about the serpents and snakes?"

"That's what Carrie said. And that's why I sort of freaked out when I heard how Carrie died."

CHAPTER TWENTY-EIGHT

DESPERADO INCOMMUNICADO

It felt like a long time had passed since my learning about Eli and Amy Green's aborted documentary *Shake, Rattle and Roll*, but in reality, it had been days. A second meeting with them was overdue. Snakes would be part of our conversation.

I called the Church of the Gate's administrative offices and asked to speak to Elijah. It was like trying to talk to a Hollywood star; there were lots of individuals who were paid to put buffers between me and the person with whom I wanted to talk. It was only because I identified my association with LAPD that my request was not refused outright, but I was passed up the line from one Church of the Gate-keeper to another.

Finally, I heard a familiar voice. "Detective Gideon, this is Sister Hannah. I was told that you were asking to speak to the returned prophet Elijah."

"I don't know about that," I said. "I do know I need to talk to Eli Green regarding police business."

"I am afraid he's not here," she said. "Might I help you?"

"No," I said. "I need to talk to Eli."

"As I explained, Elijah isn't here."

"What about Amy Green?"

"Sister Joan isn't here either."

"When do you expect them back?"

"Not until the day after tomorrow," she said.

"Explain that," I said.

"Elijah and Sister Joan are out of town on a spiritual re-treat."

"What is the location of this spiritual retreat?"

"I'm not privy to that information. No one in our flock knows exactly where they are."

"How about inexactly?"

"I don't understand."

"Sister Hannah, you're aware that lying to a police officer carries severe penalties, right?"

"I'm not lying. The death of Sister Carrie has left both Eli-jah and Sister Joan distraught, and they have gone in search of spiritual sustenance during this time of grief. All of this was an-nounced earlier today to the media."

"I'll try and be respectful of their retreat," I said, "but I'll need a phone number where I can reach them."

"I was told that their retreat prohibits the use of cell phones. They are incommunicado."

"Is that another word for 'conveniently absent'?"

"In many monastic orders, silence is the norm," she said.

"If they've gone silent, how are they going to pull off the show this week?"

"At this week's *services*," said Sister Hannah, "there will be a guest speaker. As for the broadcast, there will be a retrospective of Sister Carrie's devotionals and songs."

"Will that include 'Union of the Snake' by Duran Duran?" I asked. The musical reference was too old for her, so I added, "Or maybe 'Snakes and Ladders' by Joss Stone?"

"Can I be of any other help to you?" she asked.

I refrained from saying that she hadn't been of any help yet. "It's important that I get a message to them, and I am not asking. I am insisting. You can't tell me there isn't an emergency number."

Sister Hannah didn't answer right away. Finally, she said, "It's possible I might be able to get a text message to Sister Joan, but I'm not sure when she will be able to pick it up."

It was my turn to not answer right away. "Detective Gideon?" she asked.

"What time will they be returning the day after tomorrow?"

"They said they would be coming into work that morning."

"And what time do they usually arrive?"

"They're always here by eight thirty in the morning."

"Tell them they'll need to meet with me at that time."

"And what will you be meeting about?"

"Among other things, speaking in tongues; forked tongues, that is."

"Excuse me?"

"You can reference the Garden of Eden," I said, "and the knowledge of good and evil, and let's not forget snake, rattle, and roll."

"Did you say, 'shake, rattle, and roll'?"

"That's close enough."

There is that fine line between pushing too hard and not pushing hard enough. Dr. Frank still didn't have any news for me on the autopsy. Given the backlog of work at the medical examiner-coroner's office, that wasn't a surprise, but it made it more difficult to aggressively pursue the investigation into Carrie Holder's death. Rattling cages—or was it more a case of rattling the rattler?—was about as much as I could do. For now, I had to wait out Dr. Frank, as well as Elijah and Sister Joan.

There were other question marks on my agenda that needed tending to anyway, among them the status of Mack Carter. When I called the hospital, I found that he hadn't yet been discharged, and I asked to speak to him. A weak and uncertain voice answered the phone.

"Mr. Carter?" I said. "This is Michael Gideon. I stopped by to see you yesterday and we talked about Cricket."

"Yes," he said, his voice taking on a note of alarm. "I remember. Is something wrong?"

I spoke in as soothing and reassuring voice as I could manage. "Everything is just fine, Mr. Carter. The reason for my call is to check on when you'll be going home. Yesterday you were of the opinion that you might be discharged soon."

"That's what I hoped," he said, "but the doctor said I needed to stay here another day. Is Cricket all right?"

"She's doing great," I said, and mentally kicked myself for not having checked on her condition. After we finished talking, I would call Angie's Rescues to make sure she was doing as well as I'd said. "In fact, why don't I bring her by your house late afternoon tomorrow?"

"Thank you," he said. "Thank you. I didn't know what to do or who to call. This has all been so confusing."

"I'm sorry for your troubles," I said. "But I don't want you worrying about Cricket. She's in good hands."

"You're a very kind person."

There were a lot of people who would have told him differently, but I didn't.

"I can't wait to see her again," Carter said. "Can I pay you for your troubles?"

"It's no problem," I said. "We're actually neighbors. You only live about two miles from my house."

"I'm glad to hear that."

"I'm glad to have you and Cricket for neighbors, Mr. Carter."

CHAPTER TWENTY-NINE

A LITTLE BIRD TOLD ME

The dogs and I both needed to get some exercise, so I decided to combine that with a training session and took them on an outing to the Sherman Oaks rec center. The park is dog friendly, and offers enough space for us to go about our business unhindered.

As we walked the park grounds, I ran the dogs through their drills. Because Sirius is the advanced student, he gets more assignments. Like any good elementary school teacher, my job is to make sure he's grounded in the basics, while at the same time always adding new coursework. What's good for the goose is also good for the gander. Keeping the dog sharp keeps the handler sharp.

Working with two dogs at the same time was as much of a challenge as this handler could handle. Because the dogs were at different levels in their training, I used the divide-and-conquer method. Emily was my up-close pupil; Sirius went long distance. From afar, I used a combination of voice commands and hand signals to direct him through his paces.

Both dogs came together for the main event. I positioned them facing away from me while I set up the props that I'd kept hidden from them. Sirius was curious about what I was up to and kept turning his head to observe me.

"No cheating," I told him. Like most overachievers, given the opportunity, Sirius will gladly game any kind of *Kobayashi Maru* test.

As I was finishing up my prep work, he gave another furtive glance my way. "Peek-a-booer," I muttered. He pretended not to hear.

I called the dogs over. In the middle of a circle that I'd marked with duct tape was a realistic-looking coiled rattlesnake. The tape had been laid down to approximate the distance a snake could strike.

The dogs were intrigued by my setup. As they came close to the snake, I yelled, *"Lass es!"* Leave it!

Sirius froze, and Emily responded to his cue. Then I called both dogs over, rewarded them with a treat, and we repeated the training until I was satisfied with their response to the command.

After that, we worked on the dogs being comfortable with me doing collar grabs on them. Sirius and I have been partners for so many years, and his trust in me is so complete, that he doesn't even blink when I grab his collar. Emily is still a work in progress. She was mistreated and abused, and has every reason to distrust the human race. Despite that, she allowed me to invade her space and grab her collar in different ways and at unusual angles, including making grabs from her blind spots.

The collar grabs were done to condition the dogs in the event I needed to suddenly pull them away from a potential danger. I wanted to be able to grab their collars if a threat presented itself, and they had to be okay with my doing that even without offering up any warning.

I ran Emily through her paces again. She maintained her composure against all my intrusions. "Good girl!" I told her, rewarding her behavior with a treat.

She didn't decline the bit of jerky, but it was the praise she relished even more. Her body was this large, quivering mass of happy. To be acknowledged as a good dog, she told me in her posturing, was rapturous.

I had one more snake-charming trick. This time I was the one who turned my back so as to prepare a piece of training equipment that I'd retrieved from storage in the garage. As I readied my demonstration, it was my turn to be the observer. With a surreptitious swivel of my head, I could see Sirius's interest in trying to figure out what I was up to. His ears were raised; he could hear the ratcheting sounds as I turned the key. Years had passed since the last time I had sprung this one on him, and I wasn't sure if he remembered his former training.

When I turned around to face the dogs, I released a slithering mechanical snake. It began crawling toward them in a wavy series of serpentine movements.

"*Aus!*" I called.

The command is intended to get the dog's attention. Essentially it tells them to be alert and get moving. Sirius jumped out of the path of the mechanical snake, and then ran over to my side. Emily didn't respond with his alacrity; the shifting snake in the grass had her transfixed.

"*Aus!*" I called again.

The second time around Emily awakened to my command. She came running to me and I told her, "Good dog."

That got me a lean-in and a whole-body dog wiggle, which I find much more enjoyable than a snake wiggle. When Emily heard me say, "Good dog" again, it made her world a happy place.

And for a few moments, it made mine as well.

We were still on the grounds of the park when I received a phone call from Walt Schmitt.

"I don't mean to bother you, Detective," he said, "but my wife, Evie, wanted to know the latest on Old Man Carter."

"If the doctor gives his okay," I said, "Mack should be home tomorrow. And the vet told me Cricket should be well enough to go home to him."

"That's good to hear. Evie and I will stop by to make sure he gets settled back in."

"I know that will be appreciated," I said. "Don't be surprised if you see me at the house in the late afternoon. I'll be the one dropping off Cricket."

"That will make for a good homecoming," he said.

I agreed, and was about to click off when he said, "Oh, one more thing. I just saw Sara Lazarus. She's Matilda's owner. And I remembered how you said you wanted to talk to Sara or Gary."

"Matilda's the other dog on your street who got sick?"

"That's right. Sara told me she was taking a mental health day today, and I mentioned our conversation to her."

"And she's home right now?" I asked.

"As of five minutes ago," he said. "You still got her phone number?"

"I do. Thanks for the heads-up."

Even before Schmitt's call, I had given some thought to walking Mack Carter's neighborhood prior to his return. There was this nagging feeling that I had overlooked something on the street, and I wanted to put my mind at ease. Having the chance to talk to Sara Lazarus was an added incentive to visit.

It was only a ten-minute drive. Normally, I would have played music, but the songs that came to mind would have brought me no pleasure, at least considering the current circumstances. I didn't want to listen to "L.A. Woman" or "Riders on the Storm." And I really didn't want to hear "Falling Slowly."

Lisbet still hadn't called. That bothered me a lot, but I had to give her the space she'd asked for.

We pulled into what any casual observer would have thought was a quiet, pleasant residential cul-de-sac. Jeff Jefferies probably wouldn't have seen in that way. He and his cameras might have come up with pictures that showed something darker than the mostly manicured gardens and the freshly painted houses. The homes told one story, the people in them another. And where there were people, there were secrets.

"Just a little dog," I told my dogs, echoing the line from *Rear Window*. But I didn't say it dismissively like the partygoer had. It was the whole reason we were there.

I parked in front of the Lazaruses' home and thought of the poem "The New Colossus" by Emma Lazarus. It was difficult to think of the image of Lady Liberty without remembering the poem and its words: *Give me your tired, your poor, your huddled masses yearning to breathe free.* Now it seemed that those words should be prefaced with "once upon a time." I hoped that wasn't the case. I prayed that wasn't the case.

Leaving the dogs in the Explorer, I walked to the front door and applied hand to wood. My knocking drew an immediate response from a dog who began barking from what sounded like the backyard. The top of the door had tinted glass that blurred and obscured but still allowed enough light through to distinguish movements. A form silently approached the door and stood before it, as the dog continued to bark. It was possible that whoever was there didn't realize I was tall enough, and the glass revealing enough, for me to be aware of their presence.

"Mrs. Lazarus," I said, speaking loudly enough to be heard through the closed door and over the dog noise. "I'm Detective Gideon from LAPD, and I was hoping to ask you a few questions."

The door opened a few inches, enough for me to see one eye and half a face. I smiled and extended my wallet badge, which was enough to get the door opened a few inches more, although a security screen continued to separate us. Unseen but not unheard, the dog kept up its loud barking.

"Shut up, Matilda," yelled the woman.

The dog took it down a notch, and the woman shrugged. "We love her," she said, "but she's a knucklehead."

Sara Lazarus appeared to be in her early forties. She was of average height with a full head of frizzy brown hair and dark brown eyes. Those same eyes were red, and I wondered if I'd woken her from a nap.

"You the cop who talked to Walt?" she asked.

"I am."

"He said you'd probably be contacting us, but I wasn't sure whether to believe him."

"And why is that?"

"Dog-eat-dog world," she said. "I'm surprised that what happened to our neighborhood dogs would even make your radar."

Matilda took that moment to start barking again. "Quiet," Sara yelled.

"I'm not here on what you would call police business," I said. "I'm doing this more as a courtesy for a friend. Since I live in Sherman Oaks, I agreed to tour your neighborhood to see if there was any obvious cause for the dogs on your street getting sick."

She nodded but made no move to open the screen door, as if happy to keep that distance between us.

"As I understand it," I said, "Matilda was one of the dogs that recently became very sick."

I got another nod.

"When did this happen?" I asked.

"Last week," she said.

"Mr. Schmitt said that Matilda got sick while in your own yard."

"Things aren't always as they appear," she said.

"I'm not following."

"My kids were afraid of getting in trouble, so they didn't spill the beans right away. As it turns out, Matilda wasn't in the backyard the whole time like they said. She got out of the house and made a run for it."

"Where did she go?"

"The kids caught her on the next street over."

"Did they mention if she stopped along the way to eat something?"

Instead of answering, Sara said, "You want to tell me what this is really all about?"

"I'm not sure . . ." I said.

"Has someone complained?"

"No," I said, not hiding my puzzlement.

"It's legal," she said. "I've checked. And just to be sure we were within the law, we only have four plants, not the six that are allowed. And the area is cordoned off, so the kids can't get to it. They don't even know about it. And we did our best to make sure it couldn't be seen by others."

I finally figured out what she was talking about. Her red eyes and suspiciousness should have clued me in to her condition.

"Mrs. Lazarus," I said, "it's fine with me if you're growing pot. I couldn't care less. Really."

That surprised her. "So much for my conspiracy theory," she said. "Right? I've been stressed big-time lately. Work has been crazy. That's why I took a mental health day. I guess you can tell I needed it."

"Like I said, no judgment."

"It's not like I'm a pothead," she said. "I hardly ever smoke during the day. And today I made sure the kids wouldn't be home until later. I try and not be one of those 'do as I say, not as I do' parents. You got kids?"

I motioned with my head. "Two fur babies," I said. "They're out in the car."

"At least they don't talk back," she said.

"You'd be surprised."

She smiled. "So, you're really here about sick dogs?"

"I really am."

Sara looked past me to the street and beyond. "I thought the neighborhood watch lady was trying to bring me to justice for my crimes."

"That's not the case."

"You want to come inside then? It's kind of a mess."

"Then I should feel right at home," I said.

She unlocked the screen door and motioned me in. "The kids will be home in about half an hour," she said.

"I'll be long gone by then," I said. "I promise to only take up a few minutes of your time."

We sat in the living room, but it had enough of a view to the backyard that Matilda could see us and started barking. Sara's shouting to her didn't stop her.

"You mind if I let her in?" she asked. "Her mute button has never worked very well."

"No problem," I said.

Moments later, Matilda came bounding into the living room. She was a mostly black dog but had the "feathers" often seen in setters or spaniels. From the first, Matilda decided that we should be best friends.

"You're a pretty one," I told her, giving her an ear massage.

"We haven't done her DNA," said Sara, "but we think she's part Australian shepherd, and retriever, with maybe some Afghan and border collie mixed in."

"And all lovable," I said, keeping up with my scratching.

"All lovable," she agreed.

"Why don't you tell me about Matilda's getting sick?" I said.

"What I remember most is the vet bill," she said.

"After your kids caught up with her, how long was it before she started showing signs of being ill?"

"My husband and I got home from work at about the same time, which was a little after six, and from what I now know Matilda made her great escape a little after five. I noticed something was wrong with her not too long after getting home."

"What did the vet say?"

"He said she got into something. And if we wanted to know more than that, the tests would cost us a bundle, and even then, there wouldn't be any guarantees we'd learn its cause."

She opened her mouth to say something else, but then closed it.

"What?"

Sara decided to come clean. "Because the kids hadn't told me about her getting out, I was afraid Matilda had found some way to get to our balcony off the master bedroom."

When it became clear I wasn't following, she added, "That's where those plants I told you about are located. Our room is off-limits to the kids, and the shades to the balcony are closed, but Matilda has always had a talent for getting into what she shouldn't."

"But your plants were okay?"

"Mother's little helpers—that's what I call them—were untouched. Every now and again, Mama needs a little help from her potted friends."

Sirius, Emily, and I began our stroll around the neighborhood. I was glad Sirius didn't seem to feel the need to constantly pee like he had the night before. At least I no longer had to worry about him having a urinary tract infection.

The dogs showed no interest in snacking on any plants along the way, nor did any scent seem to be particularly attractive to them. Even though it appeared few of the residents on the street were home, I couldn't help but feel as if our every movement was being monitored. That probably had something to do with all of the home security cameras on the street, and the warning signage to would-be home invaders that came with them. The thumbprint of Patricia Gaspar and her neighborhood watch could be seen in most of the homes.

Neither the cat woman nor her cats came outside to stare us down, and Captain Gaspar could not be seen either tending to her garden or rooting out evil. Emily paused to sniff at something just off the sidewalk in Gaspar's yard, and I decided to incorporate one of the day's lessons.

"Lass es!" I said, and Emily immediately responded to my command to leave it by retreating a few steps.

"Good girl," I said.

With Emily's big head no longer in the way, I was able to see the object of her interest. In death, the hummingbird's plumage was no longer vibrant. What struck me most about the small corpse was the bird's long, distended tongue. Having never seen a hummingbird's tongue, I was surprised at its length. The tongue was easily as long as the bird's body.

I wondered if a cat had gotten the bird, but could see no apparent wound on its body. Nature does not usually provide animals with the luxury of death by old age, but there was no ready explanation for the hummingbird's death.

During my previous visit to the yard, there had been hummingbird aerial battles taking place all around. That wasn't really surprising. The diving rituals of the males are done to attract a mate. And for a hummingbird, protecting a food source can be a matter of life or death. Hummingbirds can starve to death in a matter of hours.

Mrs. Gaspar had filled the front yard's hummingbird feeder, but at the moment there were no takers. The yard seemed preternaturally still without the aerobatics of the tiny dynamos. Flying forward is one thing; hummingbirds can fly backward and upside down. They're also masters of hovering. There was no dive-bombing taking place today, and I wondered if the dead hummingbird had been a victim of one of those skirmishes. That seemed as good an explanation as any. Even the world's best aerialists suffer accidents. And had a predator killed one of the little birds, it would likely have fed upon it.

Unbidden, the words came to me: "A little birdie told me."

Why the expression came to mind, I didn't know. And neither did I know what the little bird had told me.

"Let's go," I said to the dogs.

CHAPTER THIRTY

HOPE

Before setting out for home, I called Heather Moreland at Angie's Rescues.

"How's the patient?" I asked.

"Cricket ate most of her dinner," Heather said, "but that was with a lot of encouragement from one our volunteers. Still, that's a good sign. With old dogs, having the will to live is half the battle."

"I think it's the same with old humans."

"Oh?"

"Long week," I said.

"That used to be my refrain. Nowadays I'm lucky, and that's thanks to you."

I made some dismissive noises, but Heather wouldn't hear them. She offered up her words, and her gratitude. "If not for your intervention, I would have been dead, and I know a lot of these animals wouldn't have survived without this shelter. That's your legacy."

"You give me far too much credit," I said, "but thank you anyway. I actually didn't call to bellyache, but to tell you that Cricket's human is supposed to be going home tomorrow. If it works for you, I told Mr. Carter that I'd bring Cricket home in the late afternoon."

"That shouldn't be a problem. I'll tell Dr. Misko your plans in the event she needs to write out any care instructions for Mr. Carter."

"I just finished walking Cricket's neighborhood again," I said. "I was hoping something would stand out the second time around, but I'm at a loss to explain what made all those dogs sick. There are some plant hazards, to be sure, but I daresay you can find most of those same plants in virtually every Sherman Oaks neighborhood."

"Maybe there was a toxic bloom that came and went, or some standing water that was tainted. It's possible a chemical spray was applied to a lawn, or there was some kind of chemical spill. Dogs are often attracted by the smell of antifreeze, which can be fatal."

"I thought of that," I said, "and checked the driveways and the street. Nothing."

"Whatever the danger was," she said, "maybe it's gone."

I made hopeful sounds to be polite, but I don't think Heather believed them any more than I did. We finished our conversation, and I set out for home.

I was putting down the dogs' dinner when my phone rang. The display told me Lisbet was finally calling back. Before picking up, I took a deep breath. Her call felt long overdue, but then usually I'm the one making the tardy phone calls. Knowing that was enough for me to do a little swallowing of my tongue.

"Hey," I said, pretending my cheery best. "Long day?"

"The longest," she said, sighing. "Today we put on a celebration of life at the Garden of Angels."

The Garden of Angels is part of the Desert Lawn Memorial Park in Calimesa, a small town about half an hour west of Palm Springs. For more than twenty years, the Garden of Angels has been the final resting place for Southern California's abandoned babies. I have participated in other "celebrations of life" held there, and know only too well how much work Lisbet puts into those gatherings. The best thing about the celebrations is that they don't happen too often; the worst thing is that they happen at all. Since California passed the Safely Surrendered Baby law, newborns can be left at any hospital or fire station with no questions asked. For years Lisbet has been working tirelessly to make all expectant California mothers aware of this law. Knowing Lisbet, this latest death would prompt her to redouble her efforts to get the word out.

I wondered why I hadn't been invited to the gathering, but all I said was, "I had no idea the funeral was today."

"I should have told you," Lisbet said, "but I know how busy you've been."

I hoped that was the real reason I hadn't been included. "I'm sorry I wasn't there for you," I said. "I know how stressful those events can be."

"It was a beautiful ceremony," Lisbet said. "I'm feeling more at peace now than I have in days."

"I'm glad," I said, "but I'd still like to do something for you. I just finished feeding the dogs. How about if I bring over some food?"

"The same food you just served the dogs?"

We both laughed a little. "You should be so lucky," I said. "They got chicken breast, green beans, sweet potatoes, and salmon-and-brown-rice kibble."

"That does sound delicious, except for maybe the kibble."

"You are fussy."

The vise wasn't squeezing so hard against my chest now. Lisbet and I were talking again. My world didn't feel so out of balance.

"All right, I'll hold the kibble," I said. "If the traffic gods cooperate, I can be at your place with food in an hour."

"Rain check?" she asked. "I think the day just caught up with me. All I want to do now is take a nap."

"I have that effect on women."

I was disappointed but pretended otherwise. It was worth it to hear Lisbet laugh.

"Before you go Rip Van Winkle on me," I said, "when are we going to see each other?"

Lisbet was quiet for a moment before saying, "I'm still working through some things."

This is what limbo is like, I thought, but refrained from saying that. "How about working through things over dinner tomorrow?" I said.

I held my breath waiting for an answer; the wait proved worth it. "Okay," she said. "Let's eat in at my place, though."

"Is seven o'clock too late?" I asked, remembering that I had to deliver Cricket to her home.

"That's actually perfect. The last few days I haven't been able to get any work done. Tomorrow I'll be playing catch-up all day."

"What suits your culinary fancy? Pan pizza? Sushi? Carne asada? Tuna subs?"

"No, no, no, and no," she said. "You okay with a wrap?"

"If it's you in the altogether, and if it's Saran Wrap."

"Very funny," she said. "You know that sandwich place we like? They've also got a whole line of wraps. Lately I've become a fan of their Pocket Health Rocket."

"I hope it tastes better than it sounds."

"Try it and you'll become a believer."

"You want fries with that?"

"Fruit cup."

"Chocolate shake?"

"No thanks."

"So, the pod people got to you?"

"I'm just trying to improve my diet."

"Dieting is a *piece of cake*," I said.

She groaned, and then said, "Lord help me, but I've actually missed your wordplay."

"There's hope, then?"

My words sounded flippant but were anything but. It took Lisbet a moment to answer; during that moment I could feel myself breaking into a sweat.

"There's hope," she said.

That was all I needed to hear.

At quarter past six it was still around seventy-five degrees. The front door was open so as to catch a breeze, with the security screen door latched. The dogs heard something out front, and while running to the door they started doing their vocalizing. On this planet there are only a few people who are the recipients of such love calls.

I went to the door. My shaman next-door neighbor was getting out of his car. Sirius was studying the latched screen door like someone who was contemplating a B&E. I didn't want him teaching Emily any bad habits, so I unlocked the door and opened it. The dogs were off in a shot, and I followed behind.

Seth was holding one of his Yanomami baskets that he uses for shopping. The Yanomami are an indigenous tribe that live in Brazil and Venezuela's Amazon rainforests. The baskets are made from woven palm fibers and feature lots of unusual designs incorporating a berry ink.

"They've already been fed," I said, "so don't believe their lies."

"What about you?" he asked, shaking his basket as an invitation.

I was tempted to look at the contents but was afraid of what I might see. Seth's diet tends to be health-food-store eclectic, emphasis on kale and flaxseed.

"I have a pizza that's ready to come out of the oven," I said, "and I actually made a Caesar salad to go with it. Since you haven't had dinner yet, why don't I bring everything over? There's more than enough for both of us."

"Pizza," he said, making my usual staple sound as if it were some kind of exotic dish.

"I won't even object if you want to tinker with your half of the pizza and salad," I said. "You can add grubs, or crickets, or whatever is in your bag of tricks."

"I only put crickets in your salad that one time."

I did my best cricket-sound imitation; Sirius immediately grew concerned for my health.

Seth must have heard enough. "If it's not putting you out," he said, "I'll gladly take you up on your offer."

The dogs followed Seth inside, while I returned to the homestead to get the pizza and salad. The timer went off just as I entered the house, and I was able to pull the pizza from the oven without it burning. Pepperoni, naturally. I wondered if Seth was familiar with that unusual topping.

I balanced the pizza atop the salad bowl and carried everything next door. The dogs were on their beds eating some steamed broccoli and pretending to enjoy it.

"Apparently, you're not acquainted with dog flatulence," I said. "Within the hour I'll have to put up crime scene tape."

"Then you had best not overstay your welcome," he said.

I put the pizza and salad down on the kitchen counter, and while I divided up the food, Seth made our drinks. As was usual, my libation was served with a toast.

"May we get what we want," Seth said, "but never what we deserve."

The two of us clinked glasses, and then Seth returned to the kitchen to adulterate his food. I took a big bite of my pizza slice, and with a little channeling of Dean Martin said, "'That's amore.'"

Seth smiled. "Things are better?" he asked.

"There's hope," I said.

CHAPTER THIRTY-ONE

EVEN EDUCATED FLEAS

I went to bed at around half past ten, and as I was dozing off became aware of a lonely mockingbird's persistent singing. Male mockingbirds without a mate will sometimes sing all night in the hopes of attracting the lady of their dreams, so I wasn't surprised that my mockingbird was still singing when I got up the next morning. His luck apparently hadn't changed during the course of the evening.

Harper Lee had warned the world that it was bad luck to kill a mockingbird, but I'm pretty sure the nocturnal antics of bachelor male mockingbirds have set many trigger fingers to twitching. Luckily for me, I'd slept the sleep of the dead and gotten my second consecutive good night of slumber.

"'Birds do it, bees do it,'" I told Sirius and Emily. They seemed okay with that.

"And as we all know," I added, "'even educated fleas do it.'"

Neither dog began scratching. None of us like fleas, even educated fleas.

Quoting Cole Porter, I thought, put a good start to the day. I made breakfast for me and the dogs, then began working on the Carrie Holder file. There were lots of questions that still needed answers, and I hadn't yet worked up a timeline leading to her final breath. On a notepad I jotted down some of the significant omissions in my casebook that needed answers. We were still dependent on the medical examiner-coroner's office establishing the time of death, as well as the cause of death, but in the meantime, I wanted to know the last person to see Carrie alive.

According to the security footage that detectives Duarte and Grier had gathered from Carrie's neighbors, she'd only had one guest on the night of her death. Elijah had driven over to her Bel Air residence and arrived at a little after seven. He hadn't stayed long, leaving the house at quarter of eight. His short visit, and Taylor Romano's belief that the physical affair was concluded, made me doubt any kind of romantic interlude had taken place. Forty minutes seemed more like the amount of time needed for a good fight. That was something I would press Elijah on when we had our face-to-face.

To try and get a pattern on the comings and goings of visitors, I decided to document all of Carrie's callers during the prior week, including the times they had arrived and left. Most of the names were based on vehicle registration information gathered from the footage. Tomorrow I'd add to the timeline by synching Carrie's work calendar, along with her time away from work. Before getting too far ahead of myself, though, I needed an accurate window into when she had died. Dr. Frank had given me a guesstimate of the timeframe when we'd talked in Bel Air; by now she should be able to provide me with a more definitive answer. Maybe she could even tell me if the case looked like a nonstarter, and if she believed my LA woman had died an accidental death.

I called the LA County medical examiner-coroner's office, entered Dr. Frank's extension, and got her voicemail. After leaving my name and number, I decided to try my luck with a human and dialed their switchboard. The receptionist told me, "Dr. Frank is occupied. Do you want her voicemail?" I declined the invitation.

While waiting for Dr. Frank's callback, I made an overdue call of my own. Andrea Charles sounded a lot better than she had on the night she was attacked.

"Hollywood," she said.

"How's the patient?"

"In half an hour I'll be a former patient, and it will be none too soon."

"You being sprung for good behavior?"

"You know better than that, Hollywood. My doctor decided he'd had enough of my asking to be released."

"Cops make the second-worst patients," I said.

"Who are the worst?" she asked.

"Doctors," I said. "If you don't believe me, ask a nurse. They all say the same thing."

"I'm not surprised."

"I hope you're going to take a few days off," I said.

She laughed. "Try telling me you'd be taking a few days off if someone had tried to kill you. Come this afternoon, I'll be back on the Weatherman's ass, putting a microscope on every minute he spent in Nevada. And now that the cat is out of that bag, everyone at LVMPD wants to help me nail that bastard."

"Nail away," I said, "just as long as everyone at LVMPD has the even bigger priority of covering your back."

"Back, front, and side," she said.

"Anything on your assailant?"

My unsaid worry was that her attacker might make a second attempt on her life, as unlikely as that seemed.

"Nothing that our department has been able to nail down," she said. "But I couldn't tell you if the Feds have had any success. They seem to think their cards need to be held close to the vest. What the fuck, right? Why the hell hide your cards when we know two sevens have already been played?"

I decided not to mention my doubts about her attacker not being the All-In Killer, and instead referenced the two sevens with poker lingo: "Double hockey sticks."

"Like most sisters, I don't know the first thing about hockey other than that it seems like a good excuse for a coupla white guys to be throwing punches."

"I once went to a fight and a hockey game broke out," I said.

It got a little laugh out of her, which isn't bad for a joke that's been around for a century or more.

"I'll call my contact at the Bureau and remind him we're on the same team. I'll also see what I can learn about their investigation. It's past time your bad guy got tossed in the sin bin."

"'Sin bin'?"

"Hockey slang for the penalty box. Ely State Prison will work just fine."

"Since you're calling your friendly Fed," she said, "ask him about the number seventy-seven Golden Knights jersey that his colleagues appropriated for tests."

"What do you want to know about it?"

"They need to be reminded it has to be returned. I've got a personal interest in getting it back."

"You want it for tests?"

"Nah," she said. "After we nail the killer, I got plans for that jersey to hang on the wall of my living room."

When Ben Corning answered my call, I asked him, "Were your ears burning?"

"That's a permanent condition," he said.

"Andrea Charles doesn't think the FBI has been exactly forthcoming with her, or with Vegas law enforcement."

"I hope you told her that the Bureau discourages its agents from commenting on cases prematurely."

"How about doing it off the record?"

"Off the record, her assailant is believed to be in his mid-thirties, and stands five foot nine to five foot ten inches tall. We think he has short, dark brown hair, although he wore several different wigs in the footage we have. He's white, and weighs approximately one hundred seventy-five pounds. Now, would you like to guess the age, height, hair color, and weight of the average American male?"

"You tell me."

"According to national demographics, you're looking at a white male who's thirty-six-point-eight years old, stands about five foot nine and a quarter, has dark brown hair, and weighs one hundred ninety-five pounds. In other words, the attacker qualifies as an everyman."

"With those parameters, how many suspects are we looking at?"

"In the US alone, more than six million white males fit that profile. But that assumes, of course, the assailant is an American."

Corning's comment seemed to imply something more. "You thinking he's a foreigner?"

"We haven't ruled that out, which is why we're being very careful in what we say or release. Right now, we're working with not only domestic intelligence, but foreign law enforcement. We're reaching out worldwide with the surveillance pictures of our suspect."

"You think the assailant is still in Nevada?"

"Officially, I don't have a comment."

"Unofficially?"

"We think he managed to get the hell out of Dodge."

After calling St. Joseph Medical Center, I confirmed Mack Carter would be leaving the hospital later that day. My next call was to Dr. Misko, who told me that she had no objections with my returning Cricket to her home. Dr. Misko said Cricket's discharge papers would include the meds she needed to be given, as well as her dining menu.

"Cricket needs to be on a bland diet," she said. "For the next few days it's chicken breast, cooked white rice, and that's all. Tell the owner that means no snacking."

I promised to do as she advised, and then we both clicked off to take other calls. Dr. Linda Frank was returning my call.

"Didn't your mom ever tell you a watched pot never boils?" she said. "Patience is a virtue."

"Or it masquerades as one," I said. "I'm the vulture who is saying to the other vulture: 'Patience, hell, I'm going to kill somebody.'"

"As I'm sure I don't need to tell you," she said, "the autopsy report is not complete."

"I'm okay with incomplete."

"My boss isn't. You know we're not supposed to comment until all the tests come back, which they haven't. In fact, your very call to this office is at least a month premature."

"Mea culpa," I said. "But now that I've offered my contrition, I'm still getting the vibe that you have something."

"That sounds like wishful thinking, Detective."

"Throw me a bone."

"I have some *preliminary* results. On a hunch, I submitted some hair samples, in addition to blood and urine. Because of that, we got lucky."

"What are you telling me?"

"I don't have anything definitive. And what I do have is not something I want to discuss over the phone."

"In that case," I said, "I'll see you in about an hour."

The LA County Department of Medical Examiner-Coroner is located in East LA in the Boyle Heights neighborhood, an area of town with plenty of visible wrinkles and battle scars. More than 85,000 residents live within Boyle Heights's six and a half square miles. The densely populated area is shaped roughly like a boot and is almost exclusively Latino. It's a poor, working-class neighborhood. While Boyle Heights might not win any beauty contests, what it does have going for it is relatively inexpensive rents, at least compared to most of LA. Because of that, for some in Boyle Heights *gentrification* is a bad word. In recent years, new coffee shops and art galleries have been picketed and boycotted by some of the locals.

The medical examiner-coroner's office has more than 200 employees, but those numbers aren't enough to keep up with LA's dead. Every year their department accepts more than 8,000 cases for review. The work backlog—and the backlog of bodies—has been something the county has been contending with for many years. When the phrase "bodies piled up like cordwood" isn't a cliché as much as it is an endemic problem, the heads of the living have been known to roll. More than one chief medical examiner had been fired.

Like every other cop, I was trying to push to the front of the line. Usually that doesn't work. Even celebrities—or more accurately, former celebrities—have to wait to be processed. It was months before the Tom Petty toxicology report was released, a timeframe that was not at all unusual. I suppose it was a near miracle that anything at all had been determined about the death of Carrie Holder.

Luckily for me, Linda Frank's office wasn't in the basement. That's where the autopsies are performed. My job has required me to witness several autopsies. So far, I haven't gotten sick, but it's been a close thing. Despite what's shown on television and in the movies, I've never seen a forensic pathologist try to mask the smell of the dead using menthol or peppermint oil. They deal with the reek as you might expect—with cast-iron stomachs and gallows humor.

Dr. Frank's office was tiny, or at least felt that way because of the stacks of books and papers that dominated the space. I found her using one hand to tap at her computer keyboard, and the other to finish eating an apple. She didn't seem to have any qualms about eating the core. It was already half gone.

"Living dangerously?" I asked.

She studied the remaining apple core, looked at me, and then finished it in a bite.

After swallowing, she said, "The seeds in that core contain a trace amount of cyanide. It would take several hundred seeds for them to be fatal. So far, we've never had a suicide by apple, or a homicide traced to apple seeds."

"Something to look forward to?"

She wiped the hand that had been holding the apple with a tissue before answering. "Such a death wouldn't be run-of-the-mill. In an average year this office processes roughly six hundred homicides. Most of those—around ninety percent—are a result of gunshot wounds and sharp- and blunt-force trauma. In case you're wondering, we've never had a snakebite homicide."

"Is that what we've got now?"

"I'm not ready to make that determination, and you had better not expect my findings for at least another six weeks."

I looked at my watch and said, "Starting five minutes from now, I'll have the patience of Job. But before then, you did mention something about preliminary results."

"You do know what *preliminary* means?"

"It's not cast in stone and I can't hold you to it."

"And you understand what I say is off the record and unattributable?"

"What? Who?"

Dr. Frank rolled her eyes before responding. "The time of death for your victim, give or take an hour, was at eleven at night. I thought that was a strange time to be bitten by a rattlesnake, but as it turns out I was wrong about that. In summer, rattlesnakes avoid the direct heat of the sun and choose to be out and about at night. Because of those early suspicions, though, and the presentation of the body, I decided to include hair samples to be tested along with her blood and urine. I did this because certain drugs aren't detectable in blood and urine after eight to twelve hours."

I did a mental calculation. "If your time of death is accurate, then the body wouldn't have been discovered until more than thirty hours after her death."

Dr. Frank nodded. "The state of the body made me suspect the victim might have been in some kind of narcotized sleep when she was bitten by the rattlesnake."

"And the tox screen showed this?"

"The hair samples I submitted *preliminarily* showed this. We'll need further testing to confirm that."

"What was the drug?"

"Gamma-hydroxybutyric acid," she said, and then offered up its acronym. "GHB."

"Liquid X," I said, citing one of the street names for liquid ecstasy.

"It's a potent relaxant," said Dr. Frank. "And it's abused by some as a very powerful sleep aid."

"Would you call it a knockout drug?" I asked.

"It didn't earn its reputation as a date-rape drug for nothing, so yes, it most certainly is a knockout drug. But in most cases, it's a drug that is self-administered. That's why it's known as a club drug. Do you know if the victim went to raves or dance parties, or if she abused drugs?"

"I think her busy schedule precluded raves," I said. "And there were no drugs found at her premises, including liquid X."

"Despite its street name," she said, "like most synthetic drugs, GHB also comes in powder form, or as a capsule or tablet."

"I'll recheck the inventory that was done at the house," I said, "to see if the GHB might have been guised as something else. You didn't happen to find any needle marks on the victim, did you, or anything to suggest that the GHB could have been introduced involuntarily?"

"No needle marks," the doctor said, "nor any indication of trauma."

"So, after taking the drug, it's possible the victim might have fallen asleep on her chaise longue out in the garden, awakened from her slumber, stumbled off in the direction of her house, and while doing so stepped on a rattlesnake."

"Given a narcotized sleep, that's entirely possible."

"And after being bitten by the snake, you're telling me she just decided to go to sleep on the ground?"

"My long answer would involve a lecture on brain chemistry, and how certain synthetic drugs can impact receptors and alter temporal awareness."

"And your short answer?"

"She could have been bitten by the snake and thought nothing of curling up and going to sleep on the ground."

That wasn't the Sleeping Beauty story, I thought, but maybe it was the LA woman version of it.

CHAPTER THIRTY-TWO

TO KILL A HUMMINGBIRD

I was mindful of the clock, wanting to get everything done in a timely manner so nothing would interfere with my plans to see Lisbet. After feeding the dogs and getting them settled, I retrieved the perfect card for Lisbet, one I'd squirreled away a month earlier. That card, I decided, needed just the right accompaniments, which is why I made a few stops along my route. At the florist's, I picked up a dozen red roses, and then it was off to See's Candies. Lisbet has a sweet tooth that only See's can satisfy, and I came out of the store with one box each of nuts and chews, peanut brittle, and molasses chips. She would complain about my sabotaging her diet, but only until she started sampling the selections. Studies have shown that an endorphin-like peptide in chocolate works like morphine on the brain. You can even argue that chocolate is a drug, but it's hard to do so when your mouth is full.

Because Lisbet had been specific about her choice of wrap, I stopped at our favorite sandwich shop and left with three Pocket

Health Rockets. The third wrap was to be my homecoming present for Mr. Carter.

The next stop was Angie's Rescues, where I discovered someone had decided to make good on the expression "put a bow on it." Cricket had been carefully groomed, with a pink bow affixed to her collar. One of the volunteers had even prepared a few "to go" meals for her that consisted of boiled chicken breast and white rice.

I coaxed Cricket into her carrier, picked up her meds, and then set out for Sherman Oaks. As we drew nearer to her home, Cricket suddenly perked up. I wasn't sure which of her senses alerted her to where we were, but she started shivering with excitement.

"Yes, you're almost home," I said.

I parked on the street in front of the Carter house. As I exited the Explorer, I sensed I was being watched. Maybe I imagined it, but it looked as if there was movement behind Patricia Gaspar's living room curtains. As captain of the neighborhood watch, she seemed convinced her nosiness was all for the good of the street, if not the public.

"Is my princess there? Where is my sweet girl?"

Mack Carter was out on the front porch, leaning on a walker. His voice was much stronger than the last time I'd heard it, and he looked as if he were ready to vault from the porch to get to Cricket. Next to him was a woman I didn't know, who was urging Carter to be cautious.

I yelled, "I'll bring Cricket up, Mr. Carter. Stay where you are."

The woman reached for the old man's elbow and made sure he stayed put while I pulled out the carrier. Cricket's small silver-and-gray tail was wagging furiously, and she was whining. I don't know who was more anxious to see the other, but man and dog were ready for their reunion. For a few moments, at least, the years seemed to fall off both of them. I hurried up the pathway. When I reached the porch, Cricket was doing her whirling dervish imitation inside her kennel. The woman with Mr. Carter steadied him as he reached his thin fingers through the carrier's opening to make contact with Cricket.

"Why don't we go sit down in the living room, Mack?" said the woman. "That way we can get Cricket out of her cage."

The dog was licking every one of his available fingers. "Yes, yes," he said. "Let's go inside."

The old man surprised me by turning his walker around and taking off at a fast clip.

"I'm Evie Schmitt," said the woman, offering me her hand. "You've talked with my husband, Walt."

"Michael Gideon," I said.

"I'm glad to see you," she said. "Ever since Mack got home, he's been staring out the window watching for your arrival. During the last hour I've had to talk him out of calling nine-one-one to see what was taking you so long."

"I'm sorry I didn't get here sooner," I said, smiling.

She motioned for me to go ahead, and I brought the carrier into the house. Mack was already seated in the living room, making impatient sounds for me to set Cricket free. I opened the door to the kennel, and Cricket was out like a shot. For an old dog, Cricket still had hops. She leapt into Mack's lap and started kissing his face.

"I missed those kisses," Mack said. "Yes, I did, I surely did."

Evie and I watched the happy reunion, our smiles stretching our faces. There was a lot of baby talk and kissing, and we both soaked it in. Evie wiped away a tear; the lump in my throat wasn't quite as visible.

"I have a few things I need to get from the car," I said, my voice brusque and official. It was a good excuse; it was also a way for me to avoid being seen as a mushy sentimentalist.

As I walked out of the house and started down the walkway, I was again convinced that I was being monitored. I looked for the source, and saw Marjorie Jensen—the woman with the "catitude"—staring at me from a bay window inside her house.

"Is anyone on this street not monitoring me?" I muttered.

I returned to the house carrying Mack's wrap sandwich and Cricket's takeout containers from Angie's Rescues. Things hadn't changed during my short absence. Cricket was settled in Mack's lap, and their reunion was still going strong.

Evie Schmitt had seated herself on the loveseat, and I took a seat in a chair across from her. She was a middle-aged woman with a slightly crooked smile made all the more apparent by her beaming expression.

"The shelter provided Cricket with meals for the next three days," I said, trying to get Mack's attention. "During that time, they want her on a *bland diet*, which is pretty much what it sounds like—boiled chicken and rice. The patient isn't supposed to be snacking either."

"Did you hear that, Mack?" asked Evie.

He reluctantly turned his head away from Cricket. "What's that?"

"Detective Gideon has brought Cricket her food for the next three days. It's a special diet. And that means no snacking."

I waved the containers for him to see. "There's a carton for each of the next three days," I said. "Do you want me to put them in the refrigerator, Mr. Carter?"

"Yes, that would be nice," he said.

"Was Cricket fed today?" asked Evie.

"Earlier this afternoon," I said. "Don't let her acting like she's hungry fool anyone into feeding her."

"Are you listening, Mack?" said Evie. "Cricket was already fed today. Don't go feeding her a second time."

Mack acknowledged her instructions with a nod and wave of the hand, before turning back to Cricket.

As I got up, Evie said to me, "Why don't I go write on each container which day they're to be served up?"

"Makes sense," I said, and the two of us walked out to the kitchen. After searching for a marker, Evie settled on a highlighter and began writing on the cartons.

The kitchen looked just as it must have when Carter was taken to the hospital. There were unwashed dishes in the sink; on the floor were crusted dog bowls, one blue and the other pink. Evie noticed my looking around.

"There's a maid who comes here once a week," she said. "I made sure she would be cleaning tomorrow."

"Mack is lucky to have neighbors like you and your husband," I said.

"We do what we can," she said, "but the truth is that both of us are feeling a little guilty about this entire situation. Mack hasn't had the option of letting his dogs out into the backyard because there are holes in the fence, and the yard backs on to a busy street. For months, Walt has been promising to fix the fencing, but he never got around to doing it. Today he bought the materials he needs, and tomorrow he's going to finish those repairs. That will mean Mack can let Cricket out back when he's not up to walking her."

"And it should save him from having to worry about her eating something she shouldn't."

"That's the hope," said Evie. "I wish I could be as confident about our Barney. He eats anything that's not glued down." Then she added, "And that includes glue."

I put Cricket's marked containers in the refrigerator. There wasn't much competition for space. Inside, there were only a few scant items, including a block of cheese, some salad dressing, and mayonnaise. Once again, Evie responded to my unspoken scrutinizing.

"Mack gets his groceries delivered," she said, "and senior services brings by his meals. I'll make sure everything starts up tomorrow."

"Tonight's taken care of," I said. "I brought him a wrap."

"That saves me from having to bring something over," she said, "which will make both me and Mack happy. Mack's always made it clear he prefers his can of soup to anything that comes out of my kitchen."

The two of us returned to the living room. Evie stood in front of Mack and said, "Detective Gideon was nice enough to bring you your dinner for tonight."

"I hope it's better than hospital food," I said. "I brought you a wrap."

"A what?" he asked.

"It's like a chicken sandwich," I said, "with avocado and tomato and greens and things."

"That sounds very tasty," he said.

"Are you hungry, Mack?" asked Evie.

He considered the question, then seemed surprised by the answer. "I am," he said.

"Then why don't I bring you your sandwich on a plate?" she said.

"I don't want to eat," he said in the direction of her retreating back, and then turned to me to finish, "in front of others."

"Please don't give that a second thought," I said. "I'll be going over to my girlfriend's apartment for dinner in just a little while. If you don't mind, I'd like to keep you company while you eat."

Evie returned with a tray and a napkin, and set them up on an end table next to where Mack and Cricket were sitting.

"You heard Detective Gideon, Mack," she said. "You need to eat. I've got to leave now anyway, but I'll stop by tomorrow to make sure Mariana is here. And Walt will be over to fix those holes in your back fence. I promise."

Mack looked as if he was thinking about trying to get up, but that would have meant discommoding the sleepy terrier that had claimed a spot on his lap. Evie made sure he didn't rise by leaning down and giving him a hug.

"I'll let myself out," she said.

After the two of us said our goodbyes, I was left in the company of Mack and a lightly snoring dog.

"Are you sure you don't want to eat some of this?" he asked.

I raised my palms. "It's all for you."

The wrap had been cut in half. Mack took a napkin, diapered one of the sections, and then raised it to his mouth. After taking a bite, he brightened.

"It's very good," he said, sounding somewhat surprised.

"I'm glad to hear that," I said, "because I ordered the same thing for me and my girlfriend."

He took another bite and made more appreciative noises. Cricket awakened to his sounds, or maybe to the aroma of what he was eating, and raised a hopeful head.

Mack looked at me. By his expression, it was clear he remembered Evie's admonition about not giving Cricket any snacks. By his same expression, he appealed to me for some wiggle room.

I brought my forefinger and thumb close enough to one another that they were almost touching. "Just the smallest piece of chicken," I said.

Mack mostly complied with my guidance on portion control, and Cricket happily inhaled the snack. It was evident that the two of them were longstanding coconspirators, something Mack confirmed.

"I'm afraid Cricket and her brother got quite used to eating this way," he said, and took another bite.

"It's hard not to succumb to the charms of a dog's beseeching eyes."

Mack nodded and said, "She is an artful beggar."

He took another bite, and once more shook his head appreciatively while chewing. "I'm not used to food tasting this good."

"You don't like your home delivery meals?"

Mack looked around, acting as if he were mindful of being overheard. In a mock whisper he said, "Those deliveries have always been more for my friends than for me."

"I'm not following," I said.

He winked at me and said, "Maybe I shouldn't say anything, what with you being a police officer."

"You needn't worry about that, Mr. Carter. Your secret is safe with me."

He seemed satisfied that I was to be trusted, and said, "That old-folk food hasn't been going to me as much as it has my dogs."

"Really? Why is that?"

"It just sort of happened," he said.

"Then what do you eat?"

"I usually open a can of soup."

"So, your two dogs have been eating your delivery food?"

"When the service started, at first we kind of shared," he said. "But they're such good beggars it wasn't long before they were getting the whole thing. All I did was mix in a little dry dog food."

I'm sure my face showed my surprise, but Mack must have interpreted it as something else.

"It wasn't like I was giving them sweets," he said. "They were eating like royals. My usual delivery meal is chicken, rice, and green beans. That's a healthy meal, especially with some dry food."

"Yes, it is," I said. "That sounds like a balanced diet for either the two-legged or four-legged."

Mack nodded, and took another bite of the wrap. He looked from me to Cricket, then back to me. I made the same gesture I had before, and he passed over some chicken to her, which disappeared without demur.

"Next time I'll bring Cricket her own sandwich," I said.

The thought of that tickled the old man. "You like the sound of that, don't you?" he said to his dog, and then ran his free hand down Cricket's back. She looked at him expectantly, and Mack appealed to the referee. This time I shook my head.

"No more begging," he said to Cricket, pretending firmness.

Neither of us believed his words.

"It's easy to see how you were sweet-talked out of your dinners," I said. "Did anyone suspect your food deliveries weren't going to you so much as they were to your dogs?"

Carter shook his head. "I never told that to anyone doing the deliveries. That might have hurt their feelings. But I wasn't ever really put on the spot, because it was Patricia who usually brought over my food."

I showed my puzzlement. "Why weren't the deliveries made directly to you?"

My question seemed to surprise him. "I guess because she arranged for it," he said.

"That still doesn't explain why the food was delivered to her instead of directly to you."

"I'm not very fast to the door," he admitted, "and Patricia said the delivery people didn't want to be kept waiting. That's why she asked for a key to my front door. Patricia is able to put the food in my refrigerator without me having to get up to let her in."

"Are there set days and times for the food deliveries?"

"Monday and Thursday," said Mack. "Patricia always brings the food over before four o'clock."

"And what time do you and the dogs eat dinner?"

"Late afternoon," he said. "And I also feed them first thing in the morning."

"You and the dogs were found on Tuesday morning," I said.

"I don't remember much from that day," said Mack.

"Assuming you got your delivery on Monday afternoon," I said, "why is it I didn't see any delivery dinners in your refrigerator? There should have been at least two uneaten dinners."

Mack shook his head. He didn't have an answer for me.

"Is there special packaging for your meals?" I asked.

"They come in reusable containers," said Mack, "so that you can microwave them."

I went out to the kitchen to look for the container that should have been there, but found nothing that matched its description. In the kitchen trash there wasn't much besides opened cans. Near the top of the trash bin was a big can of beef stew. I brought the can back with me to the living room.

"Do you remember when you ate this?" I asked.

"Dinty Moore," he said. "That's one of my favorites."

"Big can," I said.

"The dogs like it too," he admitted.

"Do you remember if you shared its contents with your dogs?"

"I'm not sure," he said.

"But what do you think?"

"I seem to remember that was the case."

"And that would have been Monday night, right?"

That got a tentative nod. "Let's assume that's the case," I said. "That big can of beef stew would have been enough to feed the three of you. What do you think might have happened to the food that was delivered?"

"I seem to remember I fed them the next morning."

"But you don't remember specifically?"

"I'm sorry," he said.

"What time do you usually get up?" I asked.

"Always first light," he said.

"And that's when you feed the dogs?"

He nodded.

I walked across the street. This time I found two dead hummingbirds, both with distended tongues. I took pictures of their tiny corpses, and then I used my phone to do a search on the most likely cause of their deaths. A cursory read of several articles was enough to convince me I was on to something.

"What are you doing?"

I didn't answer directly, but instead turned to face Patricia Gaspar. Her glower, and the angry set of her arms on her hips, bespoke her unhappiness at my presence.

"I'm reading about dead hummingbirds," I said. "I was curious as to how you killed them. I suspect you used honey as a sweetener, because honey solutions are notorious for fermentation and mold growth. That's why anyone with a hummingbird feeder is told to never, ever use honey. The mold often causes the tongues of the poor hummingbirds to rot. Essentially, they starve to death. But I'm sure you were aware of that and are an old hand at killing off hummingbirds. That's the only reason you would ever have a feeder. You didn't put it up to feed them; you put it up to kill them. Hummingbirds have such a high metabolism that they need to constantly feed. But you didn't like the way they invaded your garden. And that resulted in their death sentence, the same death sentence you meted out upon any uninvited guests."

"I don't have to listen to your nonsense," she said.

"As a matter of fact," I said, "you do. If what I'm saying is nonsense, then why don't you hand me your bird feeder? I'd like to run some tests on it."

Her eyes narrowed, and her voice turned low and nasty. "Get a search warrant," she said.

"I think that would be a waste of time," I said. "I'm sure you would destroy the evidence. And besides, I'm sorry to say that your violating the Migratory Bird Act doesn't carry the kind of penalties that would make it worthwhile to prosecute you. However, attempted murder, along with felony animal cruelty, does carry the kind of penalties very much worth pursuing. You're under arrest, Mrs. Gaspar."

For a few moments she was speechless with anger, and during that time I used my phone to make a recording of me reciting the Miranda rights to her. After finishing, I said, "Do you understand these rights as I have explained them, Mrs. Gaspar?"

"I will have your badge," she said.

Once more I repeated, "Do you understand your rights?"

"I understand," she said. "And I also understand you won't even be working as a dog catcher when I'm done with you."

"Would you like a lawyer present during questioning?" I asked.

"I don't need a lawyer," she said. "But you will. Oh, yes, you will."

"Thank you for your concern on my behalf," I said. "And I'd also like to thank you for being the block watch captain. I'm sure you convinced most of your neighbors to put in security cameras. In fact, I don't remember ever seeing any street in Sherman Oaks with so many security cameras. After I go around and gather that footage, I'm sure it will provide evidence of your crime."

She took a step back, as if I'd delivered a blow. "What do you mean?" she said.

"You took Mr. Carter his food on Monday afternoon. That's why you were keeping watch even before first light on Tuesday. I imagine you were prepared to use your key to get into his house. After you cleaned up any evidence of your poisoned dishes, you were going to make your terrible discovery. But then, unexpectedly, you saw his front door open early Tuesday morning. Mr. Carter and his dogs were in distress. Still, everything might have worked out for you if Walt Schmitt hadn't been leaving early for work."

Her angry flushed face turned white and pinched, and her eyes began moving from side to side, as if she were desperately seeking an escape.

"This is all ridiculous," she said.

"The security videos will show you going to the house after Mr. Carter and his dogs were taken away. You would have disposed of the delivery food, and any evidence of the poison."

"I went over to the house to clean up," she said, "like any good neighbor would have."

"The hospital will have samples of Mr. Carter's blood," I said. "Tests will show what you used to poison him."

I watched her face as she considered my words. She knew the story that the videos and the blood work would tell, and decided to plead to a lesser crime.

"Not him," she said, offering the words up triumphantly, "his dogs! I knew about his dirty little trick. His fraud, that's what it was. He told me all about it. You should be arresting him. He was the one who was giving the food meant for him to his horrible dogs."

"So, you're saying you were only trying to poison Cricket and Crocket, is that right?"

She nodded. A small smile even came to her face.

"Did you use the same poison on Cricket and Crocket that you did on Barney and Matilda?"

With clipped words, she said, "Trespass at your own risk. Isn't that what the signs say? It's certainly not my fault that those dogs ate something that didn't agree with them."

"Just like the hummingbirds, right?" I said. "You just left some enticing object out. But you poisoned Cricket and Crocket. There was no trespassing on their part."

My words provoked her. "Oh, there was," she said. "Last week, those curs left their awful little droppings all over my garden. I came out too late to stop them, but did the old man do anything? He was yelling at his dogs from across the street, but those horrible little mutts ignored him."

"And they ignored whatever poisoned treats you left out. So instead of making them just a little sick like the other dogs, you had to see them die."

I brought out some flex cuffs, and as I moved to apply them to her hands, the very proper Patricia Gaspar spat in my face.

"Go to hell," she said.

I turned in the direction of her security camera, made a point of wiping away her spittle, and said, "I'm going to add assaulting a police officer to your list of charges. Something tells me this street is going to need a new neighborhood watch captain for at least the next five years."

CHAPTER THIRTY-THREE

DUCK, DUCK, MONGOOSE

I found a quiet spot at the station and called Lisbet. Our evening together wasn't going to happen.

"As much as I hate to cancel," I said, "I'm not going to be able to make it over tonight."

I stopped talking, hoping she would jump in, but that didn't happen. "I already picked up the food and the fixings, but you know what they say about the best laid plans . . ."

I paused a second time. Her sigh wasn't what I wanted to hear. "What happened?" she asked.

"I had to make an unexpected arrest. And now I'm trying to get a judge to sign off on a search warrant. Even if there are no hiccups, all the paperwork is going to keep me working until late tonight."

"I understand," she said.

"I want you to know that I'm as frustrated as you must be."

"You need to do what's right for you," she said. "That's what I need to do as well."

I wasn't sure if Lisbet was simply being considerate, or if she was considering walking away from our relationship. Maybe she didn't know either.

"I know I keep saying that I want to make it up to you," I said, "and I know I keep failing whenever I try to do that."

"Maybe one of these days we'll get it right."

I heard every word she said, but the only one that kept sounding off like an alarm in my head was the word *maybe*. It was a fifty-fifty word. It wasn't probably, it was possibly.

"Tomorrow night?" I asked.

"Tomorrow is crazy," she said.

Then let's make it sane. That's what I wanted to say, but decided I wasn't in a position to be pushy.

"If that changes," I said, "or if you can free up your schedule, I'd really like to see you."

"I'll keep that in mind," she said. A moment later she added, "I didn't mean it to sound that way. I must be low blood sugar."

"You're not sick, are you?"

"No," she said. "Like my nana used to say, I've got a bit of a dicky tum. A bowl of oatmeal and a cup of herbal tea should set me straight."

"You sure I can't send you a pizza?"

Her refusal was emphatic. "Thank you, but *no*," she said, "although I do appreciate the thought."

"We have to stop not meeting like this," I said.

She made a sound I interpreted as amusement. I suppose that was as good an end to our conversation as I could have hoped.

There is an art to writing up arrest reports that extends beyond crossing your t's and dotting your i's. Clarity is essential. It's important to document who, what, when, where, and why, because you know some defense attorney will be studying your

words with a jaundiced eye in the hopes of pouncing on any perceived shortcomings or omissions in your statement. I am not of
the "less is more" school when it comes to writing reports. It has
been my experience that it's easier for lawyers to misinterpret
brevity than it is excess. When you arrive on the witness stand, a
good defense lawyer will feign suspicion and misgivings over
your including or embellishing upon details that weren't in your
initial report. Because of that, I try to note anything relevant, or
that might be relevant, in the write-up.

And because of that, I ended up working until two in the
morning.

My late arrival home roused two sleeping dogs. Their slow-
motion greeting at the door bespoke their emerging from a deep
slumber. "Sorry to have gotten you up," I said.

They accepted my apology. Sarcasm is lost on dogs.

Sirius and Emily did a lot of sniffing of my person and got
to know Cricket through their noses. As they became more alert,
their body language suggested they were hoping for a walk.

"I promise to take you out in the morning," I said.

The dogs took me at my word. My goal was to get four
hours' sleep. That would leave me with just enough time to prepare for my morning meeting with Eli and Amy Green, aka
Brother Elijah and Sister Joan.

We all went into my bedroom. Within a minute, both dogs
were asleep. I was the one who was exhausted, but I was unable
to sleep. My thoughts raced from Lisbet, to Patricia Gaspar, to
Sister Carrie, to my morning meeting with Elijah. Every so often
the All-In Killer joined the party. There were lots of people talking, and they were all demanding I listen.

In the middle of the night it's all too easy to imagine worst-
case scenarios. I did my best to change the formula and tried to
consider best-case scenarios. When that Pollyanna approach
didn't work, I tried rhythmic breathing. It sounded good, but I

remained awake. Sometimes you get to the point of being so tired it's impossible to sleep.

I got out of bed. The dogs smartly kept sleeping. I went out to the living room, collecting a pen and pad along the way. Making a list is how I organize my world. I decided to prepare questions for my morning meeting, and began reviewing my case notes. After talking with Dr. Frank, I had meant to call Taylor Romano, but that was another good intention waylaid by Patricia Gaspar. I'd have to call Taylor in the morning. She could probably tell me better than anyone whether Carrie ever used drugs, and in particular, liquid ecstasy.

My list grew. My world became more orderly, and that allowed me to feel more relaxed. If the end of the world is imminent, you'll probably find me making a list. It's how I would prepare for the long sleep.

I came across a scrawled notation that said *Jake the Snake*. For a few moments I wondered what the hell I'd been thinking when I wrote down those words, and then I remembered its source. I'd been talking about snakes with Detective Duarte, and he'd started telling me some story about a wrestler named Jake the Snake. Then he'd said something about Jake and a cobra, and recommended that I look up the old footage on YouTube. At half past three in the morning you do things like that, and I did.

The video was everything I hate about so-called professional wrestling. There was bad acting and lots of posturing, and worst of all, there was a real king cobra. It was a huge snake, and I watched tens of thousands of people in the arena going crazy as the cobra clamped down on the arm of the wrestler known as Macho Man.

The human race likes to think we're far removed from the spectacles of carnage and bloodshed that went on in the Roman Colosseum. I wish that were true, but I don't believe it. Kipling's story "Rikki-Tikki-Tavi"—in which the snakes are pure evil and the mongoose is good—notwithstanding, I came away from watching the footage feeling sorry for the cobra. The snake had been used as a living prop to entertain the groundlings. The silver lining to that disturbing spectacle was that the footage prompted me to explore some new avenues of inquiry.

It was four a.m. when I finished scratching at my various itches. The dogs were still asleep when I finally crawled back into bed.

I woke Taylor Romano up when I called her at seven a.m. "Sorry to bother you so early," I told her. "This is Detective Gideon."

"Oh, hey," she said, trying to pretend to be awake.

"The reason for the call is that I need to know if Carrie ever used illegal drugs."

"What?" Taylor definitely sounded more awake now.

"Carrie tested positive on her tox screen," I said.

"For what?"

"For a schedule one controlled substance. That's why I'm asking if you have any personal knowledge of Carrie's using drugs."

"No way," she said. "Her biggest vice was an occasional glass of wine."

"No illegal drugs?"

"None."

"Do you know if she had trouble sleeping and ever took any meds to help her do so?"

Taylor thought about that. "I don't think so. Sometimes Carrie didn't get as much sleep as she would have liked, but only because she was so busy. I never heard her complain of insomnia."

"Thanks for talking to me," I said. "And speaking of sleep, I'm sorry for having disturbed yours."

The dogs came with me on my trip over to Ark Studios. I had promised them a walk, but there hadn't been time. My troubles with Lisbet were making me rethink how to better follow through with promises that I made to others. It was all too easy to let my work life destroy my personal life, and I needed to do something about that. The night before, I'd told the dogs I was going to give them a walk in the morning, and one way or another it was going to happen. I would show Lisbet—and myself—that I wasn't a lost cause.

At the entrance to the studio I was stopped by a Latino man whose name tag said *Miguel*. The guard was in his mid-twenties and had the bearing and jargon of someone who'd recently served in the military.

"What is your business here, sir?" he asked.

"I have an appointment to see Eli Green," I said, "aka Elijah."

Miguel found my name on his list and handed me a visitor's badge on a lanyard. I remembered what had happened the last time I'd toured the grounds with the dogs, and flashed him my wallet badge as a preamble to my request.

"I'm with LAPD," I said, and hitched my right thumb toward the backseat. "My K-9 team will be working alongside me today. Will they also need visitor's passes?"

Miguel's mouth opened, but no reply emerged. He looked away from me, as if searching for an answer. When he didn't find one, he excused himself to go and make a call from inside his booth. Even though I couldn't hear what was being said, Miguel's body language spoke for him. There were several headshakes and a few "how would I know?" open-hand gestures. The upshot of the conversation was that he returned to my window with two more lanyards.

He handed them to me, and I thanked him. Then with a lowered voice he asked, "Drug dogs?"

"We prefer to call them detection dogs," I said in an equally hushed tone.

"Got it," he said. The barrier arm rose, and we drove through.

With their lanyards looped through their collars and their presence made official, the dogs finally got their walk. I didn't hurry them along. A promise was a promise, whether to the two-legged or four-legged.

There was a guard I hadn't encountered before working the entrance to the world headquarters for the Church of the Gate; lurking in the background was Sergeant Collins, the same supervisor I'd dealt with previously. After I'd stated my business to the guard, Sergeant Collins emerged to provide backup. This time the sticking point to my visit wasn't my gun, but the dogs.

"Only guide dogs are allowed in this building," Collins told me.

"K-9 officers, like guide dogs, have the legal right to go anywhere that people do," I said. "And since that is the law, at this time the three of us need to exercise our right to proceed."

The supervisor rubbed his neck, let out some air, and after deflating, capitulated. He turned to the guard who had initially stopped us.

"Officer Williams," he said, "please escort Detective Gideon and these K-9 officers upstairs to the third-floor meeting room."

Officer Williams offered his sergeant a serious and officious nod. He kept up his grave front until the elevator doors closed behind us. That's when a big smile emerged. His perfect white teeth were complemented by his dark skin.

"How you two *K-9 officers* doing?" he said, offering both Sirius and Emily a hand. Sniffing and wagging followed.

"I got a pittie myself," he said, giving Emily a little scratch. "Never heard of a pittie police dog, though."

Whatever suspicions Officer Williams might have had were only exceeded by his good humor at our having prevailed over the bureaucracy. As we reached our third-floor destination and the elevator doors opened, Officer Williams withdrew his hand from Emily's back and lost his smile, once more becoming the serious guard. The Church Lady was at her post. She looked at me and the dogs disapprovingly, but then again, I was pretty sure she looked at the world the same way.

"Hello, Darlene," I said. "Please inform all concerned that I'll be in the meeting room."

She offered me the barest nod, and Officer Williams and I continued down the hall.

"You like being a cop?" he asked.

"Like any job, there are good days and bad days."

"At least you get to hang around with your *K-9 officers*," he said. "It's a good thing you didn't claim they were therapy dogs. That wouldn't have gotten you in the door."

"Maybe not," I said, "but I'm pretty sure the best therapists in the world have wet noses."

That got another smile out of him. "Truth," he said, and then stood guard outside the meeting room.

I went in and took a chair, and the dogs stretched out on the floor next to me. My hands propped up my chin, and I closed my eyes. A minute or two passed, and then I heard the voice of Officer Williams saying, "Good morning, sir. Good morning, madam."

My eyes opened, and Brother Elijah and Sister Joan walked into the room. They made a point of closing the door behind them. During their time of grieving, both had managed to get some sun. Their makeup was perfect, and they looked well rested.

"Detective Gideon," said Elijah, extending a hand. We shook.

Joan didn't press the flesh, but she did give me a friendly nod. Elijah waited for Joan to sit down before taking a seat next to her. It was then that he noticed the dogs and gave a little double take of surprise.

"I hope you didn't think there was a need for police dogs at this meeting," he said.

I offered up a weak smile and said, "You never know."

In front of me were the notes I'd written up during the wee hours. I considered where best to start, and then turned my attention to Eli Green. "From what we've determined," I said, "you were the last person to see Carrie Holder alive, other than her murderer."

The couple offered surprised looks to one another. Either that or they had just learned there was gambling in Casablanca. "'Murderer'?" said Joan.

My nod answered.

"What makes you think Carrie was murdered?" asked Elijah.

"Lab results indicate the presence of GHB in her system," I said. "Gamma-hydroxybutyric acid, or GHB, has a variety of street names, including liquid ecstasy. According to individuals I interviewed, Carrie did not take drugs. It should also be noted that we didn't find any drugs in her Bel Air house. That begs the question, then, as to how that drug got into her system."

Another look passed between husband and wife. Was it a knowing look? I still wasn't sure.

"Sometimes people have secret lives of which everyone is unaware," said Joan.

"Very true," I said, wondering if she was voicing her own biography. She met my eyes for a moment before averting her glance.

I turned my attention to Elijah. "Why don't you tell me what went on during your last visit to Carrie's house?"

He shook his head and shrugged. "There's not much to say. It was a social call."

"Was she expecting you?"

He hesitated a moment before answering. "I can't recall. We had the kind of relationship where it wasn't necessary to plan everything."

"You're saying you still maintained that kind of relationship even though the two of you were no longer on intimate terms?"

"Who told you that?" he asked.

"Various sources," I said.

Choosing his words carefully, he said, "We were in the process of working things out."

"Your visit with her only lasted forty minutes. I'm assuming you didn't work things out during that short time."

Before Elijah could comment, his wife said, "This is beginning to feel more like an ambush than an interview. Perhaps it would be better if we had our lawyer present during questioning."

I shrugged, pretending indifference, while at the same time trying to come up with the best strategy for keeping them talking. Elijah beat me to the punch, though, becoming my surprise ally.

With his voice cracking and upset, he turned to his wife and said, "You don't think I had anything to do with Carrie's death, do you?"

She touched his arm. "Of course not, but if the detective is right about Carrie having been murdered, then it would only be prudent to not say anything else before consulting with counsel."

"That is certainly your right," I said, "but I was hoping we could straighten out some of these details without having to make this a very public matter. As far as I know, most of your followers aren't aware that your husband has been leading a—what did you call it the other day?—polyamorous lifestyle."

The couple looked at each other. "I had nothing to do with Carrie's death," Elijah told his wife. She nodded reluctantly, apparently accepting his words and giving him tacit permission to keep talking to me.

"Tell me about those forty minutes," I said.

"Our conversation was strained," he admitted. "I was trying to win Carrie back, but that wasn't what she wanted."

"When did the two of you stop having a physical relationship?"

"Around a month ago," he said.

"Did that put a strain on your work relationship?"

It was Joan who answered. "It put a strain on all of us."

"I'm curious about something Carrie told her best friend. She said that she was excluded from some of the goings-on at the church. According to Carrie, the two of you were conducting what she called secret ceremonies."

Husband and wife offered side-glances to each other, but said nothing.

"Ceremonies that involved rattlesnakes," I added.

Joan looked at her husband and shook her head, motioning him to silence.

"I know about the documentary the two of you were working in Kentucky," I said. "It had the working title *Shake, Rattle and Roll*, but you abruptly aborted that project despite the considerable amount of work you'd already put into it. That was a decade ago. In the time since, you've made what would seem to be a radical vocational change, going from filmmaking into religion."

Since neither of them was talking, I continued speaking for them.

"But then again, the change might not have been as far afield as it seemed. The job of a filmmaker is to tell a visual story, and all you did was transition from one stage to another. You knew better than to make snake handling the cornerstone of your religion, but you realized how captivating that visual could be. It would be hard to imagine a more gripping spectacle than your putting your life on the line to showcase your faith—and power. You reserved those performances for the very elite of your flock, those with the money. There's something about snakes, especially poisonous snakes, that's always had a great impact on the human psyche. Moses and his brother, Aaron, had staffs that supposedly turned into snakes, and then back into wood again. Since both of you are master storytellers, I have no doubt your secret snake service was particularly compelling."

I paused to take a long breath. Neither of them offered up denials, nor did they meet my eyes.

"While working on your documentary," I said, "you would have learned the fatal flaw of snake handling and preaching. True believers put their lives on the line in order to show their followers that God is working through them by giving them dominion over poisonous serpents. That's why the careers of snake-handling preachers are often short-lived. Even if preachers survive a bite, or multiple bites, their limbs end up gnarled and scarred, and most lose fingers to snakebites.

"You don't have those marks, Eli. There's a simple reason for that. In the middle of the night I was reading about a procedure called venomoid surgery. That's a term you are quite familiar with, isn't it?"

When he didn't answer, I continued. "Venomoid surgery is the removal of the venom glands of poisonous snakes. When a serpent can't produce venom, you don't have to fear its bite."

The night before, I'd watched tapes of Jake "the Snake" Roberts talking about using a twelve-foot cobra to bite the wrestler known as Macho Man. It was the centerpiece of their show. Before they went out into the ring, Macho Man had insisted that Jake prove the cobra was devenomized. To demonstrate, Jake had been forced to let the cobra bite him on his leg. It was only after Macho Man was satisfied that the cobra was harmless that the two of them agreed on how to best choreograph their battle. When they met that night in the ring, even though the cobra was devenomized, it was still able to bite hard enough into Macho Man's arm to break the skin and cause bleeding.

"Since your snake show has been going on for years," I said, "it shouldn't take me long to find out who's been responsible for tending to your serpents. In fact, I have a witness who said that Carrie recently heard Sister Joan asking a staff member if 'the snakes were ready.' I'm assuming that was a euphemism for asking if they'd been devenomized. In addition to being a longstanding and trusted staff member, logic would suggest your snake keeper has a background in herpetology."

I had been watching the body language of Mr. and Mrs. Green; a few involuntary flinches made me confident that I was scoring some direct hits.

Looking at Elijah, I said, "I'm assuming you didn't murder Carrie, and that when you left her, she was alive and well."

That got him talking. "I would never have harmed her! She was very—special—to me."

"As you know, we obtained security footage from Carrie's Bel Air neighbors, and while we don't have complete coverage of her house, we were able to determine which cars traveled along the road that fronts the house. As far as the footage shows, yours is the only vehicle that parked in the vicinity of the house on the night she died. Can you explain that?"

Eli looked helplessly at his wife. "Say nothing," she said, and raised her index finger to her lips.

"That isn't some kind of trick question," I said. "My intent is not to entrap you, but to establish a timeline for your whereabouts on the night Carrie Holder died. The coroner's office has estimated her time of death at between eleven and midnight. You left her house hours before that time."

Sister Joan spoke before her husband could. "You say that you're not trying to trick us, but didn't you just finish telling us that Carrie didn't have any other visitors after Elijah?"

"What I said is that it appears his car was the only vehicle that parked in the vicinity of Carrie's home. However, there were no cameras with a view to the walkway leading to the home, or its front door. Or what I suspect is of even more import, out to the backyard and beyond."

"I don't understand," she said.

"There's a trail that goes from the backyard of the house into the canyon," I said. "It's not a formal walking trail, but there is a path of sorts that extends from one side of the canyon to the other. Using aerial imagery, I was able to follow that trail to where it came out in a distant cul-de-sac. If anyone parked on that street, they could have hiked the mile or so through the chaparral into Carrie's backyard."

Sister Joan was studying her husband and looking relieved. Maybe he wasn't a murderer after all.

"By determining your timeline for the night of Carrie's death," I told Elijah, "I believe we can potentially rule you out as a suspect."

"Elijah came home at around quarter 'til ten that night," she said. "I'm a witness to that. And he didn't go out again. There's a security system at our house that can prove those things."

"Assuming that timeline is correct," I said, "that means you didn't get home until almost two hours after you left Carrie. During that time, where were you, and what were you doing?"

"I was discouraged," he said. "Despondent, even. I had doubts both personal and professional. In popular jargon, I needed to vent."

"And who heard this venting?"

"Sister Hannah," he said.

"Did you do more than vent?" I asked.

"What do you mean?" he said.

"Were you and Sister Hannah lovers?"

"She's an important part of my life," he said, "and ministry."

Sister Hannah had been my first interview in the Carrie Holder case. She had spoken to me and the other detectives about the picture Carrie had texted of the western diamondback rattler in the canyon just off her backyard. When I'd watched footage of the Church of the Gate service, I should have paid more attention to Hannah's being as moved as she was by Elijah's words. It was her flawed prophet, even more than his message, that she had been focused upon.

I should have recognized the look of a woman in love.

"The two of you were lovers before Carrie came on the scene?" I asked.

He nodded.

"And all the while you were smitten by Carrie," I said, "Hannah was forced to watch from the sidelines."

No one answered. They didn't have to.

After being spurned by Carrie, Elijah had gone to Hannah looking for solace.

"What happened that night between you and Hannah?" I asked.

"She comforted me," he whispered.

"Mentally and physically?"

Elijah nodded.

"In the throes of rejection," I said, "I'm sure you were bemoaning your lot."

"I was hurting," he said.

"Did you sound as pitiful that night as you do now?" I asked. "Were you threatening to give up your ministry?"

He avoided my eyes again. "I might have said something of that nature," he conceded.

That would have been reason enough for a jealous Hannah to act. She could have convinced herself that something needed to be done about Carrie for the good of Elijah and the church; it's easier to pretend sanctity than to acknowledge jealousy.

I turned to Sister Joan. "When you asked if the snakes were ready," I said, "it was Hannah you were talking to, wasn't it?"

"I think both of us are done answering your questions without our attorney present," she said.

"That's your choice," I said, "although I doubt whether either one of you wants to be charged with being an accessory to a homicide."

"We're completely innocent," Elijah said.

My expression didn't hide my skepticism, which prompted the returned prophet to say, "With God as my witness, I never wanted any harm to befall Carrie."

"I'm going to need to hear from Hannah," I said. "Without mentioning what we've discussed, I'd like you to call her and ask that she join you in the conference room."

Elijah pulled out his cell phone and made the call. After four rings, his call went to voicemail. He turned to his wife and asked, "Do you know where she is?"

Joan shook her head. "I haven't seen her since early this morning, which would have been the better part of an hour ago."

"Best guess," I said, "as to where I might find her."

CHAPTER THIRTY-FOUR

DEATH RATTLE

"The womb chamber," said Elijah, "has always been her private retreat."

"The what?"

"It's a hidden refuge loosely based on the *garbhagriha* of Indian temples. Think of it as an inner sanctum."

"Where?" I asked.

"Inside our sealed sanctuary."

"You mean the Wedding Chapel?"

He nodded. "To get inside, you'll need to enter a code into the electronic touchpad that's to the right of the entrance doors."

"What's the code?"

"Four digits," he said. "Twenty-five, twenty-five."

I started for the door. "I'd better go with you," he said.

"No time," I said.

It wasn't only that he'd slow me down. I was afraid security might think I was abducting him.

"If she's inside the inner sanctum," he said, "you'll need to access a second keypad and code."

"Where's it located and what's the number?"

"There's a lectern to the side of the center stage. In the back of the stand is the keypad. Enter seventy-five ten."

"Seven, five, one, zero?"

As he started to nod, the dogs and I ran out of the meeting room.

"Emergency," I yelled to Officer Williams, motioning for him to run with me. "Fastest way out of this building where I won't get shot?"

"Stairwell," he said.

We ran to it, and all four of us began bounding down the stairs. The dogs thought that was great fun.

"Where we going?" he asked.

"Wedding Chapel," I said.

We hit the first floor running, sprinted down a hallway, and pushed through a door with a sign reading, *Emergency Exit Only! Alarm Will Sound If Opened!*

Half the time such warning signs are meant to be deterrents only. Often the alarms are disconnected or nonexistent. In this case, there was truth in advertising. Multiple alarms went off, and the beehive was disturbed with a vengeance. Shouts were directed our way.

"Stay and explain," I yelled.

Officer Williams reluctantly nodded, and then came to a stop so as to face the fallout from the alarms. The dogs and I continued on our bell lap. The logical thing for me to do would have been to wait for backup, but my gut told me there was no time to waste.

The consecrated chapel was getting closer. I suspected the chapel was sealed not so much for sacred purposes, but as a venue for the special shows that went on inside of it.

"'Going to the chapel,'" I told the dogs.

I couldn't sing the words like the Dixie Cups had. My breath was already too ragged. But it wasn't a chapel of love we were going to anyway. The dogs and I vaulted up the steps, and I punched in the numbers on the keypad. I knew one thing that I imagined no one else did: Someone had programmed the codes for the End of Days, and I was suspecting that someone was Sister Hannah. She'd referenced the Zager and Evans pop-culture-classic song "In the Year 2525."

The electronic deadbolt disengaged, and I threw the door open. The chapel was dark. There were no lights on in the building, and nothing to suggest anyone was inside. There was an old-world feeling to the interior, a combination of Asian influences and Middle Eastern. It didn't feel like a chapel as much as it did a pharaoh's grand tomb.

With a dog on each side of me, I ran along the stone flooring. My footsteps echoed off the walls. There were steps that led up to an elevated center stage, and in the middle of that there was a pulpit of sorts. To the side of the stage was a wooden lectern draped in colorful prayer flags adorned with ancient symbols and drawings. I ran over to the lectern. If I hadn't known to look for an electronic keypad within the recess of the space, I never would have seen it.

I punched in 7510. I suspected the lyrics that followed those numbers had been significant to Sister Hannah. They were familiar to me as well. Some tunes just stay in your head. *In the year 7510, if God's a-coming, he ought to make it by then.*

But it was the final line in that verse I was thinking about: *Guess it's time for the judgment day!*

Judgment Day.

The hidden door, camouflaged within the grouting and cracks of what was revealed to be a stone veneer, silently opened. The secret passageway reminded me of something out of *The Da*

Vinci Code. I ran over to it and peered inside. What Elijah had called "the womb chamber" had no windows. Inside was darkness.

"Sister Hannah?" I called.

Even though I couldn't see far into the gloom, the sound of my voice carried, making me believe the sanctum was much larger than I'd expected. There was no response from inside the chamber, or at least no voice responded, although I thought I heard faint movements.

"Hannah?" I said.

I strained to hear. In the distance I could hear a sprinkler-like sound. I turned on my phone's flashlight and extended it through the opening. With its light, I could make out a narrow passageway leading into the sanctum.

The doorway was small, forcing me to hunch down, but after stepping through, the space opened just enough for me to be able to stand up straight. With my phone raised like a modern-day lantern, I started along the corridor. The confines of the passageway forced the dogs to walk behind me. Sirius didn't seem happy with that and stayed right on my heels. As we turned a corner, the space let out into a chamber, and my eyes went to a lone candle burning on a far wall.

"Hannah?"

Again, no response. And the candle didn't offer enough light for me to see if she was even inside the room.

Shush.

And then the sound again, but this time a little longer: *Shush, shush, shush.* Was I being told to be quiet? I stepped forward to try and better hear. That's when Sirius blocked my way, not allowing me to proceed.

My impatience could have been the death of me. I swept the light toward Sirius, wondering what was wrong with him. There was movement a few feet beyond where my partner was positioned. The eyes of the serpent only slightly reflected the light, but it was enough for me to know the danger.

The snake's rattle was shaking, and I was frozen in place by the castanets of death. Its movements—its warning—sounded like a chorus of maracas shaking around the room. I felt as if I were in the midst of a snake pit. In my panic I wanted to flee, and might have but for Emily. She was creeping forward to investigate the nearby sound.

"Steh!" I said. *"Bleibe!"* Stand! Stay!

The words were offered with an urgency that stopped Emily in her tracks, at least for the moment. Her tense posture and fixed attention showed her desire to further explore the cause of the rattling.

"Lass es," I said, and then repeated the command in English: "Leave it!" With great reluctance, Emily turned her attention away from the rattling and back to me.

I extended my light all around, made sure nothing was lurking in the shadows, and then took an unhurried backward step.

"Hier," I said.

As the dogs began their retreat, the sound of warning rattles echoed around the chamber. At least three snakes were announcing their presence. My pounding heart matched the staccato rattling beat for beat, but it was my partner who was in the greatest danger. He was still between me and the nearest snake. Not even daring to breathe, I took a slow and easy second step backward, and as the dogs followed me the rattling eased up.

"So ist brav," I told the dogs, my voice as shaky as my suddenly trembling limbs. "You're both such good dogs."

I put a reassuring hand on each of them. The absence of rattling brought a preternatural quiet to the chamber, punctuated only by my deep breaths. I was about to retreat yet another step when I was stopped by a woman's voice in the darkness.

It sounded as if she said, "I'm ready."

"Hello?"

I raised my phone light but wasn't able to see anyone.

"Sister Hannah?"

There was no answer.

I desperately tried to remember her birth name. "Annamae?" I said. "Annamae Buckley?"

"Annamae," she said, almost as if sighing. Her words were spoken softly, but the room's acoustics were exceptional. "When I was a girl, I never liked that name. I was glad to lose it. But now it has returned."

Her altogether too relaxed voice rose up and down, a singsong cadence that seemed unable to settle on a note or rhythm. Her words sounded as if they were coming from beyond the sanctum. I suspected what I was hearing resulted from a dose of GHB, and worse.

"I'm going to call for help, Hannah."

"Too late," she said.

Her words proved prophetic.

CHAPTER THIRTY-FIVE

YES

Once again, I was working late at my house trying to prepare my case notes. Filling in the many remaining blanks would take weeks. My determining the guilty party had been more luck than not. Cases don't usually get solved so expeditiously. In most circumstances they're built slowly and painstakingly. Sister Hannah, aka Annamae Buckley, had died in the same way she had killed. She had chosen to take a life by snake.

It was her familiarity with poisonous snakes that had first gotten her hired at the Church of the Gate. As a teenager in Florida, she had milked venomous snakes, and then had gone on to become a veterinary technician.

In the end, it wasn't handling dangerous snakes that killed her. It was love, or what she thought was love. Sister Hannah had long loved the man she had built up as a god. My suspicion was that she'd contemplated acting against her rival for some time. That would have explained her having the GHB, and knowing how to get through the canyon to where Carrie lived. When the opportunity presented itself, she'd acted. Maybe Hannah even interpreted Carrie's picture of the rattlesnake as a sign from God that she should act.

Sister Hannah had wanted the death to look like an accident. That's why she'd been mindful of not driving up to the house. She'd parked on the other side of the canyon and crept across it in the darkness. The walk would have discouraged most, but she hadn't been deterred by the possibility of encountering snakes. In fact, she was used to going out into the wild to procure them. That had been one of her duties at the Church of the Gate, something known only by Elijah and Joan.

It was impossible to reconstruct everything that had happened on the night Carrie Holder died, but I suspected that after Hannah reached the house she knocked on the front door. She would have explained that she was there to discuss Elijah; Carrie would have had no reason but to assume she had driven to her house. The night was balmy, and the two of them would have proceeded to the backyard to talk over a glass of wine. When the opportunity presented itself, Carrie's drink would have been doctored with the GHB. The rattlesnake Carrie had photographed provided the perfect culprit. No one would have any reason to suspect that Hannah had carried in a different snake that she had secreted in a bag.

Much of that was supposition, but what wasn't guesswork were the rattlesnakes kept in the church's inner sanctum. They'd been collected and cared for by Sister Hannah. Most had undergone the surgical removal of their venom glands. That was Sister Hannah's specialty. But a few of the rattlesnakes, she'd left intact. It was just a matter of getting one of those snakes to bite Carrie. Hannah knew how to pin the fangs, thanks to the many serpents she'd milked; you held them firmly and forced them to bite into a rubber surface. Human flesh would have proved much more yielding than hard rubber.

Hannah had loved Elijah, who loved Carrie. That was the vicious cycle that had left two dead and one wannabe prophet exposed. Ouroboros, I thought, remembering the symbol of a snake swallowing its tail. It was supposed to represent the cycle of life, of birth and death. There had certainly been enough death.

I yawned. Coffee can only take you so far. I stretched back in my chair. It was time to go home. Everything would still be waiting for me in the morning, and it was past time for me to attend to the dogs. Brother Elijah and Sister Joan were now speaking through a lawyer. Ditto Patricia Gaspar. I would be talking with lots of lawyers in the weeks and months to come.

Another yawn. I looked at the time. Almost midnight. It was too late to call Lisbet. We'd talked briefly earlier in the day. At the time she had sounded preoccupied, which was probably a good thing. It was lucky she had put off our getting together even before the events of the day unfolded. I was glad to have not had to disappoint her yet again, but that didn't unburden me from the void of her absence.

I stood up. The dogs gave me a reason to put one trudging leg in front of another. It was dark outside. It was dark inside. Halfway to the SUV, I came to a sudden stop. By some miracle, my synapses came to life, the neurotransmitters sparked, and belated connections crystallized.

"No," I said.

There was no one in my vicinity, but that didn't stop me from carrying on a conversation.

"Can't be," I said.

My legs started working again. I found myself running. I wasn't tired anymore. There was somewhere I needed to be.

I knocked loudly on the door and identified myself. The dogs and I were on the landing. They had my back. A light came on.

A light.

"Michael?"

A concerned Lisbet was standing in the doorway clutching at her robe. I extended the flowers that I'd bought for her the day before. They were in need of a vase and a drink of water. Lisbet took them from me.

"Are you all right?" she asked, clearly mystified.

"I was going to give you those flowers along with a special card last night. This card," I said, holding it out to her.

"Actually, I was going to give you the card months ago. But then I decided I couldn't be that selfish. The All-In Killer had me twisted in knots, and I was afraid to involve you in my life, even though that's what I wanted more than anything."

Lisbet tucked the bouquet under her arm and took the envelope from my hand. It wasn't sealed, allowing her to easily remove the card. That's when she saw what was taped to it. The ring went with the card. I had wanted to propose to Lisbet months earlier. Better late than never. By then, I had dropped to one knee.

"Marry me," I said.

She looked from me to the ring, and back to me.

"Please marry me despite everything," I said. "Despite my PTSD, despite my work."

"We need to talk," she said.

"You need to say, 'Yes.'"

"You don't understand."

"How far along are you?" I asked.

There was an intake of breath, and tears welled up in her eyes. "You know?"

"For at least half an hour," I said. "I finally put it together."

"Eleven weeks," she said.

"Wow," I said. Once was not enough. "Wow," I said for a second time.

Sirius decided to take advantage of my being down on his level. He put his face on top of my shoulder, and both of us looked at Lisbet expectantly. She started laughing, and crying, and with her nose running had to wipe away the snot on her robe.

She was beautiful.

Lisbet bent down, and we kissed. Uninvited, Sirius licked our faces. All of us were laughing when Emily joined in as well. Being on one knee in the presence of dogs was apparently cause for celebration.

As a young man, I had assumed that one day I would be a father. And then my world had been turned topsy-turvy by Jenny's death and my time in and out of hell, and it had seemed as if I was never destined for fatherhood.

"Why on earth didn't you tell me?" I asked.

"I was afraid," Lisbet said. "At about the time I learned, there was this—divide—between us. And the more I tried to bridge it, the more it seemed to grow. I wasn't about to have you stay with me out of some sense of obligation."

"What you call obligation I call the best news I ever could have imagined."

"Really?"

"Cross my heart. And speaking of heart, will you marry me, Lisbet Keane?"

"Yes," she said, "yes, yes, yes."

I was still down on one knee. Lisbet bent down and kissed me.

CHAPTER THIRTY-SIX

THE PORRIDGE IS JUST RIGHT

The excited cries of the dogs alerted me to Seth's appearance even before he arrived on my doorstep. I had invited him over for what I had described as an "evening of toasting." I had also promised him that we would be doing so with a special offering, a bottle of Pérignon.

"I'm ready for a night of celebration!" he said.

"That's two of us."

"Where is the Dom Pérignon?" he asked.

"The Pérignon is chilling," I said. "I thought we would start with an aperitif of Campari and soda."

"That ought to whet the palate perfectly," Seth said.

I went and prepared our drinks. After handing Seth his, I extended my glass. For once, I was the one who made the toast.

"To the best man," I said.

"And let's not forget the bride-to-be, and the groom," he said.

We clinked glasses.

"And speaking of the bride-to-be," Seth said, "where is Lisbet?"

"Her friends have shanghaied her for an evening out," I said. "The morning sickness—or the twenty-four/seven sickness, as Lisbet refers to it—seems to have abated enough for her to celebrate, at least within limits. While her friends are drinking, Lisbet will be having green tea and crackers."

Seth was beaming. "Wedding bells," he said.

We joined glasses.

"A baby."

More smiles, more clinks, more sips, more toasts.

Seth said, "'To keep your marriage brimming / With love in the loving cup, / Whenever you're wrong, admit it; / Whenever you're right, shut up.'"

"That would make me a Trappist monk," I said.

"That would make you a chatterbox," he said.

Lisbet and I had agreed to get married in a month's time. My future wife was hoping her pregnancy wouldn't be showing too much when we walked down the aisle. I had left it to Lisbet to decide what kind of wedding she wanted. Luckily for me, she said she wanted an informal outdoors wedding, and the sooner the better. I was glad she'd decided to not delay our nuptials. That limited her time to back out. Did I know that I was getting the better end of the deal? I sure did.

Seth's smile wasn't fading, and darned if it wasn't contagious. In fact, my face started to hurt. My facial muscles weren't used to this kind of workout. For too long the smiles had been absent.

"It wasn't much more than a week ago," said Seth, "when you thought Lisbet was breaking up with you."

"It just goes to show you that I'm not as good a detective as I'd like to believe."

"We all have blind spots when it comes to those things close to home."

"I thank you for that reasonable-sounding excuse."

I made a hand gesture for Sirius to leave his uncle Seth's side and join me. He came over and I rubbed his nape back and forth. Now that Seth had one free hand, he took the opportunity to drink deeply. Emily insisted that he continue putting his other hand to good use.

"In fact," said Seth, "when it comes to the professional detecting front, as of late you've had quit a run."

I shook my head. "One of my father's favorite expressions was 'blind pig finds acorn.' That old chestnut—or acorn—pretty much applies to the death of my LA woman, as well as the Sherman Oaks poisoning. Things pretty much fell into my lap."

"If you hadn't been doing a lot of shaking," he said, "things wouldn't have been doing their falling."

I accepted his appraisal, even if I wasn't convinced it was true.

"What's happening with those cases?" he asked.

"There are a lot of people who are proclaiming themselves martyrs," I said, "even though they're not the ones who went and did the dying."

"That's usually the case."

I nodded. "Both Patricia Gaspar and Elijah are claiming that they're the victims in all of this. Gaspar says she never meant to poison Mack Carter, and that the food she doctored was only supposed to give his dogs some harmless payback for their having 'fouled' her yard on numerous occasions. As for the other two dogs on her street that almost died, she denies any responsibility. According to her, their getting sick was just a coincidence, much like the dead hummingbirds in her yard."

"She's not going to get away with it, is she?"

I shook my head. "The surveillance tapes show her going in and out of Carter's home after he was taken to the hospital. It's clear she was removing evidence."

"What about Elijah and Sister Joan?"

"I don't know if they'll spend time in prison," I said. "At the moment the only indisputable charge is that they were illegally housing poisonous snakes without a permit from Fish and Wildlife. But even if we can't nail them on a substantial felony, the Church of the Gate has taken a big hit. Their celebrity parishioners are doing a disappearing act, and some of their big names have very publicly called Elijah a fraud."

"You mean he's not really divine?"

Seth doesn't usually do sarcasm, but when he does, it's invariably devastating.

"I wonder if anyone ever really believed that," I said. "My suspicion is that even his most devout followers didn't ascribe supernatural powers to him. When you watch a magician, most people don't come away believing in magic. Does the audience believe in faith healers and the miracles that they supposedly perform, or is it more that they view the show as compelling theater?"

"One thing is sure," said Seth, "he was a snake oil salesman."

Seth tilted his glass, drained it dry, and then said, "That Dom Pérignon ought to be nicely chilled by now."

I pretended to not understand his heavy-handed hint. My smile disappeared, and I feigned confusion. "Dom Pérignon?" I asked.

"You told me we'd be celebrating with a bottle."

"I am afraid you must have misheard," I said.

I should have prepared for that moment with a camera. I should have immortalized Seth's befuddled expression. He took the bait—hook, line, and sinker.

"You distinctly told me that we would be celebrating over a bottle of Dom Pérignon tonight," he said, sounding positively testy.

Straight-faced, I said, "Now I understand your confusion." Then I got to my feet and said, "I'll be right back."

Half a minute later I returned with a bottle on ice, but it wasn't a magnum of Dom.

"*Dog* Pérignon," I said, showing Seth the bottle.

There was a drawing of a dog on the bottle, along with the words *Dog Pérignon*. I opened the bottle and poured it into two bowls.

"Very funny," said Seth, sounding unusually churlish.

Sirius and Emily came over to check out what I was pouring. Each of them took a tentative lick, decided that they liked what the bartender had served, and continued drinking.

I held out the bottle to Seth. "Want some?" I asked. "It's non-alcoholic. I think the main ingredient is infused salmon water."

"No, thank you," said Seth.

His momentary disappointment at being denied bubbly had already passed, and his smile returned as he watched the dogs sucking down their Dog Pérignon.

"Thanks for being a good sport," I said. "But the subterfuge was not without purpose."

"You mean it was done for some reason other than your being cheap?"

"I'm sure your presence here was not predicated upon some trifling sparkling wine."

"Maybe not," he said, "but substituting Dog Pérignon for Dom Pérignon seems to be the very definition of bait and switch."

Not entirely changing the subject, I said, "I met one of our neighbors yesterday."

"Oh?"

"Maybe you know him? Noah Wester. He lives two blocks over with his wife, Pearl."

Seth shook his head. "I don't think I know either of them."

"Mr. Wester came knocking at the door to tell me that he was planning to take me to small claims court, where he intended to sue me for the maximum amount of ten thousand dollars."

"That sounds like quite an introduction."

"He had incontrovertible evidence proving my guilt," I said, "but I didn't even need to see the evidence to know he was telling the truth."

Usually it's Seth who's the raconteur. For once, he was the one who looked spellbound. "I'm listening," he said.

I lifted my glass and looked at it regretfully. It was empty. In a moment that would be remedied, but for now I continued talking.

"Normally Sirius greets all guests. But when Mr. Wester came to the door, Sirius was nowhere to be found. After hearing Mr. Wester's intentions about lightening my wallet, I called Sirius, who reluctantly skulked into the room. He knew the jig was up."

I pointed to Seth's empty glass and asked, "Ready for a refill?"

"Get on with the story," said Seth.

"You might not know the Westers," I said. Instead of continuing my thought, I offered a parenthetical diversion. "Good people, by the way."

Seth glowered at me.

"But I'm sure you've seen their beautiful golden retriever, Goldilocks, or Goldie, as she's known. She has these beautiful, glowing golden feathers that shimmer when she walks. In fact, both her mother and father were AKC champions, but I digress."

"You sure do."

"The intention was for Goldie to be bred to some muckety-muck highfalutin' golden boy. But Sirius had other ideas. A six-foot fence? Child's play for Sirius. A closed back door? A trifle for the Houdini of the dog world. Evidence of the crime? Not my partner. After his visits to Goldie, he even closed the open door behind him."

"Come on."

I raised my right hand. "Did I mention the CCTV? That's how Mr. Wester tracked me down. The cameras caught Sirius before, after, and during the act."

"During?"

"I had him fast forward that part. The only reason he got caught was because either Mr. or Mrs. Wester remembered to deadbolt the back door one night. That forced Sirius to impro-vise—he was able to pop a screen, and then use his nose to push open a window. The day after his visit, Pearl noticed the screen on the ground and thought her husband had removed it for some reason and not put it back; similarly, Noah Wester also noticed the downed screen and imagined his wife had been cleaning the windows. Eventually they compared notes. Eventually they re-viewed the security footage."

"You dog, you," said Seth to Sirius. The words were spoken with genuine admiration.

"When Mr. Wester came to visit me, he told me his inten-tion was to terminate the pregnancy and collect damages from me. I'm glad to say we were able to agree to an alternative. I will be paying Mr. and Mrs. Wester five thousand dollars, and Goldie will have her litter of pups. From those offspring, I'll get the pick of the litter."

"You're not kidding?"

"I am not kidding."

I walked over to the cabinet and pulled out the wine cooler and bottle of Dom Pérignon that I had secreted inside, along with two champagne flutes.

"Forgive me for ever doubting you," said Seth.

I carefully poured our glasses. With what the bubbly cost, I didn't want to spill a drop.

"To fatherhood," said Seth.

"To life," I said. "And to hope."

Our glasses came together. We sipped and appreciated. Since it was a celebration, I refilled the dog bowls, but made sure they got the Dog Pérignon and not the Dom.

"He really closed the door behind him?" asked Seth.

"Mr. Wester provided me with the footage," I said. "Care to watch?"

"You got any popcorn?"

"As a matter of fact, I do."

CHAPTER THIRTY-SEVEN

TYING THE GORDIAN KNOT

One week prior to our wedding day, I decided to have a heart-to-heart with Lisbet. I didn't want to enter our marriage carrying the baggage of my apprehensions and concerns, and it took me about fifteen torturous minutes to spell out my worries to her. That's a lot of angst, and I didn't gloss over anything. For too long I'd downplayed my PTSD, along with the other dark clouds hanging over me. There wasn't only Lisbet to take into account. A baby was going to be entering the world. I wanted Lisbet to do what was best for both her and the baby, and if that meant our not being together, I would accept her decision. When I finished with my too long litany, Lisbet reached for my hand.

"Michael," she said, "do you love me?"

That was a no-brainer. "Yes," I said.

"Then that's the only thing I needed to hear."

"But what about—*everything*?"

"We will face *everything* together. That's what couples do. Since time immemorial, babies have been born in the midst of

wars, and epidemics, and famines, and disasters natural and un-
natural. We can hope those things don't happen to us in our life-
times, but it would be unrealistic to think that we'll be unscathed
by adversity."

"You make it sound so easy," I said.

"Not easy," she said, "but why make it any harder than it
has to be?"

The two of us kissed, and she asked, "All better?"

The knots that had been tying me up melted away, and I
said, "All better."

On the morning of my wedding day, Ben Corning called. For a
moment I considered letting his call go to voicemail. Anyone but
a cop would have done just that. I knew the timing of the call
wasn't coincidental. I also knew what Corning was going to say,
minus a few details. When I'd come clean with Lisbet, I had
warned my wife-to-be of the impending storm.

And in particular, the rider on the storm.

"I'm guessing the homicide occurred last evening," I said.

Corning sounded surprised. "Yes," he said.

"What was the seven-seven connection?"

"The homicide occurred at a residence located on Sunset
Strip."

I allowed myself a sigh. "Explain," I said.

"Back in the fifties and sixties, there was a popular television show called *Seventy-Seven Sunset Strip*. The location referenced Sunset Avenue in LA. That's why some of the older poker
players call two sevens Sunset Strip. I looked up the show on
YouTube. It had a real catchy opening jingle. Bluesy, with finger
snapping and people singing, 'Seventy-Seven Sunset Strip.'"

Corning's version wasn't catchy, but I didn't tell him that.
"And yet I'm assuming that since I didn't hear any police or me-

dia reports about a homicide occurring on Sunset Avenue that it must have happened elsewhere else?"

"Correct," said Corning. "Our victim lived on a road named Sunset Strip in Willcox, Arizona."

"Which is where?"

"It's a small town about eighty miles east of Tucson and forty-five miles west of the New Mexico border. It sits in an area that's known for producing most of Arizona's wines, but that's not saying it's Napa Valley. For a time, it was probably best known for Wyatt Earp's brother Warren being shot and killed there."

"Was the victim shot?"

"He was," said Corning. "Seven times."

The good news was that Willcox, Arizona, was a lot farther from Los Angeles than Las Vegas was. The bad news was another innocent individual had died.

"Okay," I said.

"You don't sound surprised by any of this."

"I'm not. I've known for some time that the man who attacked Detective Charles in Las Vegas was not the All-In Killer."

Corning didn't immediately respond, and when he did, he didn't sound happy. "And how did you know something that we weren't sure of until a few hours ago?"

"All the other victims have been killed in isolated spots," I said. "And we had the picture of Flattop Jones left in the mojo bag. The All-In Killer was advertising the fact that Flattop Jones was an assassin hired to kill a detective. My mistake was thinking that I was that detective."

"It would have been nice if you'd passed along that theory to us," said Corning.

"I'm sure within a day or two of the attack on Detective Charles you'd already determined the same thing. Right?"

When we're kids, most of us have parents encouraging us to share. The FBI was not an organization that liked to share.

"Some—inconsistencies—between Detective Charles's attacker and the All-In Killer surfaced early in our investigation," he admitted.

"Have you identified her attacker?"

"Officially, no," he said. "But we've been trying to track down a hired killer known as the Ghost. What little information we have on him seems to match the description of Detective Charles's assailant. Our Ghost is believed to have born in Eastern Europe, but has no accent to betray his country of origin. His greatest skill is his ability to blend in wherever he goes. And somehow, despite his occupation and the many people he's suspected of having been paid to kill, he's managed to stay off most law enforcement radar."

"If he can be hired, he can be found."

"We're proceeding with that same belief."

"Thanks for the update," I said.

"You interested in the particulars of the seven-seven homicide?"

"I'd like to hear about it another time," I said. "Today, I'm going to a wedding."

CHAPTER THIRTY-EIGHT

THE UNINVITED GUEST

Imagine the perfect wedding. That's what ours was. If a male makes that statement, you know it must be true. For most men, me included, the idea of a romantic evening is ordering out delivery pizza. It's a good thing Lisbet organized our big event.

My most significant contribution was selecting the ring-bearer and the flower girl. Yes, it was one of those dog weddings. Sirius wore a doggie tux that had a zippered pocket where the rings were placed. We knew those rings were in good paws. My partner looked dashing, and he knew it. But in time-honored tradition, the male did not upstage the female. Emily wore a beautiful pink bow that covered her mangled ears. The bridesmaids, all old friends of Lisbet, had also seen to Emily's nails, which were painted to match their own. Our pittie looked runway-model good, and our guests showered her with attention.

If it hadn't been for a late cancellation—Providence must have intervened—we never would have secured the perfect wedding location, the Los Angeles River Center and Gardens. It's in the middle of Highland Park in northeast Los Angeles, and lots of LA residents aren't even aware of its existence. It is a true urban oasis, a garden and natural setting in the midst of one of the most populated neighborhoods of the city. Because the River Center is part of the Mountains Recreation Conservation Authority, it tries to operate in a manner befitting its land conservation status. As they are quick to tell you, if you don't like the idea of leaves and spiders, the River Center might not be the ideal place for your gathering.

We were okay with leaves and spiders because they came with such things as beautiful gardens, fountains, decorative wrought iron, and Spanish tile. The Arroyo Seco—which means *dry stream* in English—runs through Highland Park. And even though it was summer, I'm glad to say the Arroyo Seco did not live up to its name; water was still flowing.

Father Pat officiated. He invoked God's blessings upon us, but at the same time knew we didn't want a church wedding, and so he personalized the ceremony. Naturally, that meant retelling the story of how the two of us had first met. When he finished, there wasn't a dry eye.

My mom might have been the happiest attendee of all. When she and my father had gotten married in 1968, the groomsmen had tied on the biggest trail of beer cans any wedding getaway car ever had. My mother had kept half a dozen of the cans as mementos. They weren't the light aluminum cans that people drink from today, which might be why they had so nicely withstood the test of time. Mom had tricked out her wheelchair, tying those old Schlitz and Hamm's cans to it.

Anyone who wonders where I got my warped sense of humor needn't look far. A couple of my cop friends threatened to give Mom a speeding ticket. They also asked if she'd been drinking and driving. Mom loved it. She told everyone she couldn't wait to spoil her grandchild. Her only regret was that Dad wasn't alive to join her in that spoiling.

Did I dance? They say tough guys don't dance. I danced. I even managed not to step on Lisbet's toes. For one night at least, I was glad not to be a tough guy.

At the reception, it fell upon my best man to make a speech. In addition to being a shaman of renown, Seth is a raconteur nonpareil. He knows many ways to mend a soul, and doesn't rely only on herbs and potions. His observations and one-liners made everyone feel better. I've always found it easy to be skeptical of Seth's clients who call him a miracle worker; now I know they might not be so off the mark.

The final words of his toast were classic Seth. He asked everyone to raise their glasses, and then he saluted Lisbet and me and said, "To love and laughter, and happily ever after."

It was an evening of hugs, friendly pummeling, laughter, and the recounting of histories and stories. We went from table to table, and from invited guest to invited guest. We were swept along in what felt like a most wonderful dream.

As the outside vendors broke down the bar and hauled off the trash, Lisbet, Seth, and I began filling up the SUV with all the offerings that had been left on the gift-and-card table.

"I thought we were specific about no gifts," I said, "other than requesting donations to Angie's Rescues."

"Some people don't feel right about not bringing a gift," said Lisbet.

I was surprised at the extent of the haul. It took us a number of trips before the table was empty. The three of us looked around. The staff had left the area immaculate, leaves and spiders notwithstanding.

"It has been as memorable a wedding as I've ever had the pleasure of attending," said Seth. "And though I wish this evening never had to end, it's time to bid adieu to the two of you. If I don't see you in the morning, have a wonderful honeymoon."

He embraced Lisbet, and then me, and then bent down and said his goodbyes to the dogs. Naturally, Sirius and Emily were going with us. There was no way we were leaving our ring bearer and flower girl behind. In fact, our honeymoon had been tailored with them in mind. All of us would be driving up the coast. Dog-friendly hotels had been booked up to Vancouver and back. We'd even managed to find a few honeymoon suites that allowed dogs.

As we started out on the drive home, Mom's little surprise revealed itself. Hidden from view, but not from our ears, was the beer can collection that had been tied so many years ago to her honeymoon getaway car, and that she'd arranged to have tied to ours. I carefully gathered the cans. One day I might be lucky enough to do the same favor for my son or daughter. The very possibility of that made me feel warm all over.

When we arrived home, I grabbed a wheelbarrow and started filling it with all of our gifts. It only took me four trips to bring everything inside. Being the organizer that she is, Lisbet wanted to make an inventory of what we had been given so that she could send out thank-you notes from the road. We were most of the way through our booty when she encountered an unsigned card with a stenciled message. Lisbet read it aloud:

"My invitation must have gotten lost in the mail, but present circumstances precluded my attendance anyway. Please enjoy the wine and think of me when you drink it. Best wishes for the future?"

Her reading emphasized the question mark that had concluded the writer's last sentence.

The card had been taped to a case of wine. As Lisbet turned her attention to the box and its contents, I came over to her side and said, "Let me."

Using a cloth napkin to avoid contaminating any potential evidence, I secured the card in a baggie. Then I pulled out one of the wine bottles, and then a second. After looking at them, I returned them to the box.

"What is it?" asked Lisbet.

I didn't want to start our marriage off by deceiving or equivocating, although I would have rather not answered her question.

"The wines are selections from Willcox, Arizona," I said. "That's where the latest victim of the All-In Killer was found. I know the handiwork of Ellis Haines all too well, know his taunts and his insinuations. He's the author of our note; he's the one who arranged to have it delivered to us along with the wine."

I was afraid the news would upset Lisbet, but when I dared to meet her eyes, I was surprised to see she didn't look fazed.

"Are you okay?" I asked.

"Absolutely," she said. "That's one less thank-you note that I have to write."

I imitated her nonchalance. "Arizona wine," I said. "As if any self-respecting Californian would drink Arizona wine."

"Major *faux pas*," Lisbet said, nodding her head.

My wife's exaggerated French accent made me laugh. *My wife.*

"Your French is *très bien*," I said.

My French wasn't *très bien*, which is why she joined me in laughing.

Still, I was concerned. "We can talk about this, you know."

"If you want to," she said.

"I'm going to call Rick Shea right now," I said, "and have him investigate this." The LAPD detective had the nickname Ricochet. He was the best investigator I knew.

"Not tonight you're not," said Lisbet. "We have plans, and we're not going to let this intrusion put a pall on our special day, or on our future together."

"Someone might have seen something."

"Someone might have," she said. "But don't you think it's more likely that some delivery person was paid to leave the package and note on our gift table?"

I found myself nodding.

"You know those fairy tales?" said Lisbet. "When the witch or sorceress shows up uninvited at the grand wedding and takes great offense at not having been asked to attend, and as a result casts some nasty spell?"

"Sounds familiar," I said.

She looked at me and most emphatically said, "Wrong."

"Wrong?"

"That's not our fairy tale. In our story, the couple lives happily ever after. We're not going to let an uninvited guest ruin our wedding, or our honeymoon, or our lives. And we're especially not going to let this uninvited guest ruin the rest of our evening. Does that sound okay to you, Mr. Gideon?"

"It sounds perfect to me, Mrs. Gideon."

She took me by the hand, and I let her lead me. For years I'd wondered if I would ever completely escape from the fire, or if in the end it would consume me. In her company, it felt as if I had finally found a way out.

THE END

GIDEON, SIRIUS, EMILY, AND LISBET
WILL RETURN IN
THE LAST GOOD DOG
IN SPRING 2021

To be notified when Alan's books are available for preorder
and/or sale, follow him at:

https://amazon.com/author/alanrussell

https://www.bookbub.com/authors/alan-russell

https://www.goodreads.com/alanrussell

https://www.facebook.com/AlanRussellMysteryAuthor

LOOK FOR ALAN'S UPCOMING RELEASES:

No Sign of Murder
A Private Investigator Stuart Winter Novel
On sale October 1, 2019

The Forest Prime Evil
A Private Investigator Stuart Winter Novel
On sale October 1, 2019

Political Suicide
A Thriller
On sale November 5, 2019

AUTHOR'S NOTE

Whether they be real or imagined, the dogs in my life have always been very important to me. I grew up with dogs, and dogs made me grow up. When I was a junior in college my mother died. One of the things I remember most about her was the love she had for dogs, and in particular, German shepherds. At the time of her death, there were two family shepherds, Samson and Delilah.

My mother's death wasn't easy on any of us. At the time, my siblings were spread out, and we were all renters. For several months my father coped as best he could, but then he announced that he was unable to take care of both dogs and planned on relinquishing Samson to an animal shelter. He made this choice because Samson was the younger of the two dogs and required more care. (On a parenthetic note, Delilah died only six months later. She was still a relatively young dog at the time; I'm convinced she died of a broken heart. German shepherds are known to be unusually devoted to one human—my mother was Delilah's human—and in her absence she was lost.)

Because I was afraid that my father's intention to give up Samson might result in his death sentence, I said I would take him. Keeping a shepherd while attending college (where I was the editor of the school newspaper, as well as working a part-time job at a hotel) involved a lot of complicated logistics, including trying to keep Sam out of sight whenever the landlord visited (the lease I'd signed to the house I was living in said "no pets").

After graduating from college, my girlfriend (who later became my wife) and I found a rental where Sam was allowed. I always called Samson our "difficult genius." When I write about the intelligence of Sirius, it's easy for me to conjure up stories of Sam. Doors and windows were no obstacles for him. On several occasions when Sam thought he wasn't being observed, I watched him turn door handles with his mouth and open windows with his nose.

Sometimes Sam was too smart for his own good. On one occasion, I was working in my room and doing my best to ignore the shrieking of Shannon, a neighbor girl who kept rollerblading up and down our driveway. Sam's patience must have worn thin from all the noise (and invasion of space he considered his). He opened the door, went out to the driveway, shook Shannon from behind, and then returned into the house. Not only that, Sam apparently closed the door to cover up what he had done.

Only after being summoned to the door by Shannon's father did I learn of Samson's transgression. I was mortified, especially when I was told he had shaken Shannon by the backside. My difficult genius was only too aware of his guilt, and slunk away during my conversation with Shannon's father.

It's easy to write about Sirius opening doors when you have shepherds who have done the same. I think German shepherds are the engineers of the dog world. They see an obstacle and find a way to surmount it. We have had the privilege of having a variety of dogs and dog breeds in our lives. All have been wonderful in their own way, but when it comes to being escape artists, our shepherds have been in a league of their own.

Lady is our current shepherd. All of our other dogs have found the backyard gate to be an unbreachable barrier. A short time after she joined our pack, Lady learned how to paw the gate open whenever it wasn't latched. And when we recently had wrought iron fencing put in around our patio, it took Lady only two days to figure out how to work the latch (shake railing with paw, push with head) to open the door.

It's easy to write stories with dogs, because my life is full of dog stories. Thank you for going on this journey with me. The grand finale of the Gideon and Sirius novels awaits us both.

If you have enjoyed these books, please tell the world. For more personal stories, please like Alan Russell Mystery Author on Facebook. And if you can take a moment to write a review, or express your satisfaction, your five-star reviews on Amazon, Audible, BookBub, and Goodreads mean a lot to me. As always, I can be reached at alanrussellauthor@gmail.com.

Until next time!

Alan Russell
July 30, 2019

ABOUT THE AUTHOR

 Critical acclaim has greeted bestselling author Alan Russell's novels from coast to coast. *Publishers Weekly* calls him "one of the best writers in the mystery field today." The *New York Times* says, "He has a gift for dialogue," while the *Los Angeles Times* calls him a "crime fiction rara avis." Russell's novels have ranged from whodunits to comedic capers to suspense, and his works have been nominated for most of the major awards in crime fiction. He has been awarded a Lefty, a Critics' Choice Award, and the Odin Award for Lifetime Achievement from the San Diego Writers and Editors Guild. A California native, Russell is a former collegiate basketball player who nowadays plays under the rim. The proud father of three children, Russell resides with his wife in Southern California.

Author photo credit: Stathis Orphanos